CONFESSIONS OF AN
ACCIDENTAL LAWYER

MICHAEL STOCKHAM

Whistling Pigs Press LLC
Paperback ISBN: 978-1-7379584-0-6
Ebook ISBN: 978-1-7379584-1-3
Audiobook ISBN: 978-1-7379584-2-0
Hardcover ISBN: 978-1-7379584-3-7
First edition revised 01.31.2023

Book shepherd: Aurora Winter, www.SamePagePublishing.com

Book cover designer: Richard Ljoenes

Front cover photographs: prison cell by Mopic / Shutterstock; crib by Shevchenko Nataliya / Shutterstock; Teddy Bear by RACOBOVT / Shutterstock

Author photographs by: Jamie House

Disclaimer

Although inspired by some real-world events, this is a work of imagination. It is a work of fiction. No character is a representation of anyone who has lived.

BOOK REVIEWS

BOOK REVIEWS REQUESTED

Please leave an online book review! Your review will help other readers discover a new book by a new, award-winning author. You will also be encouraging Michael Stockham to write more novels for your reading enjoyment. Please leave your book review online on Amazon or Goodreads.

This book has already attracted many 5-star reviews and book awards.

INTERNATIONAL IMPACT BOOK AWARDS, Gold, 2022

AMERICAN FICTION AWARDS, Finalist, Thriller & Mystery/Suspense, 2022

LITERARY TITAN, Silver, 2022

AMERICAN WRITING AWARDS, Finalist, 2022

FIREBIRD BOOK AWARDS, 2022

#1 NEW RELEASE, AMAZON, Legal Thriller, 2022

SYNOPSIS

Battling against a Texas prison, a young lawyer fights for a fair trial in a prison-friendly town as witnesses and evidence evaporate.

Scarred physically and emotionally by a botched delivery, his wife struggles to realize their dream of a healthy baby and a happy family.

Trapped in solitary confinement, an inmate fights for medicine to keep his failing heart pumping.

Torn between career and family, with the lives of a prisoner, his wife, and his unborn child on the line, the young lawyer struggles to ensure that his client, his family, and his integrity all survive.

MICHAEL STOCKHAM takes us on a page-turning journey in this novel inspired by actual events. He is a litigation attorney, award-winning author, and speaker.

———

Thank you in advance for taking a moment to leave a starred review on Goodreads or Amazon.

Significant credit for this book goes to my family for their infinite love and unwavering support.

Special thanks to Aurora Winter for her editorial wisdom and unlimited patience.

CHAPTER
ONE

LATE SUMMER. Outside Haskell, Texas. State Highway 277.

Autumn has been slow to arrive. Speeding tires make the blue van vibrate until the only sound is a loud, pervasive hum. As a state-prison vehicle, it possesses the bare essentials. A tepid stream of air conditioning funnels to the back of the van. Off to the east, the sun rests above the pecan trees on the horizon, its heat piercing the van.

The acrid smell of sweat from the prisoners surrounds Prisoner No. 4483214, Emmett Kendrick, who glances out the window. Exit 308A slides by—only seventy miles to go to the hospital facility at the Robertson Prison in Abilene. Emmett started counting highway signs twenty miles ago. The pain started where it always does, in his jaw, then it inches its way down his neck, and seeps into his chest and arm. Now it constricts his breath, chokes him.

Each bump on the highway slams through the old shocks on the van and jackhammers his ribs, causing a fire-burst of agony. Two prior open-heart surgeries left his chest weak, stapled together with wire mesh. Never a large man, the decades in prison have weathered and wearied Emmett, now pushing seventy.

Emmett glances at the only source of help—two Corrections Officers in the front seat, behind a cage of expanded steel mesh. Ominously, as a reminder of their power, a shotgun, mounted vertically, rests between them by the dashboard. Their starched, creased uniforms and protective vests make them appear formidable. They smirk and turn up the radio loud enough to drown out any prisoner complaints from the back of the van.

"Boss, I need my Nitro," Emmett says as loudly as he can, but his voice leaks out in only a hoarse whisper. The guards focus on the road, not the prisoners, and the sound from the air conditioning, the hum of the van, and the radio drown out his voice. Other prisoners glare at him because asking for help stirs the guards' ire.

Nitroglycerin would relieve the pain, calm down the angina. But even if he had it in his shirt pocket, he could not reach it. During transport between two solitary-confinement units, prisoners wear manacles that lock their wrists to a leather belt around their waist. A chain from the belt connects to the leg irons around their ankles, which are then cuffed to a U-bolt in the floor. Locked down so tightly, he could never reach the Nitro in his pocket. His supply has been spotty lately—the prison always makes excuses. He cranes his neck and peeks through the windshield. Exit 312 slides by on the Texas landscape.

Emmett gasps as another angina attack squeezes his heart like a vise. Will this crushing weight on his frail chest turn into his final heart attack?

"Boss, I need my Nitro," Emmett croaks again, desperate.

But no one helps him.

CHAPTER
TWO

MARCH. Ithaca, New York.

Winter shows signs of finally letting up. I glance out the hospital room window and see grimy snowbanks melt in a constant trickle. Inside the hospital room, a chill permeates every word uttered as Dr. Brown covers the Informed Consent paperwork. His bony hand protrudes from a wrinkled set of green surgical scrubs and points at words on the page. My wife, Hannah, rests exhausted under a pile of blankets, while our newborn daughter, Lilly, sleeps in the crook of her arm. A monitor on a pole behind Hannah calls out her vital signs. She squeezes Lilly more tightly and closes her eyes against the conversation.

"We must stop the bleeding," Dr. Brown says.

His direct statement hits me in the gut.

"You've been doing the same thing for weeks," I grumble. "You pump her full of IV antibiotics, stop the fever, and then send us home, and claim the blood should stop on its own. But it doesn't."

"We thought it would. But something else is going on. We need to find the source. If we can't figure that out and stem the bleeding, then the infection will never resolve." His tall, six-foot frame seems to shrink as he talks to us.

I stare at Hannah. My wife stares at me, her gaze pale and drained, her usually vibrant features ashen. Her blonde hair limply frames her feverish face. She holds our weeks-old baby like a life preserver as the storm rages. I must protect her. Somehow. My hands clinch into fists as I turn on the doctor.

"Shouldn't we get a second opinion?" My question more of a snarl that betrays my lack of confidence in anything he says. "Surely someone here or down at the Women's Hospital in Elmira knows how to fix this. Her fever spiked to one hundred and six degrees yesterday. . . . One hundred and six!" I protest, my voice loud enough for the nurses in the hallway to hear me.

Dr. Brown holds his palms as if in surrender, blowing some of his long, gray hair away from his cheek. "Look, I've consulted with my partners, and we all concur. The best option is the procedure. We go in, scout around . . . ."

Hannah's eyes flash open and she gives Dr. Brown a piercing look. "So exploratory surgery?"

"It could be a tear in the uterine lining or perhaps we find a foreign body we're able to remove."

"You mean something you left behind," I say. My voice bounces off the hospital room walls.

Dr. Brown points a finger at me and signals me to be quiet. "It's called retained products of conception. Look, we were very careful during the delivery. Pathology confirmed the full placenta, but sometimes it's not so simple. It's possible some remnants escaped discovery. If they did, we must remove them immediately before the infection deteriorates into sepsis, an infection in her bloodstream."

"And if it's a tear in the uterine wall?" Hannah asks, her voice cracks. Anger and fear tinge every word.

"It depends on the severity." Dr. Brown takes a deep

breath. "If the tear is significant, we might not be able to repair it. Then the only cure is removal."

"That means no more kids . . . ever," Hannah says, her voice drained and exhausted, as if watching a dream implode before her eyes.

I know how much my wife wants children to fill our home, how much being a mother means to her. I squeeze her cool hand reassuringly. She has lost so much blood that it's near impossible for her to keep her body temperature up; the nurses continuously bring her blankets from the warmer.

Dr. Brown takes off his glasses, closes his eyes, and pinches the bridge of his nose. "We may already be at that point, Ms. Simmons," Dr. Brown sighs, the normal timbre of his clinical tone evaporates. "With the severity of the post-partum infection, profound scarring is a real possibility."

"You're telling me . . ." I start, pacing like a wild animal caged for the first time.

Dr. Brown interrupts me, his normal ramrod posture now stooped over. "I'm saying you need to focus on two things: your beautiful, healthy baby girl, and saving your wife."

He turns his focus away from me, his eyes lock on Hannah's. "Ms. Simmons, we must stop the bleeding, and that requires surgery. You already need a blood transfusion. You must consent to the procedure." Dr. Brown looks at both of us, then lets out a long sigh. "I'll give you two some time alone. Sign the forms," he barks.

Dr. Brown exits, leaving me alone with my wife and baby girl under the sterile lights of the hospital room.

Hannah's fever has raged on and off for weeks. She closes her eyes again, and dark circles accentuate her fatigue. Lilly, our three-week-old daughter, shifts in her arms and yawns.

"Daniel, I hate the thought of surgery," my wife grumbles. "I hate how anesthesia makes me feel—always so nauseous."

As much as I hate the doctor, I can't risk losing my wife. "Let them try, Buzz."

"I'm not risking it," she barks, her voice sharp and stubborn. Her anger rises, and her hair flares as if full of static.

I try to project calm, an argument will cause her to dig in her heels, "We've got to get you better. We have to stop the infection."

"Not if they're going to take me apart . . . leave me barren," she says, a subtle thunder in her tone. My wife hated being an only child and is determined our daughter won't have a lonely childhood, bereft of siblings. Hannah doesn't want to give up the future she's always dreamt of. She's always wanted a big, happy family with four children. For years, Hannah has imagined our sons and daughters laughing and playing together in our backyard. Now that dream may be over forever.

Moments tick by. Hannah's voice breaks. A tear trickles down her cheek. She brushes it away, too proud to let me see her cry.

I feel helpless to reassure her, to make this problem go away. I'm not a doctor! "Maybe they're right, maybe it's as simple as finding something left behind and removing it."

She tries to check the fear growing in her voice. "And if they can't find something? What then? What if the doctors panic, and they decide they have no choice—just rip out everything?"

"That won't happen," I try lamely.

"I don't want the surgery or the transfusion, Daniel," Hannah says obstinately. She's understandably afraid, and that makes her even more stubborn than normal.

I take a breath and sit down next to her in a chair by the bed. I grab her small, cool hand and wrap it in mine, hoping the warmth might help. Her grip seems weaker this morning than last night, as if her life is leaking out.

Lilly stirs, yawns again, and dozes off. Avoiding my wife's piercing gaze, I stare at the monitor that dings off her low blood pressure. Finally, I whisper in desperation, "If we don't get your infection under control, I'm going to be raising Lilly by myself."

My statement hangs in the room as the clock ticks off the seconds. Hannah shakes. It's impossible to tell if the trembling stems from the fever or her fury with the situation. I instantly regret the hurt my words caused, but my closing argument is powerfully persuasive. It must be. She can walk forward with Lilly and me or not.

I wait, staring at the numbers on the monitor behind her. Hannah chews on her lip. After a few moments, she nods in reluctant agreement. She hands our baby to me.

I kiss the top of our daughter's sweetly scented head. Her downy blonde hair is fine and incredibly soft. Lilly's tiny hands grasp my finger. Our baby is a miracle—but I can't let this one small miracle cost me the life of my adorable, but stubborn, wife.

Hannah grabs the clipboard and scribbles her signature on the dreaded consent form, frowning. Then she presses the buzzer and calls the nurse.

"What if I'm not whole when they finish?" Hannah murmurs fretfully, her eyes slightly moist.

"Positive thoughts, Buzz," I say. The statement is flat, but it's all that I have.

"Four kids," she says, jutting out her chin.

"What?" I respond, baffled.

"Four is the number of kids I want to have. Don't let them take that away," she whispers fiercely.

"I won't."

"Promise me!" she says, her defiant voice laced with fear.

"I promise," I vow—clueless how much those words will eventually cost.

CHAPTER
THREE

MARCH. Teton Springs, Texas.

The early March moon casts shadows. Bright beams of light penetrate the one-foot by four-foot barred window near the ceiling in Emmett Kendrick's prison cell. It must be close to a full moon because the light glows sufficiently to project the shadows of Emmett's sole companions. Two doves nest on the outside ledge of the windowsill.

A warm winter, many birds have chosen not to fly further south, hunkering down instead in the scrub brush of North Texas. The doves have been reasonable company over the last few days, and Emmett is glad they have not abandoned him.

Blessed silence blankets Emmett's cell. Johnson—two cells down—had screamed well past midnight. Solitary confinement drives most men crazy. Now in the peace of pending dawn, Emmett watches the simplicity of the doves' shadows as they flicker across the concrete. Many of those species mate for life, promised to one another. Yesterday, Emmett was worried a Red-Tail Hawk he saw canvass the skies would spook the birds, causing them to fly away, but this morning's shadows confirm they stood fast. He is not alone.

The sound of Emmett's breath fills his eight-foot by ten-foot cell. He has nearly dozed off when a drumming sound rouses him. The purposeful beat of rubber hitting concrete grows louder, warning of imminent danger. The formidable steel door next to the guards' picket opens. Riot shields smack the edge of the doorway. Emmett closes his eyes as the heavy soles pound against the concrete, coming closer. Ten… Nine… Eight… Seven… Six… Five… Four… Three… Two… One. He prays fervently that they are here because of Jackson's fit last night. But, as Emmett opens his eyes, the black riot helmets pull into view through the small, square window in his door. A key turns the lock on his meal slot. A baton jams through the now open hole. Emmett cringes.

"Inmate Kendrick!" the guard shouts. "Cell check. Back into the far corner of your cell, face the wall."

"Boss, this makes little sense. Why you tossin' me in the middle of the night?" Emmett asks. He cowers, aware he is powerless.

"Contraband. We had an anonymous report that you're hidin' stuff you shouldn't be hidin'. Be calm. Comply. Get up. Get back into the far corner. Face the wall."

Emmett obeys. The cold concrete pierces his feet—no time to put on his prison fatigues and shoes. In a threadbare pair of boxer shorts, bleached countless times in the prison laundry, Emmett backs into the cold gray walls behind him.

The key turns in the lock. The door opens wide, and the Corrections Officers flick on the blinding fluorescent light. CO Thompson's figure fills the doorway. He is an enormous man. A pitiless grin pokes out from a thick, jet-black mustache. Two other guards, both in full riot gear, stand behind him and hold their shields at the ready.

"Inmate . . . turn around," Thompson commands and points the baton at Emmett for emphasis.

"I'm just watching. I will do nothing," Emmett protests.

"Turn around!"

"I'm just standing here."

"You leave me no choice. Restrain him."

The two guards with riot gear flow past Thompson like inky water passing around a boulder in a stream. They advance on Emmett, shields up. Both move with precision and lock their shields in position, at right angles to one other, their brown eyes locked in a piercing stare. They back Emmett into the corner and pin him to the walls. The drumming of his own heart sounds like a galloping horse racing out of control, faster and faster. The fear of another heart attack strikes at his core.

Striding into the center of the cell, CO Thompson grabs the mattress with a large, beefy hand and rips it off the bed. He tears off the bedding and leaves it in a heap on the floor. He steps to the small shelf where Emmett keeps his few belongings, and he moves like a frenzied dog hunting a bone. He tosses everything off the shelf with the back of his hand. Pages of paper flutter through the air.

"You been writin' again, Inmate Kendrick?"

"Just court documents."

"Could'a fooled me. Thought you were writin' fiction or maybe some of that there pornography." The officer stops, turns toward Emmett, and gives him a cold, penetrating stare. "That will get you in trouble."

"No stories, Boss. Just what I said. I'm writing papers to the Judge." Emmett's breath fogs against the riot shield, voice muffled.

"Now why would you want to go and do somethin' like that?" the guard growls.

"I have a right to send those papers to the Judge."

Officer Thompson flicks the last pages from the shelf into the air.

"You ain't got no rights, convict." Thompson edges up to the riot shield and drums his finger at Emmett's eye level. He says in a low snarl, "You should be careful writin' stories, Inmate. Someone, someday, might be unhappy about that."

A tense moment of silence passes. Thompson's dark, foreboding eyes, like the steel all around stare into Emmett's. Emmett says nothing. He holds his breath. His heart thumps loudly, erratically. Is he the only one who can hear that drumbeat?

Thompson shouts, "Cell's clean. Let's go."

The three guards move out, kicking at his mattress on the way out. They lock the bolt. The baton jams back through the meal slot.

"It'd be a shame to toss this cell every night," Thompson sneers.

The steel panel of the meal slot slams shut, the lock turns. Emmett slides down against the wall, crouched in the corner.

"Breathe easy," he tells himself, as he anxiously surveys the chaos littering the floor. He finally spots what he's seeking —his small bottle of Nitroglycerin, his heart medicine. He grabs the bottle, his aching heart racing.

His trembling, age-spotted hands fumble and cannot open the pill bottle, and his hurtling heartbeats underscore the urgency. Emmet's unsteady fingers finally jerk open the pill bottle. Pills fly everywhere. He grabs one pill from the floor, heedless of the dirt, and pops it in his mouth.

"You'll be okay," he reassures himself.

He hopes it's true.

CHAPTER
FOUR

JULY. Dallas, Texas. Two years later.

I have graduated from law school, and we moved to Dallas so I could start a job at a law firm. My wife, Hannah, and I sit near a pond, on a blanket spread out upon the grass. It's a beautiful July afternoon in Dallas, and time lumbers lazily along. The shade from pecan trees and a soft breeze keep the Texas heat off us. Ducks manically dive under the pond's surface for small minnows, their efforts rippling rings to the pond's bank. Cicadas rumble at a high pitch in the branches, and the sweet smell of fresh-cut grass envelopes us.

Hannah's slender fingers carefully unwrap a sandwich for our daughter, Lilly, now a high-energy toddler, to lure her back from chasing a butterfly.

"Lilly. Lunch. Come get some juice, little one. It's hot out."

Hannah's skin is a soft golden brown from playing outside all summer with Lilly. Life has poured back into her, and her petite, thin, sultry frame in shorts and a halter-top is irresistible. The Texas heat suddenly seems warmer. Hannah tucks her blonde hair behind her ear flirtatiously. She tilts her head and looks up at me. Her hazel eyes still take my breath away.

"You know, if we started trying now, Lilly and her brother or sister would be only three years apart," she says, broaching her favorite subject.

I look back at the ducks in the pond and pretend I didn't hear her. I'm all in for getting busy; *getting pregnant* is flat dangerous.

Stumbling over her tiny sneakers, Lilly ambles her way back to us for lunch. Her nose wrinkles as she watches a bright orange butterfly wobble by us.

"I love flutterflies!" she squeals.

I grab her shoulder to keep her from running away again, bend down, and kiss her forehead. The summer heat intensifies the smell of baby shampoo enveloping Lilly.

"I know you do, Little Bear. Go eat with Mama."

Once she settles in next to Hannah on the blanket, I walk to the edge of the pond and pull up a blade of grass, watching several ducklings trail their mother. Hannah's statement stirs up all the old arguments with the doctors in Ithaca. I look back and take in my wife and daughter as Hannah attempts to coax Lilly to eat the sandwich. Their long, blonde hair flits in the soft wind as they laugh, and Hannah tries to keep Lilly's focus on lunch, not the fish, ducks, and pond. It's a losing battle, but Hannah's patience seems infinite.

Motherhood makes her soul shine. I can tell she is on purpose in life. Her college degrees focused on children. After college, she taught elementary school, and her passion for children deepened. The little ones were her favorites. Her energy intensified as Lilly filled her world.

Despite all that went wrong the last time she got pregnant, Hannah still dreams of four children. She refuses to let Lilly be an only child—and suffer the same fate she herself endured. Late at night, Hannah whispers to me about the loneliness of no brothers or sisters, the pressure as the sole focus of two parents. To fill the emptiness, Hannah had an imaginary friend, Corey, until she was ten. Sometimes, at night in bed, when she talks in her asleep, I catch her still whispering to Corey. Now, Hannah is talking more often of a second child.

Me . . . I am not so sure I am ready. Flashbacks of her face, pale white as the hospital sheets, haunt me. She almost bled to death. Sepsis almost claimed her. Who can say it will be any different next time?

Not just the health risk plagues me. I graduated law school three months ago. I have spent all summer studying for the Texas Bar Exam. The exam finally arrived. Today is Wednesday, day two of the three-day test. Hannah and Lilly join me for lunch to keep my anxiety from morphing into stupidity.

Cursing under my breath, I flip a small, flat pebble into the pond; it skips twice and sinks, startling a large, orange Koi fish gliding just under the surface. I can't think of food. My stomach roils from the nerves caused by the test and now Hannah brings up a second kid, but I know I should try eating something. I will need the energy as the exam consumes the afternoon with impossible questions. Four in ten fail the Texas bar exam—failure would be humiliating.

I stroll back to them, sit on the blanket, and grab a home-made turkey sandwich. It tastes delicious, and suddenly I am hungry, calm for a moment.

"Don't you think Lilly would be happier playing with a little brother or sister?" Hannah asks, pushing the subject, in her subtle but not-so-sly way.

"I'd like a little sister," Lilly pipes in.

I flinch. Now it's two on one.

"Buzz, I'm just trying to get through the bar exam. Can I just do *that* right now?" I say rougher than I intended.

Hannah bristles at my tone. "I thought it might be a good time to talk about it. Thought it might take your mind off the test."

"It's not the right time," I say, trying to cut her off.

Hannah stands and puts her hands on her hips. "Well, I didn't want to get into it, not today, but . . . when will be the right time?" Her matter-of-fact tone suggests I'm close to crossing a line. Her eyes spark a warning.

"Buzz, I'm focused on the test."

"Daniel, all you're focused on is that test!" she says and turns on me quickly. "You didn't even take two days off to go to your family reunion. You sent Lilly and me. A weekend of casseroles and answering the same questions over and over. You want to spend two days alone with my family without me?"

"Not really," I say. A twinge of guilt flashes through me.

"Look, I know the bar exam is huge, but your law books turn you into a ghost." She pauses. Her neck flushes. "It's just Lilly and me. At law school, it was that way. It's been that way all summer. And I'm pretty sure you'll be that way when you are a lawyer. So tell me, when is the right time?"

"We were supposed to wait until after law school with Lilly," I remind her.

"Ugh! . . . Well, I'm glad we didn't," she says.

Hannah's complaints are not without merit. And frankly, I am glad we did not wait for Lilly. I adore her and the time I get to spend with her.

All summer I focused solely on me—focused on the make-it-or-break-it exam and my career, the constant anxiety swamps me. Honestly, I ignored Hannah's desires. Guilt stalks me for putting career ahead of family, the proper balance elusive!

"To be honest, Buzz, it's not just the bar exam," I say.

"Then what is it?"

"The truth is—I can't risk losing you." Worry laces my voice. "Not again."

Hannah sits back down on the blanket and turns her gaze to the mama duck still paddling with all her ducklings in tow. She's quiet, but her quick, gruff movements give away her frustration. "Look, I know you love me, but honestly, you're being overly protective. Motherhood is normal and natural. Yes, there are risks. No risk—no reward. Another baby is worth the small risk. Women have been getting pregnant for millennia. Medical care is better than ever. You dream of making partner one day. I dream of being a mother with four children one day. Don't my dreams matter?"

I sigh. I love and need both my wife and daughter— they're my anchor, especially in the competitive world of the law. Law school was chocked full of type-A gunners, in it to win it for themselves. I don't think the practice of law will be much different. It's no accident there a million insulting jokes about lawyers. I'm being trained to be strong and stoic. But I'm still human. Hard shell. Tender underbelly. Without Hannah and Lilly to keep me anchored in place, it would be easy to drift away when buffeted by storms.

But am I being selfish? What about Hannah's dreams? What's best for Lilly?

Hannah and Lilly share a bag of potato chips. Lilly takes a last bite of turkey and then sprints off after another butterfly. Hannah follows her, answering every question Lilly poses. As they play in the grass, I finish my sandwich and then gather up lunch remnants and the blanket, so we can move toward the car. Lilly runs back to me, explaining a fact she learned about a caterpillar.

Hannah walks up. "I guess it's about time to get you back to the test," she says and takes the blanket from under my arm.

"Buzz…" I start.

"Bear…" she tosses my nickname back at me playfully. She touches my forearm. "It will be different this time."

I take a breath. "Buzz . . . you're right. Lilly needs a little brother or sister."

Hannah smiles a warm, knowing, maternal smile. "I agree."

I wrap my arms around her and give her a tender kiss, sealing the deal.

"Glad you finally came around to my way of thinking, counselor," she teases.

"Was there ever any doubt?"

"Only in your mind," she laughs, her face alight with joy.

"Yeah!" Lilly shouts. "I'm going to have a baby sister!"

CHAPTER
FIVE

JULY. Teton Springs, Texas.

"Medical!" The guard calls out, announcing the pudgy nurse who stands to the right of the officers' picket from which they watch the cellblock all day. Clogs that knock against the concrete floor accentuate her pale, green scrubs. "Any inmate in here need medical?"

Emmett Kendrick shuffles over to the door of his cell. He knocks on the meal slot. A guard unlocks it, opens it, and steps back, his dark gray uniform and ramrod posture visible through the gap.

"Boss. I got to talk to the nurse."

"Kendrick. We'll get to you and your big mouth. Wait quietly."

Emmett sits on the concrete floor next to the door, following commands. If he doesn't, there's no chance the nurse will check on him. He hears the nurse walk by and talk with a couple other inmates. All in hushed tones, but all sound echoes in solitary confinement.

"Ma'am," Jasper says, his voice raspy and tired. He lives a few cells down from Emmett. "Ma'am I have a mighty awful cold, been coughing all night. I can't get no sleep, no rest at all. You have some medicine to take away the cough, make it so I can rest and get better?"

"I'll see what I can do," the nurse says, her stock answer. The same pattern plays out with two more inmates: "I'll see what I can do."

Finally, the nurse knocks on Emmett's door. He rocks forward so he can see the nurse. She squats down, away from the slot, keeping a safe distance, her gaze resigned. Strands of curly black hair have fallen from her normally tight bun.

"You called medical, Kendrick," the nurse says, flatly.

"Yes ma'am. I'm just checking on my heart medicine. For the last five days, I have been without it. I'm supposed to take them every day. Last time I stopped . . . Dr. Patel stopped them, I had a heart attack pretty soon after. Can you check if Nurse Hatcher has them down in pharmacy? Each day they say maybe tomorrow."

The nurse sighs. Wearily, she says, "I'll ask. I'll see what I can do."

She turns and leaves, escorted by the guards, who have slammed the meal slot shut and locked it. The cellblock door clangs shut with hollow finality.

That was the last medical call for the day.

CHAPTER
SIX

NOVEMBER. Houston, Texas.

To help integrate us into the law firm, our department has sent Steve and me to Houston to work with our lawyers there. I like Steve—except for the fact that he's a head taller, damn handsome, and fifty pounds heavier than I am, making me feel slight in contrast. He's over six feet tall, has short blonde hair, and a devout Catholic. Since he's single, he's always attentive to pretty girls, and pays particular care to his clothing—dressed in fine new suits, and French cuffed shirts with an extensive collection of cufflinks. He chews his nails when he's worried, which is most of the time. Goes with the territory as a baby lawyer.

The Houston office is a bit more laid-back, a bit more good-ol' boy than our prim home office in Dallas. One hefty, potbellied partner greeted me in his office by spitting a gob of tobacco juice into a plant. "Son, let me give you a few pointers." Then he spent an hour telling me war stories about trials from the past twenty years. I finally escape to my little office in a daze and behind on my work.

Outside my door, a deep voice booms, "Denise!" It comes

from another old warhorse named Hitch, who offices next to me. "Where are my keys?"

"I'm sure they're right where you left them," she says.

"How is that supposed to help me at all?" Hitch says. The two of them have squabbled like feral alley cats for most of my time in Houston. Denise is a short, fireplug of a lady. She and her husband live on a farm just outside the city. Gray streaks run through her jet-black hair which she keeps in a tight, functional braid. She's a slacks-and-button-down kind of woman. No nonsense and takes no guff. She has been Hitch's secretary for thirty years, which it turns out, is his longest relationship with any woman.

Finally, I hear Denise call out, "I found them in the men's bathroom."

Hitch walks into the hallway, his tall, thin frame in a pinstripe gray suit. The top button of his shirt is undone, and his untied tie drapes down his torso. "How did you—"

"Don't ask," Denise says. "Now, let's get that tie tied," her fingers already working on his top button in an attentive and caring manner that tells me she's done this hundreds of times.

At night, Steve and I return to an apartment the firm rented for the month. In the parking lot, leaves crunch under our steps, and we can smell the wood smoke puff from a chimney on one house just behind the complex. Our apartment's furniture is practical, but clean. We will stay two weeks, then two other new associates will take our place. Hannah has called, and I wrap up my chat with her as Steve tosses out the to-go packages from dinner we picked up at the taco hut around the corner.

"Daniel, everything good on the home front?" Steve asks.

"Yep. Lilly's sleeping. Nobody seems to miss me too much. I'll be ready to get home, though."

"Two weeks is a long time."

I say, "We're trying for another kid," not sure why I

suddenly divulge such intimate facts to Steve. But it feels good to say it out loud to someone.

"Congratulations."

"Yeah, it should be wonderful," I say, my voice tense and with little enthusiasm.

"What?" Steve asks. "You're not on board?"

"I'm on board, just worried," I say. Then I tell him the story. "After Lilly was born, the doctors made some mistakes. . . . *Many* mistakes. Buzz was. . . ."

"Buzz?" Steve asks.

"Hannah, my wife. I call her Buzz her because she can't focus on anything for very long; she flits around like a bumblebee."

"Got it," grins Steve.

"Buzz—Hannah—was high-risk for preterm labor. They put her on bedrest, but they missed diagnosing her with a bilobed placenta."

"A what?" Steve's quizzical look tells me he is confused, and perhaps uncomfortable that I am revealing these personal details. But it feels good to confess my worry to someone.

"See, most of the time there's only one placenta, one lobe —a single piece. With Lilly, the placenta developed two lobes. After Lilly came, the doctors removed only one lobe. They left the other behind." Steve flinches. I continue. "They call it 'retained products of conception,' which is just a way to gloss over that they missed a piece, and that started this pernicious rot."

"That sounds awful," Steve says, still uncomfortable but now invested in the story.

"It was terrible; for weeks after, Hannah suffered bleeding and infections. And, I mean, we were clueless. We aren't doctors, you know. So we did what everyone does, we trusted what they told us. After a while, I noticed the doctors looked as clueless as we were. They hospitalized her repeatedly for observation and IV antibiotics. Then they said they might have to perform a hysterectomy. One night, her fever spiked to 106 degrees. I can still hear her beg me, '*Don't let me die.*'"

"I can't imagine," Steve says, holding the television remote and staring at a spot on the carpet.

"We kept traipsing in and out of the hospital. She kept losing blood. Soon she was so pale, so empty, they wanted to give her a blood transfusion. They couldn't figure it out." Relived anger prompts me to pace. "Twice—after delivery and weeks later—they tried a surgical procedure called a dilation and curettage, which just means you blindly scrape the uterus with a spoon."

Steve winces at my blunt picture. I feel slightly guilty at being so direct, but plow on.

"Nothing worked," I say. "Finally, they let me take her down to the Women's Hospital in Elmira, New York, a few miles down the road. The surgeon there performed another D&C, but he used a sonogram to see what he was doing. I mean, he was not going in blind. It seemed like such a simple change. Evidently never occurred to the brain trust in Ithaca."

"So it worked then?"

"Yeah. That procedure in Elmira took fifteen minutes. Then the bleeding stopped. The infections vaporized. It was funny, that night, Hannah sent me to a local pub to get her a cheeseburger and tater tots. She was back to her normal self in just a few hours."

"Now, that's a crazy story." Steve turns his gaze to the television. "She's good now? Back to normal and all?" as he flips through a couple of channels and lands on a ball game.

"They can't tell us. No one can tell us whether the infection caused permanent scarring, whether it will stop us from having more kids. Instead, they tell us, 'Wait and see. . . . Concentrate on enjoying Lilly.'"

We both allow our focus to drift into the athletes playing

on TV, and the heaviness of my story dissipates. A ballplayer hits a clean triple, and the ballpark fans go wild.

After a few minutes of silence, Steve says, "That is one of the craziest stories I've ever heard." He stops for a beat. "I really hope it works out. I'll keep you two in my prayers."

"Thanks," I say. "We're going to need them."

CHAPTER
SEVEN

FEBRUARY. Midnight. Dallas, Texas.

Outside, a soft, rare snow falls at night in Dallas. Hannah and I cuddle in bed, our toddler nestled between us. We whisper excitedly about the appointment the next morning with Dr. Phillips. Hannah's skin is warm and her voice rich in hope. She has finally found an OB/GYN she trusts, thanks to the other mothers in her circle. Incredibly, Dr. Phillips had an appointment on Friday morning. Before I drift off to sleep, I run my fingers through Lilly's downy hair. She has grown into a precocious two-year-old and insists on sleeping between my wife and me. Not for the first time, I wonder whether a little brother or sister for Lilly will take a miracle.

When we meet him the next morning, in his starched lab coat and a used stethoscope primly draped around his neck, Dr. Phillips exudes intelligence and talent. His brown eyes perch on ebony cheeks.

"Will I be able to get pregnant again?" Hannah asks, her voice full of hope.

Dr. Phillips dashes that hope with no straight answers. "We need more tests," he says. He explains Hannah needs a hysterosalpingogram. The scientific name is mysterious and scary.

Hannah glances at me apprehensively, and my heart swells. I want to do anything I can to protect my wife, but I'm a lawyer, not a doctor.

"And what exactly is that test?" I ask. "A hystero...?"

"A hysterosalpingogram." He dodges my question. "I'm going to refer you to one of my colleagues who specializes in fertility."

The fact he jumped to a fertility specialist strikes me cold. I reach for Hannah's hand to reassure her, and she takes it gratefully.

The doctor continues, "It's an X-ray procedure we use with some saline and dye to see whether the fallopian tubes are open and to measure the uterine cavity, . . . to see how open it is and its shape. It's a short outpatient procedure. Most take about fifteen minutes to perform. We have to figure out the extent of any scarring."

"Could the scarring ... could the scarring prevent me from having any more children?" Hannah asks, her voice catching. Hannah's tight, thin smile tells me the scarring may not be just physical. Motherhood runs through her identity, to amputate that dream would leave a deep wound.

In a clinical tone, Dr. Phillips says, "No rushing to conclusions. Let's get the hysterosalpingogram. Then we'll know much more. You'll like Dr. Abrams. If there's an issue with scarring, he's the one to figure it out. I've seen him do amazing things."

"Do we schedule that through you?"

"The ladies up front can help you. They'll coordinate an appointment with Dr. Abrams, and we'll go from there." Dr. Phillips closes the file on his desk. He stands and extends his hand for a firm handshake as he says, "Remember there are *many* ways to become a parent these days." The perfunctory nature of his tone pisses me off.

All the way home, I think about how sick I am of doctors. Hannah stared out the window, despondent. We went to the meeting elated, and left deflated.

A couple of weeks later, an assistant with a big smile takes our information for Dr. Abrams's files. After a few minutes of waiting, a nurse shuffles us back to Dr. Abrams's office. I look at his myriad diplomas. He went to medical school in South Africa and completed his fellowships in Israel. Hope springs up. Maybe he will have something new to say. Dr. Abrams flips through Hannah's charts. Where Dr. Phillips had been pressed and starched, a former Air Force physician, Dr. Abrams's gray hair frizzes atop his short, stocky frame, scrubs, and comfortable sneakers. He asks a few high-level questions. We tell him the story of the dimwitted doctors in Ithaca. We've told this story a thousand times.

"Look," I say. "Dr. Phillips tells us you can do some amazing things with fertility. But I need to know if you're the guy. Hannah *will* have a second baby. That's a fact. So you're either on this bus or off this bus. I need to know now."

Dr. Abrams's eyes widen and then narrow as he sizes me up. Then a big grin grows on his cherub-like face. "Okay . . . I'm on this bus," he decides. "First thing to do is have a 'look-see.' The procedure I recommend is called a hysterosalpin-gogram. Basically, we take a needle, inject some die in the uterine cavity, and then trace it with an X-ray to see where it goes. We want open fallopian tubes; we want space for a baby to grow. Let's see where we are."

Hope flashes across Hannah's face. She tucks her long blond hair behind her ears. She leans forward, attentive and eager.

Dr. Abrams, although probably seventy, is a whirlwind of energy. As Hannah and I leave his office, he buzzes back into his lab and barks orders to his team. We walk to the elevator, feeling hopeful for the first time in a long time.

"Do you believe in him?" Hannah asks, biting her lip.

"As a matter of fact, I do," I say, reflecting that doubt is destructive. Faith can bend the impossible to your will.

"And you really think Lilly will have a baby brother or sister?" Longing wells up in her large hazel eyes.

"Yes, absolutely."

Hannah's voice hitches. "I didn't want to think it was a possibility—you know—the doctors in Ithaca made it so that Lilly was destined to be an only child."

"They screwed up, no doubt about that. But now we've got Dr. Abrams on our team. Doctors can work miracles these days."

The elevator doors close, giving us privacy.

Hannah searches my face. "Do you think I'm being selfish wanting another baby?"

"No, Buzz. Dreams are not selfish. Dreams make life worth living." I squeeze her hand to reassure her. Her warm, slender fingers are interlaced with mine. She leans against me, drinking in my strength. I won't let her down.

The "look-see" procedure (or hysterosalpingogram) takes place on a Wednesday, ten days later. The hallway in the radiology department in the hospital is thirty-six steps end to end. I know this because I can't stop counting each pace in my head as I walk and worry. I worry about my wife, my work, my future. I worry about taking so much time off work so early in my job at the law firm. I am only a few months into being a lawyer, and the demands on my time are intense. The partners are brilliant, but always working. They demand precision and perfection. It will be daunting and difficult apprenticeship from Associate to Partner.

I hate hospitals. The universal pungent smell of germicide and the harsh ultraviolet light. For places of caring, they usually present as inhumane, sterile, and repugnant. Even though I'm pacing, there really is no place to go, so I plop back down on the hard hallway chair.

I stare at the red "IN USE" sign above the doorway to the X-ray room where they're examining Hannah. The red light finally goes off. My heart beats faster. Hannah will emerge soon. An MRI machine in a room behind me bangs away. The magnets spin as they develop an image. I wonder what news that patient will receive. No one comes to Radiology for a wellness checkup.

The door cracks open. I expect to see Dr. Abrams, but it's Hannah. She appears slowly, gathering her purse on her shoulder. She stares at the floor, her long, blond hair mussed from lying on the table.

"How did it go?" I ask.

"It was awful." Tears welling up in her eyes. "One of the most painful things I've ever endured. They had to stop halfway through. The needle couldn't go anywhere. The dye couldn't get through. I couldn't take it, so they stopped."

"Did Dr. Abrams say anything?"

"He said he wanted to get the radiologist's report, and we could check back in a few days."

"So it could be good or bad, we just don't know yet." I try to sound optimistic.

"It's bad. I know it's bad. I could see the X-ray technician's face as she did the test. She looked horrified, like she'd never seen what she was looking at before. Like she'd seen a monster."

"Let's hear what Dr. Abrams has to say. We have to start somewhere."

"We're nowhere, Daniel. Because of the doctors in Ithaca, we're nowhere." She pushes away some of her tears with the back of her hand. "Thank God we have Lilly. If those doctors had done anything to her . . . ," she growls. I imagine a female grizzly standing on her hind legs roaring at Dr. Brown, ferociously protecting her cubs.

As we make our way out to the parking lot, Hannah

descends into silence. I can tell she wants to withdraw, to prepare for the worst.

Fear gnaws at me, but I push it aside. I can't afford doubt. Hannah needs my strength and resolve.

When we meet with Dr. Abrams a few days later, he confirms the X-ray technician's concerns. "You have scarring inside and outside the uterus. Normally, when we do this test, the die will show a uterine cavity that looks like an upside-down triangle, an inch or two long. But in your case, the X-ray showed an area smaller than a thumbnail. No access to the fallopian tubes, to the ovaries, no space for an embryo to attach and develop. The scarring has essentially glued the entire uterus shut."

My heart sinks. Next to me, crumpled tissue in hand, Hannah dabs tears away from the dark circles under her eyes.

"How do we fix it?" I ask.

Dr. Abrams takes measure of me, and then Hannah. His eyes flash, then he says, "Surgery. I must get in there and see what I can do. I've spoken to Dr. Phillips, and we will do it together. He will perform a laparoscopy. He will blow up the abdomen with air and go in through the navel, using a laparoscope. It's like a slender lighted telescope and it allows us to see what's going on and perform surgery. Dr. Phillips will work to remove the scar tissue from the outside of the ovaries. I'll work from the inside and remove scar tissue. That's the next step if you're up for it."

Too devastated to answer, Hannah looks stunned.

"I'm up for it," I say, knowing it's a tremendous gamble. "Are you?" I ask my wife.

Hannah searches my face. She hesitates and looks at Dr. Abrams. She takes in his frizzy gray hair and old, wise eyes and risks trusting him, in spite of the fact that it was the doctors in Ithaca who ruined her healthy body. "Dreams are worth fighting for. I'm up for it."

Dr. Abrams claps his hands in triumph. "Excellent! Angela at the front desk can get you scheduled."

Hannah and I stand up to leave.

Dr. Abrams says, "I've seen a lot of dark days in this business, Hannah. You just have to believe in the next sunrise."

CHAPTER
EIGHT

MARCH. Houston, Texas.

"Now why in the blue fuck would you have done something like that in front of a jury?" Hitch barks, his long lanky arms punctuating his comments.

Steve and I are enduring a post mock-trial debrief from Hitch at one of his favorite watering holes. It's not exactly a strip club—the waitresses' corsets sufficient to make the place "respectable," which means the dinner is reimbursable as a mentoring effort. Steve and I spent most of the day going one-on-one in our firm's trial academy held offsite each spring in Houston, Texas. They assign us a mock case, and we try it before a jury of unemployed folks looking for something to do for a day. Hitch served as our Judge, and ultimately mentor. He has invited us to a "debrief" which seems more like a whipping. His eyes follow a waitress in a tight skirt across the floor. He nods, and then turns on Steve.

"You never ask a question on cross-examination to which you don't know the answer. You never ask why? Or how? Anything open ended. You lose complete control of the witness."

"I thought it was important to get out the background," Steve says.

"Look, you can't lose control of a witness on cross; they ain't your friends, and they won't do you no favors." Hitch takes a long draw off a double Old Fashioned. "Boys . . . you end screwing up like that on an actual trial, and your opponent will skin you. Clients pay us to win, no matter the facts. That's just the truth of it."

A waitress clears our plates and the remnants of our steak dinner, the only solace to what Hitch deems a piss-poor effort at the mock trial.

"Darlin', send us another round," Hitch says, touching his index finger to the remnants of his drink. He pauses a minute to take out a cigar, trims it, and places it to his lips. Then he returns to his critique. He looks at Steve. "When you do an opening, lay out a story, something the jury can follow. Almost like a fable. Yours was too many facts, too much for them to take in at one time."

"But I laid out a theme," Steve says, "A deal is a deal, and then I argued the contract."

"'A deal is a deal' is a phrase, son. Not a story. Someone is a hero, someone got wronged, and someone is a villain. That's the way it works in a story. You come out the gates with something stale like 'a deal is a deal' and you're going to lose them. These folks have a million other things on their minds; give them something to figure out, a puzzle. You got to give them the players, and you have to tell them why they should pay attention to you all week."

The waitress quickly returns with our drinks, and Hitch hands her a credit card. "Look, we do these mock trials to get y'all ready for a real court. Lord knows you need the help. These days, most cases settle. Hell, the way it's goin' right now, you might not try an actual case for years. But if you get a live one, you've gotta be ready to go. Hear me?"

Steve and I nod. Hitch is correct. As baby lawyers at a

large firm, the chances of us sitting first chair in a trial are remote, if not nonexistent. But eventually, we'll step into the well of the court with all the weight of a client's case on our shoulders. That flash of responsibility makes Hitch's critique seem less harsh. We have to hone our skills for the day when eventually we will get to go to trial. That may be years away, but better to prepare. Hitch turns toward me.

"Daniel, your directs, your cross exams were *okay*—tight in places. But you still lost that one witness—she kept rambling and lead you around by the nose. Tight! Your questions must be tight. One fact at a time. Feed it to the witness. If they disagree, smack them with what they said in their deposition or a document. But never lose the control of a hostile witness."

I take a draw off my drink and hide behind the rim of my glass of beer. I take my medicine from Hitch, but don't want to comment for fear of drawing further rebuke.

"That closing, though, *that* had promise. A few more years, and you might close with the best of them." Hitch pauses and pays for our steak dinner, leaving a generous tip for the sultry waitress. "Boys, focus on the story. Focus on control." Hitch glances at his watch. "Gents, Wife Number Four is going to be mad at me, I got to go. Now I'm an hour late for bridge out at the Country Club because of our little dinner here. Y'all enjoy your drinks."

He downs his double Old Fashioned that just arrived. He pulls a match so he can light his cigar as soon as he is out of the door saying, "Y'all could be skilled trial lawyers—just focus on the fundamentals." With that, Hitch waves a hand at us dismissively and heads for the valet. He's soon gone into the night.

After a moment or two of silence, Steve says, "I guess we should head back to the hotel."

"Shit," I say. "Hitch was our ride."

CHAPTER
NINE

MARCH. Dallas, Texas.

A few weeks after our initial meeting with Dr. Abrams, I sit in the surgery waiting room on a hard steel-blue chair. The whole place feels industrial, sterile. A dying ballast in one light causes it to flicker repeatedly. The procedures started a 7:00 a.m. and were supposed to take an hour. At 8:30 a.m.—ninety minutes in—concern washes over me. My hopes of a quick fix are evaporating. The clock in the room ticks past 9:00 a.m. I have received no word from anyone about progress in the operating room with Hannah.

An attendant sits behind a glass check-in window. "They haven't finished yet."

I gaze at a well-worn magazine, but find myself re-reading the same paragraphs again and again. The clock's second hand ticks time out loudly. Finally, forty-five minutes later, a tired-looking Dr. Phillips, dressed in his scrubs under a starched, white lab coat, walks toward me.

"How did it go?" I ask.

He sits in a chair across from me, and recounts the facts with dry, military precision. "It was a difficult surgery. The scarring was pervasive." That statement sends a chill through me. "I've not seen scarring to that extent before. Dr. Abrams will come out and tell you about his portion of the surgery. The laparotomy went as well as we could expect. I could remove a substantial amount of the scar tissue outside the uterus and along the ovaries. The incision is small, right below her navel, so the scar should not be noticeable, and there should be no complications from that. But we distended the belly with air as part of the procedure, so she will be sore from that for a few days. The abdominal muscles received a significant stretch. Any residual gas will take a while to work its way out of her system, and that will amplify her discomfort in the first twenty-four hours."

"Most of that sounds promising. Sounds like we're on a road to success?"

"We'll have to see how she heals. Dr. Abrams can give you more details and his opinion." He looks at me sternly. "I think it's important when she wakes up that you prepare her because she will probably *not* have another child."

The statement blasts through me, my heartbeat throbs in my ears.

After dropping that bomb, Dr. Phillips gets up and leaves.

I'm not a fan of Dr. Phillips's bedside manner. I fume in silence, but I can't blame him; he has done nothing wrong. He has been honest in his opinion and is trying to help. But as he walks away, fury wells up inside me. Healing is not merely science—it's also art, intention, and faith.

One of the worst parts of surgery is the helpless waiting. I'm stranded. I must sit while Hannah is unconscious and at the mercy of professionals I hardly know. It's a forced, uncomfortable trust.

In the corner near me, a woman pours a cup of coffee from a carafe set out for visitors. It smells burnt. But it's something to do while she waits for her loved-one under the knife.

Another half hour passes, and Dr. Abrams finally appears, a ball of enthusiastic energy. His surgical cap sits askew, and his hair pokes wildly out on one side. He sits down next to me and pats me on the forearm.

"How did the surgery go?" I ask.

"Splendidly!" Dr. Abrams grins, proud of job well done. "No guarantees, we'll see how she mends, but the surgery went well."

I shift in my chair, taken aback by the contrast between the assessment of the two doctors. "But—Dr. Phillips basically told me adoption would be our only choice."

"Forget about Dr. Phillips being sour in the mouth. He can be a bit of a pessimist. Brilliant surgeon. Indeed, his half of the surgery was something to watch—a work of art. Amazing set of hands. He cleaned up a significant amount of scar tissue and that will make things easier for me. But he can be a Gloomy Gus."

I nod agreement. "And your half?"

"I removed significant amounts of scar tissue from the corners, from the openings to the fallopian tubes. They may stay open; an ovum may pass through. Time will tell. We hope the uterine lining regenerates itself. I snipped away some of the scarring and then crushed—."

"Crushed?"

"Yes, with a clamp. I crushed the scar tissue on the lining bit by bit. That's what took so long. Delicate work. Nip by nip. But it should reestablish blood flow to the lining. After that, the tissue should regenerate. Remember, we just need sufficient room for an embryo to attach, to grow. A pregnancy, the natural stretch from the baby developing, will take care of the rest. There was significant scarring. Took a long time, that and an argument with Dr. Phillips. He thought I was going too far, that I was going to puncture the uterus. But I know what I'm doing. I went slowly. I could feel it; just a little further was how I needed to do it." Dr. Abrams mimes his surgical technique with his hands. "But it made Dr. Phillips a little crazy."

I smile. "So what now?"

"Now we wait. See how the body heals. The human body can do remarkable things." He stands and says warmly, "I'm off to make babies. Keep her spirits up. We may be on our way to some wonderful things here."

Dr. Abrams bounds away, grabbing a cookie from a tray on the counter. He disappears out the door, his sneakers squeaking loudly on the hallway tiles. I can't help but grin.

A few minutes later, a post-op nurse calls for me. The nurses have propped Hannah up with a pillow and her blond hair, damp from sweat, frames her face. She is foggy from the anesthesia, but peace fills her expression. I take her slender fingers in my palm, and kiss them, careful not to knock the IV line.

"How did it go?" she says, hope growing in her large hazel eyes.

"Dr. Abrams is pleased. He's optimistic," I say in a quiet, reassuring voice. I don't share "Gloomy Gus" and his pessimism. To heal, Hannah needs to believe that she can. The placebo and nocebo effects are both real.

She smiles and drifts back to sleep. I continue to hold her hand, my heart pounding in my chest. *This has to work.*

Once back home, Lilly is eager to see her mother and crawls into bed with her. Hannah runs her fingers through Lilly's fine blonde hair, and together, they watch a documentary on alpacas. A toddler does not understand the concept of surgery and recuperating. Luckily, Hannah's dad has come into town to help distract Lilly. But when not with Grandpa, Lilly rests in bed with her mother, and it's difficult to define who is comforting whom. Over time, the pain and soreness from the surgery disappears. Hope and anxiety, however, linger all around us.

CHAPTER
TEN

MARCH. Teton Springs, Texas.

Emmett looks out the barred window. With the warmer weather of March, the doves have moved on to other territory. But Emmett can't move on—he's stuck in solitary confinement. Occasionally, he still gets a glimpse of the Red-Tail Hawk through his prison glass, and its soaring freedom feeds his soul.

The State of Texas doesn't pay inmates any stipend, even if they work at the prison. Instead, Emmett receives $7.50 per month from parishioners in the local Presbyterian Church to spend in the prison commissary. The rental on a typewriter is $2.00 per day. He could theoretically purchase a typewriter for $225, but that is almost three years of saving. Today should be the day the library delivers him the three books he asked for—his limit on the intra-library loan program.

The sound of the hard rubber casters from the cart are obvious on the concrete flooring in the hallway. When you are in solitary confinement, it's like blindness as some of your senses become more pronounced. As the cart pulls up to his window, Emmett can see that Officer Larkin is the Corrections Officer chaperoning the prison orderly—another inmate—on rounds today. If she had been born in a big city rather than a prison town, Officer Larkin might have become a model. Her sultry beauty is oddly accentuated by the gray-black prison fatigues and the no-nonsense body armor she wears. She smiles at him through the window in his cell door.

The thick spine of a copy of the Federal Reporter pushes through the meal slot on his door. The library orderly holds onto it until Emmett grabs the book. Two more books pass through in the same manner. This is the case law he needs. Then a thin type-writer appears. It's a special typewriter developed for prisons—all clear housing, with no handles or parts outside the plastic frame. The simple design prevents inmates from breaking off items to create shanks to stab the guards or other prisoners. Officer Larkin uses her baton draw his attention to the meal slot.

"How long do you need the typewriter, Emmett?" she asks. "They're going to make me fill out an inventory report if you keep it past my shift. You'll help me on that point, won't you?"

"Ma'am, I think a couple hours will do. I have a short motion to type up for the Judge. Then I'll be finished and can turn it back to you."

"Fair enough. I'll come back at 1600; they make me punch out at 1630."

"I appreciate it ma'am."

"I know you do, Emmett."

Emmett sets the typewriter on the edge of his bunk and sits crisscross on the floor. His cot has been a makeshift desk for the past several years as he has tried to work his case through the court system.

After staring at the blank page, Emmett begins, one key at a time. He pecks out his request to the court. He needs a lawyer.

To the Honorable Judge Navarro.

I, Emmett Kendrick, humbly ask the court to appoint an attorney to assist me in my legal dispute against the State of Texas and the Teton Springs facility. This is the second motion of this type I have filed; the first being denied. I respectfully ask that the Court reconsider the earlier denial, as my case has now survived summary judgment, and it's headed to trial. As a prisoner in solitary confinement in the Texas prison system, I believe preparing for trial without counsel will be an undue hardship and could impact my Constitutional rights. To be blunt for the Court, I am locked in my cell twenty-three hours per day, and have little access to law library materials, and potential witnesses. Preparing a proper presentation of my case to a jury may well be impossible. Because of the severe limitations on my mobility and access to materials, and because I am a long-time incarcerated prisoner with limited funds, I respectfully request that the Court see fit to appoint counsel to represent me in the upcoming trial in October.

Emmett types an exact copy for his records, signs them both and then folds one, placing it in an envelope. Until 4:00 p.m. he reads legal cases and regularly glances at the envelope on the edge of his sink—it's his prayer for a fair trial on his claims. True to her word, Officer Larkin shows up right at 4:00 p.m.

"You ready for me, Emmett?" she prods.

"Yes, ma'am." Emmett passes the books through the door slot, then the typewriter. Finally, he hands her the envelope. "Ma'am, I'm not sure my balance in the commissary will cover the postage. If I'm short, would you make sure this envelope makes its way back to me so I can mail it next month after I get my stipend?"

Officer Larkin stares through the small window in the door.

"Emmett, I'll make sure it gets mailed," her voice sounds distant as it trundles through the meal slot. "If you're short, I'm sure I have some change in my pocket."

Emmett slides the envelope through the opening, and watches as Officer Larkin leaves the unit, flirting with the guard in the picket on her way out.

CHAPTER
ELEVEN

MARCH. Dallas, Texas.

Internal wounds are maddening because they are impossible to watch heal. *Is Hannah healing properly? Or were we at yet another dead end?* Hannah and I return to the hospital radiology department for the verdict.

The first few moments in Dr. Abrams's office are thick with suspense. Then he springs it on us like a game show host delivering a prize. "I have good news! The dye shows that we have sufficient space to implant an embryo once we get to that point."

"How soon can that happen?" Hannah asks, excitement flashing through her large, beautiful eyes.

"When the body is ready. Maybe a month. Your blood-work came back. Hormones are all out of balance, so we'll have to adjust those. That takes several injections. And we have to rectify your T-cell count."

"T-cells?" Hannah asks, concern enveloping her words.

"Your T-cells are extraordinarily high. Your ordeal in Ithaca probably elevated them. We have to get that under control. Or your own healthy T-cells will attack and kill your embryo. T-cells fight off anything the body perceives as a threat . . . virus, bacteria. Unfortunately, these cells don't distinguish between pathogens and an embryo in the early stages. So it's imperative that we reduce the T-cell levels."

"So what, a few pills?" she asks, hoping for an easy fix.

"No, I'm afraid. You need an infusion every week to negate the Natural Killer T-cells. We've had good success with intravenous immunoglobulin, or IVIG. The good news is, if we can get your T-cell count down, we can implant an embryo!"

"So . . . success?" I ask.

"Success!" he grins. "I've seen IVIG work wonders with this type of condition. I'm fairly confident we can get a solid result here, too."

"Is it expensive?" I ask. My law school debt flashes through my head.

"Unfortunately, yes, *very*. But unless we get the T-cells under control, we are at a dead end, full stop. Hannah's body will eliminate the embryo before it implants and grows into a healthy baby."

Hannah squirms at the thought of her own body betraying her cherished dream. She bites her lower lip, and crosses her arms defensively.

Dr. Abrams continues, "We've come a long way already. But we still have a long way to go. In vitro fertilization (IVF) is a complex series of procedures used to help with fertility. If you trust me, we'll likely get to the finish line successfully. That's my plan. But it's up to you."

I think of Hannah leading around a group of first graders on a Halloween parade. When she was a teacher, she dressed up as a clown—full makeup. Joy radiated out from behind her red nose. Children make her happy. Her own children define her.

"We haven't come this far to give up now," Hannah says. "But can we afford it?"

"It's usually around $5,000 per week." Dr. Abrams clarifies. "For up to forty weeks."

Hannah gasps at the staggering sum.

"Will insurance cover it?" I ask, seeking hope.

"Some insurance companies do. But most don't."

Five thousand dollars a week. Forty weeks to a full-term baby … we're looking at $200,000 of debt. *More debt.* The total amount is overwhelming. I have already saddled us with $150,000 in law school debt, we just bought a house and took on a mortgage. Car payments, utilities, insurance, it all stacks up to a sick feeling in the pit of my stomach.

I take a deep breath to steady my nerves. I take my wife's hand. Her fingers interlace with mine. "Okay. We'll make it work. Somehow."

"Great! We are still on this bus!" Dr. Abrams claps his hands together. His frizzy hair stands up with his excitement.

Hannah smiles at me, grateful. "Hero work."

"A happy wife makes a happy life," I say.

I'd better get promoted at the law firm—or this baby could bankrupt us. But I don't want her to worry about that.

CHAPTER
TWELVE

APRIL. Downtown. Dallas, Texas.

During my first year at the law firm, I have settled into a steady routine. I arrive by 6:30 am. I've taken to sharing a cup of coffee with one paralegal on my floor. John's severe military high-and-tight cut red hair frames his gray eyes full of wisdom. We sit in a conference room and watch the sunrise, trading stories about our lives before the law firm. He's nearing retirement, and he often has more interesting stories than me. Then begins the day's work.

I leave the office when my work allows. On the way out, I pass the portrait of William Paul Moore III, our Managing Partner. His cold eyes peer out from a stoic expression under salt-and-pepper hair. He controls my career. I've never even met him.

Grinding away, that's the rhythm required to advance. Only the weather has changed, which morphed from the deep chill of winter to the warmth of a Texas spring. I commute to and from work each day, thirty minutes each way. I resent the commute because it's idle time. When I am not busy, thoughts swirl through my mind. The cost of the IVF, the risk that it might not work, and what failure would mean for Hannah. As I near home, I force those thoughts away. I want to focus on the possibilities and triumphs to come, keeping only positive beliefs front of mind. I don't want to drain my wife's precious maternal energy with my worries.

When I arrive home, Hannah is talking on the phone. Her long blond hair hangs over her shoulder in an elegant, precise braid. My hard-charging toddler plays nearby, her golden hair a rat's nest. Hannah's friend Yuki sits at the kitchen table. She gives me a small, friendly wave. Yuki is our age and a first-generation immigrant from Laos. Her shiny jet-black hair falls to her waist and accentuates the bright yellow silk dress she wears.

Yuki stands and gives me a kind, platonic kiss on the cheek. "Keep her safe."

"Working on it," I say.

Yuki waves goodbye to my wife and leaves.

I set down my briefcase in my home office, where I work most nights and weekends. Credit card applications blanket my desk as I try to find the funds to cover the IVIG. I remove my blue pinstripe suit jacket and hang it in the closet—time to leave the law behind for a while. On the shelf above the clothes rod, tucked inside a stack of undershirts, rests a bag of chocolates. As I do every night after work, I take out a morsel, put it in my suit pants pocket, and go find my daughter. Lilly stands in the hallway, pushing a "car" fashioned from a large, brown cardboard box. Hannah and Lilly have crafted head-lights out of colored paper. A bright blue cotton dress with white flowers hangs above her bare feet, a baseball cap turned backward on her head. She inherited my family's pudgy little toes and Hannah's beautiful large eyes.

"I didn't forget you, Little Bear. Here, this is for you." I take the chocolate out of my pocket.

Lilly smiles with delight and curls her hands into pretend paws to take the chocolate as her alter-ego, "Little Bear." As long as I can remember, Hannah has called me, "Bear"—her protector—and Lilly naturally became "Little Bear," my cub. Lilly is a creature of patterns. She leaves the box, grabs the chocolate—excitement flashing through her eyes—and shuffles down the hall to show Hannah the tiny present. I wish I could take credit, but I can't. With all that's happening at the firm, it's easy for me to become forgetful. Hannah thoughtfully hid that bag of chocolates, making this nightly ritual effortless. This tiny custom is something I look forward to at the end of every day.

After changing clothes, I find Hannah setting the table for dinner. Lilly twirls in the kitchen, chocolate smudged on her lips. They have set out six place settings. Three for Hannah, Lilly and me. Three sit in front of stuffed animals Lilly has chosen and placed in chairs. A memory from Ithaca rockets through my mind: *"Four is the number of kids I want to have. Don't let them take that away."*

Hannah continues her conversation on the phone, the receiver tucked between her ear and shoulder. She smiles at me and runs a hand through Lilly's hair and shuffles her off to play. Hannah is a master multitasker. I watch her gracefully place a few more items on the table. I frown, seeing the bruises that cover the back of her hands—bruises from the IV needles.

The nurses ignored her yet again! I run my fingers through my thinning hair. Anger wells up in me, and my jaw clinches. In Ithaca, we learned a butterfly needle—a thin needle usually reserved for kids—was the key to Hannah's tiny veins. But the small gauge of the butterfly needle makes the IV drip take longer, and nurses don't like to waste time. As a result, they ignore our experience with hospitals and Hannah's body. Each new nurse or tech is the same. They half-listen, smile, and grab a regular needle. Most say, "I got this," or "Don't worry, I do this all the time." They then miss a vein once or twice with the large needle. A bruise soon puddles at the injured spot. The nurse will place a bandage on the puncture, and then finally reach for the butterfly needle they should have used from the start. They apologize sheepishly in a way that blames it on an anomaly. They "don't know why it wouldn't cooperate."

Hannah never says, "I told you so." I wish she would be more assertive. But I guess that's my role as her protector.

The large purple contusions on Hannah's hands reveal that today's nurse was unskilled. Once the IV starts, the drip takes about an hour. Hannah takes Lilly with her; Dr. Abrams and his staff love children.

Hannah hangs up the phone.

"The nurse really got you today," I say, motioning to her bruised hands.

Hannah ignores the opportunity to complain. "There's some good news," Hannah says, a smile perched on her face.

"Tell me."

"The T-cell count is dropping. Dr. Abrams says it's steady, almost normal. We're close, Bear."

"That's great news, isn't it?"

"More procedures," she sighs.

"No way around those," I say.

Hannah glances at the back of her hands, then shakes them as if trying to rid herself of the bruises. "They don't listen."

"Make them listen. Be more assertive."

"You know that's not my style." She yawns. "I'm tired . . . exhausted."

"Maybe two kids is enough," I say.

Hannah whips around, her eyes full of disbelief and a twinge of anger. She plants her fists on her hips. "Why would you say something like that?"

"I'm just saying, maybe we're meant to have a smaller family, a beautiful, but small family."

"Four, Daniel. Four kids."

"Two could work, though. You get to be a mom. Lilly gets a little brother or sister. It could be enough," I offer more as a question than a statement.

"Two is *not* enough. You know that!"

I add up all the bills in my head and pile on all the time and effort it is going to take to advance at the firm.

"I'm just saying, with me trying to become a partner, the debt we're racking up. Maybe we should, you know, adjust our expectations."

"It's just money, Daniel."

"*A lot* of money," I snap.

"You didn't seem to worry about money for law school."

"Buzz, that's different. That's my career; that's how we make a living. We had to spend that money to make money."

"So your dreams get funded and mine get cut because yours come with a paycheck?"

"That's not what I meant."

"*That* is exactly what you meant." Her voice is husky with the tears she holds back. Hannah plops into a chair, avoiding my gaze.

"I'm just saying that we can't do this whole Dr. Abrams thing three times. It'll bankrupt us."

"But he said getting pregnant might fix everything, get rid of all the scarring," Hannah says, with a twinge of doubt.

"I didn't mean to upset you," I sigh, exasperated. "But good work on being more assertive!"

She grins, and the argument evaporates.

"Let's focus on kiddo number two for now."

She nods in agreement. "One baby at a time."

I glance at my watch. "It's time for your shots."

Hannah glances toward the hallway bathroom where we keep all the needles high on a cabinet shelf away from Lilly.

"Let's get them over with." Fatigue with the entire process spills out in those few simple words.

After the surgery, Dr. Abrams, true to his word, turned

Hannah into a half-biology, half-chemistry experiment. Prenatal vitamins comprised the full extent of "add-ons" we did with Lilly. Now, Dr. Abrams has Hannah on a menagerie of pharmaceuticals—the wackiest being Viagra suppositories to increase blood flow to heal. Those raised an eyebrow or two when I turned in the prescription. The compounding pharmacist checked the recipe twice. We traipse off to the pharmacy regularly to pick up another white bag filled with the doctor's concoctions and stapled with receipts. Insurance covers "regular" items; anything "unique" is out of pocket. *Dr. Abrams is proving remarkably unique.* Each receipt adds dollar signs to our debt. Besides pills, creams, and suppositories, we have injections. Every night, at home at 7:00 pm Hannah receives an injection of estrogen, progesterone, or both.

"It's easy," Dr. Abrams told me, a bit of mischief in his eyes peering out at me from under his fluffy gray eyebrows. "After you do it a few times, you'll be a professional."

"Doc, I've never stuck a needle into anybody," I say.

"Don't think of it like that. Think of it as blessing her with hormones."

I watched a few videos on injections, but nothing really prepared me for the first time I stuck a needle into Hannah's tender skin. To prepare the shot, you draw the liquid into a syringe. The needles are long, really long. Time slows during the injection, and the tiny steel tubes seem to take forever to slide beneath the skin. Some hormones require a wider gauge needle to flow through; the more viscous the liquid, the wider the needle. The progesterone is oil-based and thick. So it requires a larger gauge needle, something akin to a pipeline. I joke and refer to it as a "pig sticker." When the time comes, with all my novice skill, I hold my breath and try not to hurt Hannah. It's a unique role to be a clinician and husband.

The videos warned me about all the wrong places you can hit with a needle: blood vessels, nerves, bone. That leads to analysis paralysis in the unqualified. To help, each week the nurses sketch an oval on Hannah's hip with a permanent marker. I aim for that oval over the next seven days. So, all I have to do is draw the shot and shoot the hoop. Every night. They have turned Hannah into a human dartboard. Estrogen is a friendly hormone with wonderful glowing side effects. Progesterone is more spiteful, often exposing protracted crankiness. When we give her a big dose of that, I lie low for the rest of the night.

Night after night, we hold hands and commit to pushing forward.

CHAPTER
THIRTEEN

APRIL. Downtown. Dallas, Texas.

Outside my office window, spring has slipped quickly into summer-like weather, another record-setting month in Texas. Most everyone hunkers down in the air conditioning. Draft briefs and legal opinions litter my desk at the firm.

As I do every day, I had arrived early, before the staff, so I brew the first pot of coffee. I often joke about the beauty of sunrise from my office window. Once John and I finish our communal cup of coffee, I sit down at my desk and run through my "To Do" list. After corralling some sort of order to my day, I dig into one of my projects. Today's task is a complicated discovery dispute. The other side says we owe them documents as potential evidence in a case. We say it's a "fishing expedition." They have no case. They are looking for one. The legal opinions on the issue that I am reading are detailed and difficult. The issues and legal reasoning are tough to work through. But, despite the intellectual rigor of it all, it's a long way from the meaningful impact I had dreamed of making when I entered law school. Then I wanted to change the world. Now I am a simple gear in a law firm churning out motions, trying to work my way up and bide my time until I can become lead counsel on a case years from today.

It's late afternoon, and I have been pounding away at a motion for ten-plus hours. I am craving a jolt of coffee. When I stroll back in from the break room at 4:45 pm, the phone rings. It's Lisa Ballard, the clerk for United States Magistrate Judge Navarro. I know Lisa from the local bar association. Lisa and I exchange some catch-up pleasantries on the phone, and then she asks.

"Judge wants to know if you'd be interested in her appointing you in a case."

A bolt of excitement jumps within me, but I try to keep my voice measured.

"What kind of case?"

"We've had a prisoner, a Mr. Emmett Kendrick, make it past summary judgment. It's impossible for him to prepare a trial on his own. He's locked in Administrative Segregation, you know, solitary confinement . . . AdSeg."

I look at all the work piled on my desk. Time remains a precious commodity: I am short of it, but the opportunity has my full interest.

"What's the issue?"

"It's an Eighth Amendment conditions-of-confinement case. Mr. Kendrick alleges the prison fails to give him his heart medicine regularly, placing him at risk for another heart attack. Let me give you the case number. Look it up, see if it's something you would think about doing. The docket sheet is long. He's been at this for a while. Trial starts in Wichita Falls in October."

Less than six months—a bullet train to a jury trial. I scribble down the case number.

"I'll look it up. Let me check it out and talk with the head of my trial department to see if the firm wants to do it. I'll call you back."

I hang up. A thrill fills my body. Jury trials are rare treasures to young trial lawyers. Hitch was right, less than five percent of cases ever make it to trial. When they do, the stakes are often high "bet-the-company" cases. Clients want seasoned, gray-haired lawyers like William Paul Moore III to try their cases. This relegates associates like me to years of heavy lifting behind the scenes. My firm is a big firm, trying large commercial cases. It will take years before I have any opportunity to take a witness in court, longer to sit "second chair" on a trial, probably a decade before I am "first chair," leading a trial team in court. Lisa just offered me a baby-lawyer's dream—to leapfrog forward in time. I would be first chair in a federal court trial, *unbelievable*.

I call Hannah and tell her the career-altering news. The genuine excitement of this moment seems lost on her. Or maybe it's my legalese. Oh, well. I know she is concentrating all her energy on healing so she can carry our baby. I tell her I will be home late again. She gave up protesting long ago. I hang up, still pumped.

I plug Mr. Kendrick's case number into the court's website. I scroll. The docket sheet rolls on forever. Mr. Kendrick has been a very busy prisoner. Three years ago, he sued the Teton Springs Prison in North Texas—four miles northwest of Wichita Falls on Texas Farm-to-Market Road 369. He also sued several wardens and senior medical staff. I pull up the Complaint to learn more about what he alleges. Mr. Kendrick had knocked out the Complaint on an old type-writer, the big Courier font a sure giveaway. Plus, a few typos remain—no correction tape in prison, I guess.

At the time he sued, Mr. Kendrick was a sixty-seven-year-old inmate. His heart is in terrible shape. The Complaint describes a long history of cardiovascular disease. He suffered heart attacks three times: 18, 12 and 5 years ago. He has also undergone several serious, invasive surgeries, including a five-vessel bypass after his first attack, and angioplasty with a four-vessel bypass after his second heart attack. After each open-heart procedure, the surgeons wired together his sternum. The multiple surgeries and his age make the cartilage, bone, and wire juncture frail. Certain shackles and restraints pull his arms and shoulders back, especially when transported in a vehicle. The restraints stretch his wired sternum, rendering him unable to reach any medicine he might have in his pocket, which leaves him in pain for hours.

The complaint alleges that his treatment program calls for steady doses of Isosorbide Mononitrate. It dilates his blood vessels so blood can flow through them easily, reducing the stress on his heart when it pumps. When he stops the Isosorbide suddenly, severe angina attacks overwhelm him. He needs Nitroglycerin to ease the pain of these attacks. He is supposed to have a small vial in the shirt pocket of his prison fatigues at all times. Mr. Kendrick alleges that the Chronic Care Nurse in AdSeg at the Teton Springs Prison fails to stock and deliver his Isosorbide and Nitroglycerin regularly. He details all his efforts to get the warden, the prison doctor, and others to fix the situation. The Complaint alleges they all turn a blind eye, and that he suffers regularly despite it being easy to relieve.

I lean back in my chair and mull over the allegations. Most people forget lawsuits are only accusations. Typing up a complaint means nothing. In fact, any jerk with a few bucks can sue and wreak havoc with hyped-up claims. Lawsuits then take months, if not years, to hash out. Parties exchange documents and depose one another and then facts filter down to some sort of truth that a jury will decide. Thus, healthy skepticism is the best tool for reading any lawsuit, especially a prisoner suit.

If I say, "Yes," it won't be just me, however, signing up this case. It will be my firm, and I am a brand-new Associate. Management and a partner sponsor will be required. I head down to my Trial Practice Leader, Connor McBryde, to ask about representing Mr. Kendrick. I tell him about Judge Navarro's request.

"Look, I'll get to first chair a jury trial in federal court. When else will I get the chance anytime soon? It's a great training opportunity—under live fire in a courtroom. Plus, Kendrick's a prisoner. So there is not much risk if the jury decides against us. Other than expenses, and I'll try to do it on the cheap, what does the firm have to lose?" I coax. I really want this opportunity.

Connor quizzes me with a few more questions, and then, "It's your choice. I'll clear it with the higher ups. If you have the time and want to do it, go ahead. Sign him up."

Elation hits me as I leave his office. From the hallway, I can hear Connor talking on the phone to William Paul Moore III, the firm's managing partner, who's always too busy to talk as he moves from one responsibility to another. No turning back now that the head of our firm knows about Emmett Kendrick. A twinge of panic washes through me. *What if I embarrass myself, embarrass the firm?* I try to shake the doubt from my brain. This is a huge chance for me, not only to get trial practice but also to prove I can be a trial lawyer, to raise my profile in the trial group. I call Lisa back in the Judge's chambers.

"Lisa, I'll take the case," I say.

"Great. I'll tell the Judge. You'll see the order of appointment come through in the morning."

I hang up the phone: *game on.*

CHAPTER
FOURTEEN

LATE MAY. Downtown. Dallas, Texas. Twenty weeks to trial.

Immediately after the Judge appoints me, I ask Steve if he would like to try Emmett's case with me. He jumps at the chance. Steve and I put together an engagement letter and send it to Mr. Kendrick at the Teton Springs Prison. In the letter, we remark we are coming to Teton Springs to talk about his case.

To see a prisoner is normally not a big deal. You show up at the prison during visiting hours, tell the guards the name of the inmate then wait for them to take him or her to a visiting room.

I have been to one other prison visiting room, helping a partner with a sentencing memorandum in federal court for a drug mule. That client was at a minimum-security prison in Seagoville, Texas. The visiting area is a large room with chairs and benches. Several small rooms line one side of the area, so prisoners can talk confidentially with their lawyers. During my visit, other prisoners in the room chatter and try to catch up with their families. Vending machines line the walls. Little kids eat candy, drink soda, and fill daddy in on school, sports, and other pursuits for an hour. The prison has regular visiting hours, so to speak with our mule was merely showing up and waiting.

To see Mr. Kendrick will be something different altogether. He lives in solitary confinement in a Texas prison. Most prisoners live in General Population, where they interact with other prisoners on the unit and exercise in the yard. More dangerous or violent prisoners move to High Security, where the prison limits prisoner movement and contact, and the guards keep them under close surveillance. The next, most restrictive level is Administrative Segregation, which is a fancy way to say solitary confinement. AdSeg prisoners spend twenty-three hours a day in their cell. They receive one hour for exercise alone inside a chain-link pen in the yard that resembles a dog run, complete with fenced roof. These prisoners can shower three times per week. All meals and other supplies pass through a slot in the door, known as a "bean slot." Inside, the cell has a concrete bunk with a mattress and a steel toilet-sink combination unit fused to the wall. Nothing goes into the cell without the guards' permission, and the guards often toss the cells looking for contraband or weapons. Any breach, and the warden extends the prisoner's time in AdSeg. Prisoners find it hard not to make mistakes in prison. Thus, many of these prisoners remain in AdSeg for years. Mr. Kendrick is no exception.

He is serving a fifty-five-year prison sentence for a Tarrant County aggravated robbery, which puts his release date in 36 years absent significant good-time credits. He's *never* getting out of prison alive. There have been escape attempts and incidents of having contraband intended for escape. One such incident at the Wynne Unit of the Texas Department of Criminal Justice in Huntsville, Texas cost him 7,528 days of good time credit off his sentence. The State added back *twenty years* to his imprisonment.

Because of Mr. Kendrick's confinement in AdSeg, Steve

and I must make an appointment to see him. We send the required form to the warden's office. The warden writes back to approve a date and time to visit. We must wait for that process to run its course, which takes a few days.

Teton Springs Prison is just outside of Wichita Falls, which is 180 miles north, northwest of Dallas. Our appointment is at 1:00 pm. I pick Steve up at his apartment, his short blond hair still damp from a shower. We head off in my black sedan. Over the next three hours, we mostly talk about other work at the firm. Then the conversation turns to Mr. Kendrick. It excites both of us to try a case.

"What do you think will happen when we get to Teton Springs?" Steve queries.

"I assume they will take us to the visitation area," I offer uncertainly, a picture of the other, chaotic prison visiting room in my head.

"You think they'll leave us alone with him, since we're his attorneys?"

"Not sure," I say. "He's in AdSeg for a reason."

Up to now, trial encompassed most of our thoughts, the logistics of presenting his case in court. With my excitement about the opportunity, I had thought little about alleged violent episodes cited in some of the government's court pleadings. As Steve rides quietly in my car, he chews on his pinky nail. The sun glints off the silver cufflinks in his shirt. I get the sense he, too, is worrying.

After the long drive, we pull into the parking lot with plenty of time to make our meeting. Pickup trucks fill the slots. My shiny, black, four-door sedan stands out. We get out and put on our suit jackets. We pull out briefcases with pens, legal pads, and everything we know about this case, which is very little. Looking around, it's obvious we are lawyers. We are the only ones in suits, dark suits. Everyone else we can see is in a Corrections Officer uniform or obviously civilian staff in jeans or dresses. As we walk to the entrance, I notice a few of the guards and staff point in our direction. The entire prison knows we have arrived.

Steve and I head into the lobby. The room is sparse—dull gray walls and a tile floor, easy to mop. It's lunchtime, so we wait.

"You two here to see Kendrick?" the clerk mutters. "Give me your driver's licenses and sign into the registry." We comply.

"You two," an officer says. "Take everything out of your pockets and step through the metal detector." We wait on the other side as he paws through our briefcases for contraband. Attorney-client privilege protects my files, but not my gum or bottle of water, which they confiscate. Once screened, they take us through a door to the yard of the prison. A chain-link fence surrounds us on three sides. Razor wire lines the top of the tall fencing.

"Wait right here. Another Corrections Officer will escort you to the AdSeg visiting area." The guard slams the door. We stand there, alone and exposed.

It's late May in Texas, and the power of summer is already fierce in the afternoon. Heat waves undulate off the concrete and prairie around us. We wait just outside the heavy steel door from the lobby. Everywhere we look, guards watch over prisoners. In the center of the complex juts a tall guard tower, with windows and a catwalk on all sides. Outside the perimeter, the fields have been mown flat for hundreds of yards in all directions. The cleared landscape makes it easier for sharpshooters in the tower to find and hit their target, an escapee. To our left, inmates walk the yard. Some run on a makeshift track. To our right, a few inmates cut grass and rake debris in the hot Texas sun. The smell of fresh grass clippings mixes a sweetness with the air. The sun beats down; as is usual in this part of Texas, clouds are sparse. A sidewalk stretches out in front of us, connecting to another building. A high, chain-link fence creates a corridor between the two structures. On top of the fence, double coils of razor wire loop forward. A small span of razor wire stitches together the thin vertical gap where the fences meet at a corner to our right. The triangular razors shimmer in the sun. Ever curious, Steve reaches out and touches one.

"Yep, as sharp as I thought they'd be," he says, yanking back his finger and sucking off a small drop of blood. I smile at his curiosity.

After a few minutes roasting in the heat, sweat slips down my back and into my waistline. A Corrections Officer approaches us.

"I'm Officer Larkin," she says, "Are you the lawyers here to see Emmett?"

I look around. Who else could we be?

Steve and I note this Corrections Officer immediately. Officer Larkin is beautiful—model beautiful. She has braided her long, jet-black hair into a tight rope and threaded it through her cap and down inside her body armor. She wears a wisp of makeup, her piercing eyes outlined in inky eyeliner. It's the only makeup she is likely allowed, and it announces her. Any other place, she is the type of raw beauty that any man would take a chance on. Outside she likely has a friendly smile. In here, she is all business. Her gray-black prison fatigues and the body armor she has strapped around her torso suggest she is ready for anything. She's certainly ready for Steve and me. As Officer Larkin turns to lead us, I notice the pepper spray at her hip and two sets of handcuffs in the small of her back on her duty belt. She seems mildly amused to escort us through the prison.

Steve is single, and she is stunning. Steve straightens his short blond hair with his fingers and tugs at his French cuffs to show off the shiny links. He naturally starts quizzing Officer Larkin. Most of the questions are innocuous, about the prison. How it works? Where are we headed? Then, flashing a big smile Steve probes, "How did you get into this line of work?"

"It sort of chose me. Both my parents were prison guards. So, it comes natural. Besides, up here in this town, almost everyone is a prisoner or a guard."

"What Unit do you work in, mostly?"

"AdSeg," she says and pauses for a beat. "I actually like working in AdSeg. I volunteered."

This statement seems discordant to us. Why would a beautiful woman want to work with the most violent of offenders?

"Why?" Steve asks, his surprise obvious.

She stops and looks us both up and down appraisingly, like a cat toying with mice. "Power," she says and flashes a predatory smile. She opens the door to the next unit.

Steve's face flushes slightly as he and I walk through, and she shuts the door behind us. The heavy steel slams, echoing in the space. We have entered the guts of the prison. Those in uniform around us control our every movement. I notice a guard desk across the room, staffed by two guards. On the wall sits a pegboard hung with tools. Red paint outlines each tool. The outlines make it easy to inventory, to see if any tool given to a prisoner on work detail has gone missing.

Our escort walks us through several sectors of the hallway separated by prison bars. Each time, we must stop. Larkin calls to the guard on the other side who pushes a button. The bars slip open. We pass through. The bars slam behind us with a deep buzz as a bolt slides into place. She takes us past High Security, where several small groups of prisoners play basketball in confined courts that remind me of squash courts. They have concrete walls on three sides, and heavy fencing on the fourth for the guards to watch for trouble.

Steve asks me, "You think the guards ever bet on the games?" His smirk is clear.

Officer Larkin leads us into solitary confinement, otherwise known as Administrative Segregation or AdSeg. The door is the same heavy steel, but without bars. The AdSeg building feels more like a hospital or asylum than a prison. It's all concrete walls and metal doors. No bars. We follow her into a large visiting room. It looks like what I expected. Vending machines line the walls and a few chairs sit in the middle. But no families, no children mill about. Not a single soul stirs but us. Individual cubicles that look like telephone booths line one side of the room. Thick glass with diamond shaped wire running through it separates the small cubicles on one side from a shelf and chair on both sides. Next to the chairs, on the inside and outside of the cubicle, hang identical telephones for talking with your inmate.

Larkin points us to a specific cubical. "They'll bring Mr. Kendrick shortly," she says, then turns on her heel and struts away.

Steve and I wait patiently for Mr. Kendrick. While we sit there, I stare at the telephone handset. I suffer from germaphobia—always have. I have no sanitizer or wipes—nothing to clean the phone, which I touch. It feels greasy.

We have never seen Mr. Kendrick. All we know is he is a violent felon sequestered in this most restrictive unit of the prison. Visions flash through my head of a tall, powerful man always fighting the prison system. He used a gun. He is obviously a sufficient risk that they have to lock him down twenty-four hours a day. But no matter what, he is our lottery ticket to a jury trial. Besides, the guards will watch our safety. *I think.*

Officer Larkin waits on the other side of the room. I assume she is giving us distance. But in a large, unoccupied room of hard surfaces, everything we say will echo. Apparently, safety overrides confidentiality. Her power, the prison's power over Mr. Kendrick, is omnipresent.

Ten minutes pass, then from inside the visiting room, Steve and I hear a door clang shut and the rattle of chains.

A few moments later, the door at the back of the cubicle opens. Sunlight from a large window behind him obscures his profile. Mr. Kendrick waits outside the open door as a guard places a large manila envelope on the shelf in front of the window. Mr. Kendrick kneels on the ground and a guard unlocks the manacles around his ankles; shackles bind his hands behind his back. Mr. Kendrick steps inside. The door shuts, and a large slot opens. Mr. Kendrick kneels again and sticks his hands, backward, through the opening. The guard unlocks the shackles, removes them, and slams the slot closed. The lock turns. Mr. Kendrick stands alone inside a three by four-foot box. He sits down and picks up the telephone handset on his side. He gestures to ours. I pick it up.

"Mr. Simmons?"

"Yes. And this is my colleague, Steve Davis."

"Gentlemen. . . . Have a seat."

"Thanks, Mr. Kendrick. It's good to meet you," I say.

"I'm glad to see you attorneys. . . . Call me Emmett."

Emmett is not at all what I expected. He is smart, no doubt. From his chiseled cheeks, his ice-blue eyes stare out clear and full of purpose, and belie substantial intelligence. But he looks more like an old man playing chess in the park than a violent felon who the State must lock up most of his waking hours. He has shaved his head, which he later explains is because he hates lice. His face is also clean-shaven. He rubs his palms against it.

"The guards let me shower and shave this morning. On account I was meeting with my lawyers. I got lucky, too. I got a new razor. Normally they keep the razors in a community bin, and you take your pick, and hope you're lucky. Hope for a sharp one. This time, they gave me a new one, . . . straight out of the package."

From what I can tell, Emmett stands a little over five feet tall. His bright white fatigues cover a slight paunch from the prison food. He has sneakers without laces. But mostly I notice his welcoming smile.

"Y'all had a pleasant trip up to Teton Springs?" Emmett asks. "Didn't have any trouble finding the place, did you?"

"Nope, we just followed the signs," Steve says.

Emmett says, "I saw y'all pull into the parking lot there. I have a small window, maybe one foot by three foot, near the top of my cell. If I stand just right on my bunk, I can see most of what goes on in that side of the prison." He'd been watching for us most of the day. He says he likes my car.

"Black is a good car for a lawyer," he says.

Then he talks about his case. He picks up a manila envelope.

"This holds the entirety of my legal file I'm allowed to keep in my cell. I think most of everything else is on file with the Court. If you need something else, I might could tell you where to find it."

I look at the thin envelope. Most cases that go to trial have bankers' boxes full of documents lining the pews in the court-room gallery. Emmett planned to try his case with one thin envelope. Over the next hour, Emmett explains his claims to us. Mostly, he focuses on the claims in his complaint and how the system fails to provide him regular doses of Isosorbide and a ready supply of Nitroglycerin.

"The worst part is angina attacks. I'm always out of Nitro to stop the pain. When it comes, I just have to wait it out on my bunk; I learned some deep breathing exercises somewhere that help—maybe from the doc in the infirmary."

He runs us through the way a medical call is supposed to work on his unit. A nurse should walk into the unit and yell, "Medical!" That same nurse should then walk the unit and look at each inmate through the slot in the door. If the inmate has a health issue, he can discuss it with the nurse. Inmates with regular medicines should receive their doses on these rounds. Emmett explains the nurses call out but visit only those cells where they must deliver medicine that day. If you can't get the nurse's attention, then you wait and try the next day. Often Emmett's Isosorbide is not on the cart. The nurse tells him she will get it and come back. But that rarely, if ever, happens. "They just say, 'I'll see what I can do.'" Emmett says.

We discuss strategy with Emmett.

"In my court papers I submitted affidavits from nine witnesses that will testify how the prison fails to follow the medical protocols required by the State of Texas regulations. All of them are good people," Emmett says.

Steve and I glance at each other—all nine of his witnesses are convicted felons.

Emmett walks us through the papers in his file, explaining the importance of each one. I wonder how he did any of this from his cell. He has sections of the Texas prison policies for the treatment of inmates and all his legal briefs.

Finally, I ask Emmett, "What would a win at trial look like for you?"

He ponders my question for a moment. Intelligence glows behind his blue eyes. "Mostly, I want my pills supplied regularly. It would also help if they shackled me in a way so as not to pull the wires in my sternum. Oh, I'd also like a complete copy of my medical records. I want to take them with me if I have to go back to the emergency room."

"This all sounds reasonable," I say. But I remember the State has fought him tooth and nail at every turn on this lawsuit.

"When you send a letter up here, remember to mark it, 'Attorney Mail.' Although, I'm pretty sure the guards read it anyway while they check it for contraband in the mailroom." With that, our interview naturally winds down.

"When y'all coming back?" Emmett asks with thick curiosity.

"Not sure—probably a month. It'll take a while to digest all this material."

Emmett appears pleased that a trial has arrived.

"I'll have the guard hand you this file." He pauses, then adds sincerely, "It's been a pleasure meeting you. Can't tell you how much I appreciate y'all's help." Then he says, "Goodbye," and hangs up the phone.

Steve and I watch as he performs the shackling ritual in reverse. He knocks on the door. It opens and Emmett kneels, placing his hands behind him through the slot. Once bound, he stands and the guards open the door. One shackles his ankles after he kneels again. A guard grabs his file. We hear his chains rattle as he shuffles down the hall. After the doors clang shut, a guard appears around the corner and hands us Emmett's file and leaves. Steve and I are alone in the visitors' room, except for Officer Larkin, who has kept vigil over us and now approaches to escort us out of the prison.

We sign out at the front desk and head for my car. I wonder who got my gum and bottle of water. I wonder how many men are watching us from the rows of barred windows in the prison. We must seem an oddity, and Emmett might have achieved rock-star status in AdSeg for securing a trial. Whether or not they believe his claims, he has hauled the wardens and the medical staff into court. He will accuse them in the town square of intentionally failing to treat him properly under the Constitution. I am not sure how the prisoners communicate while locked down twenty-three hours. But I have a feeling that Emmett's success, and that he now has lawyers in dark suits pressing his case, has spread like wildfire inside the prison.

Outside Bowie, Texas, on the way home from our first visit with Emmett, Steve and I stop at the Red Truck Café on the side of the state highway. No actual town exists, just a few structures. Across the street, two more buildings stand against the Texas wind. One sign says "Beef Jerky Warehouse." The other says "XXX Movies." I think, "Odd combination." Steve and I order lunch.

"What are you two boys doin' out here, all dressed up in your Sunday clothes?"

I suspect most of her customers wear a suit only for church on Sundays and for funerals. Steve tells the waitress the story of our prison visit.

"Now why would you go do a fool thing like that? You ask me, them convicts get treated better than they deserve. After all, they must've done something just awful to get themselves locked up."

After fifteen minutes, she delivers two of the largest chicken fried steaks I have ever seen, both smothered in white gravy with a side of mashed potatoes. Steve tucks his expensive tie into his shirt to avoid staining it. The size and flavor of the meal keeps Steve and me from talking much while we eat.

After lunch, Steve and I drive back to Dallas. We talk about our impressions of Emmett, make a list of things to do.

"This will be excellent," Steve says.

"I know," I say. "A real federal court trial our first couple of years in. Who would have guessed?"

"You think there's any chance we could win?" Steve asks almost as if to himself.

"We'll see," I say.

We coast back into the city as the sun drops toward sunset. I think back on the waitress at the Red Truck Café. She represents our jury pool—people who think any treatment is fair game in prison. After all, "them convicts" are wicked people. Then I think of Emmett and how he told us his story so clearly and matter of fact—as if it was a simple truth he wanted to tell.

As we near Steve's apartment, I say, "There's a chance. We *could* win."

CHAPTER
FIFTEEN

FIRST WEEK OF JUNE. Dallas, Texas.

Dr. Abrams has tinkered for weeks, working to get Hannah's bloodwork and biology just right. He's part physician, part mad-scientist, part chef, adding a dash of this and a dash of that.

These past weeks have limped by, doubt always lingers, wondering if the circumstances will ever fit what we need to make a baby by in vitro fertilization, or IVF. Dr. Abrams explained that for IVF, he will collect eggs from Hannah's ovaries, fertilize them with my sperm in a lab, and then grow the embryos in a Petri dish. If all goes well, he will transfer them to her uterus. But, everything needs to be "just so" to create a new life.

Normally, when you take medicine, it's reactive—quelling symptoms. Here we seek to create the perfect vessel—perfect biological environment—to bring another human being into the world. It takes time; the process is slow, providing ample time for worry, doubt, and debts to build.

Any long-term effort like this can become rote. The pattern of shots and treatments has lulled us into a sense that all this craziness is normal, and that tomorrow promises just another day like today, full of shots and prayers.

So, it's jarring when Dr. Abrams says, "It's time." He explains we are ready to move onto the next phase, actually creating the tiny life we ache for—the time to fulfill or break a dream. Anticipation and hope build.

Hannah checks in at the front desk. We are now moving through the first gate in IVF, claiming all the building blocks. Second gate, Dr. Abrams will see if he can grow embryos in his lab. Third gate, he will implant them. Then we wait and see if life will bless us with another child.

Dr. Abrams pulled in Hannah a couple of days ago to retrieve several eggs. It was a quick procedure—retrieval with a special needle to her ovaries. The slight soreness in her abdomen does not dampen her excitement. On this long road, Hannah has moved through all the changes with grace. Today, however, is "my collection date." Hannah sits beside me on the couch with a mischievous smile.

"Mr. Simmons." A clinical voice calls out across the room.

"Yes," I say. I'm the only man in the waiting room. All the women glance up at me. *They all know why I'm here.*

In front of the audience, the nurse holds out a small white cup. "Here's your cup. Lydia will show you where to go."

I flush with embarrassment. Lydia smiles wryly and points down the hall. I grab the cup and follow Lydia. I feel a dozen eyes burning into my back as I attempt to saunter nonchalantly down the corridor. Lydia looks like the old ladies I see when I visit my grandmother in the retirement home. For months, Hannah has been the focus. Swarms of nurses have convened around her like a queen bee, a flurry of activity, all in a wild fertility dance. I feel like a bull being led to the breeding barn.

Lydia leads me to a sterile bathroom. "Here you go, Mr. Simmons. When you have the sample, just place it on the shelf." She flashes a playful smile, places her slight hand on my forearm, dropping her voice into a whisper. "Also, there are some gentlemen's magazines under the sink that might prove helpful. You know, just in case."

Dr. Abrams did not foreshadow this oddly sterile, uncomfortable moment.

I smile politely. "Thank you."

Lydia pats my shoulder, her smile impish. "Relax. Don't worry. It's normal and natural, besides, it takes two pieces to make this puzzle, so to speak. Take your time."

I close the door, and it takes a while to get the image of grandmotherly Lydia out of my mind.

CHAPTER
SIXTEEN

TEN DAYS LATER. Neighborhood. Dallas, Texas.

The sun crests the tops of the live oaks as Hannah and I get out of the car. It rained last night, so the air smells fresh, but the humidity is thick all around us. It's the kind of day where you sweat immediately upon stepping outside. Heat radiates from the concrete in the alley as Hannah and I walk up to our friend Yuki's home to help with their garage sale.

Hannah's jeans frame her shapely figure, and she has braided her hair into a perfect French braid. Desire flares briefly in me. The IVF has been clinical, and I enjoy this moment of simply wanting my wife. She's on her cell phone with Dr. Abrams's nurse. Hannah hangs up the phone, beaming.

"What's the latest?" I ask, hopeful.

Excitement flashes through her large, hazel eyes. "We have six embryos dividing! No guarantee, but she thinks we will have at least three for Monday."

"That's wonderful!"

Three is a good solid number. IVF is not a hundred percent success activity. When we started, Dr. Abrams fertilized eight eggs that replicated into embryos. We have lost two. If none survive, we have to go through the ordeal again. *But we do not have the money to do this again.*

"Dr. Abrams thinks we should implant three at most. He likes three, says it's a good number, and he won't implant over three. Some doctors will implant five. He thinks that's unethical."

"With three, there's a higher likelihood one will take," I say supportively.

"Yes." Her smile is beautiful and impish in the morning sun. "What if all three take?" She giggles. "We'd have our family of four all in one go!"

My chest constricts, and my heart races. When you start down the IVF road, the goal is *one* healthy child. There is a chance of triplets, but you don't think about it. You leap over physical and anatomical obstacles; you swallow mountains of expense—or in our case debt. This final in vitro process and procedure will cost an additional fifteen thousand dollars.

The odds makers will tell you to play the greatest odds of success—implant the three embryos. Odds makers, however, must not have raised triplets. I think about how busy Lilly is as a toddler, all the effort to corral her when she first started crawling. Honestly, I fear all the energy it would take to chase three little ones all scuttling in different directions at the same time. Triplets would prevent sleep for a long while. But I don't share these anxious thoughts with my beaming wife.

"Three, huh?"

"He says three is the most likely number for us to have at least one more kiddo." A lilt of hope in Hannah's voice.

Hannah is beguiling, but only a smidge over one hundred pounds. They say babies come earlier and earlier each time. Lilly was two weeks early. Triplets notoriously come as preemies. Preemies are notorious for birth defects or developmental issues. Bearing triplets carries an enormous risk. She smiles at me expectantly, her expression radiant.

I swallow. "What's the worst that can happen—they all have weddings in the same year?" I smile at her. "Three it is."

The next week we arrive at Dr. Abrams's office. This is it. This is where all the fanfare, shots, and effort lead. Only three embryos survived the weekend and continued to replicate—getting bigger, cell-by-cell.

One could think, "We're down to three," or "Three is the perfect number." The reality is three is the only number. We implanted all of them. It's the most likely pathway to success, to have one take and a baby to grow. But . . . if it does not work, then we slide back to the beginning. We would have to travel the long road to get back to this place again. But with all the ballooning costs, this is our one and only chance.

We're broke and drowning in debt.

Dr. Abrams's assistant props Hannah up in the "insemination chair." This resembles a 4-H experiment more all the time. The nurse inverts the chair at over 45 degrees. Hannah's golden hair drapes off the bottom edge; her socked feet poke up in the air like two weird antennae. When making babies, gravity evidently counts, a lot.

Dr. Abrams waddles in, humming a Frank Sinatra song, His comfortable sneakers squeak on the polished floor. When you think of IVF, you think about Hi-Tech machines and growing little humans in Petrie dishes in the lab. On a surgical tray to his right, Dr. Abrams has our children—potential children—under a small drape of fabric.

"Are we ready?" he asks.

"Ready."

"Where are we? Where is our mind? Are we ready to conceive—to make life?!"

My mind flashes to Dr. Frankenstein, atop the tower, swinging in the lighting and thunder, a maniacal glow in his eyes.

Hannah takes a deep breath and whispers, "Yes."

I swallow and feel the nervous electricity in my chest. "Yes."

Dr. Abrams sings a tune to Hannah and reaches under the draping, to show me our children, and pulls out a glorified turkey baster. Not a real turkey baster, mind you, but one that looks like a professional, medical-grade turkey baster. The room is calm and full of positivity. The nurse keeps the banter light. Then it's time.

Dr. Abrams's focus is total as he squirts the embryos into Hannah. And then . . . we wait. Two hours. IVF is a long game of patience. I'm not sure what type of chit chat you engage in while they suspend your wife upside down like an odd little maternal bat, hoping to conceive.

"Do you think they might all be girls?" Hannah wonders, her face flushed from inversion.

"I don't know. Let's not get ahead of ourselves." The joke in my family has always been that I would have four girls to raise and stress over as a father. I did not expect to try for three out of four all in one shot.

"I hope it works. I want it to work," she says, like a soft prayer.

"Let's focus on good thoughts."

Dr. Abrams finally releases us to head home. The ride home is quiet. Hannah smiles with her hand on her belly, eyes closed, focused on a fertility mantra. We walk into the house, and she collapses on the bed, emotionally spent. Lilly runs in, hops on the mattress, and snuggles up with her.

"Where's my baby sister," Lilly says, a giant smile on her face.

"Patience, little one," Hannah says and then places Lilly's palm on her tummy. "She has to grow for a while." Lilly seems satisfied with that answer and tells Hannah what games she played while we were gone.

I survey the scene in the bedroom. Over the past few months, she and Lilly have made the bed a peaceful refuge of pillows, blankets, and stuffed animals. They have created their own barricade against the world.

After a few minutes, Lilly gets up and goes to the refrigerator and grabs a grapefruit, and then crawls back into bed with Hannah. A few days ago, I jokingly told Lilly that sleeping with a grapefruit keeps away monsters. She has taken my silly advice to heart and has carried a grapefruit to bed ever since. She holds it up, so Hannah can see.

"Don't worry Momma, I'll keep the monsters away." Lilly says.

Hannah looks at me and rolls her eyes. I shrug.

"How did I know?" I say, as Lilly curls up with the grapefruit between them.

Hannah's discharge orders require her to lay down quietly and wait. She takes Dr. Abrams seriously, as if entering a fertility meditation, not allowing anything to force a hiccup into her rest. We will return to Dr. Abrams in four days to see if the bloodwork shows any signs of pregnancy. I watch Hannah close her eyes. Hope fuels the soul.

Each day Hannah rests, and I head to the firm. The constant work of the law distracts me, and that reprieve is welcome. I have legal memos to write, briefs to write, and an endless number of documents to read and re-read, trying to understand the legal arguments. Every evening I walk past the portrait of William Paul Moore III. On the commute home, in the waning sunset, I wonder if this pace of work is what I have to look forward to for the next forty years. The thought unsettles me.

While I bury myself in work, several of Hannah's friends come by and play with Lilly or take her to do things. You can't tell a two-year-old to hold on and lie down for four days, especially a bright blonde bolt of energy. I come home, Hannah rests. I leave, she rests—locked in a still, fervent maternal appeal for more children.

When you undertake IVF, it's its own kind of prayer. We

have invested everything, including a huge part of any future income, into Dr. Abrams's magic. But no way exists to know instantly if it worked. No windows. No constant monitoring. No transparency. We could rest on the precipice of an utter IVF failure, and we would have no insight.

Then superstition takes over, and we don't want bad news. All has gone well these past few days; we don't want to jinx any part of the process. So, we smile. Whisper positive sayings. Hope. It's the closest thing to a prayer.

Possibility wraps itself around us.

CHAPTER
SEVENTEEN

JUNE. Downtown, Dallas, Texas. Nineteen weeks to trial.

In my office at the firm, I think through Mr. Kendrick's case. For prisoners, cruel and inhuman punishment violates the Eighth Amendment of the United States Constitution. 42 United States Code § 1983 provides for a civil lawsuit when a government actor violates a citizen's Constitutional rights. The Fourth Amendment protects against warrantless searches and seizures, or excessive force by a police officer. The Fourteenth Amendment protects "pretrial detainees" against abuse once arrested but before conviction. To win under these pretrial cases, the individual must prove the official acted "unreasonably."

In contrast, the Eighth Amendment protects convicts. To win, a prisoner must prove the official acted "maliciously and sadistically"—a nearly impossible standard. But courts have held that some conditions of confinement violate the Eighth Amendment. For example, United States District Judge William Wayne Justice held that Texas jails violated the Eighth Amendment through "pernicious" conditions that led to extensive pain and squalor of the inmates. In 1980, he ordered federal supervision of Texas prisons. That oversight lasted over twenty years. In a wicked irony, however, medical negligence does not violate the Eighth Amendment. Rather, if the surgeon lops off the wrong foot, that is not cruel and inhuman. That is just life.

Mr. Kendrick complains about not receiving drugs. I doubt how to prove that is malicious or sadistic. It may just get lost in the crush of day-to-day activity of a prison system: mere negligence.

At the federal courthouse, sheer volumes of prisoner suits work their way through the system. Prisoners have endless complaints and all the time in the world. Plus, lawsuits are a way to cause mischief. Prisoners typically file lawsuits *"pro se,"* without counsel. The system must process them like any other lawsuit. Many Judges have staff attorneys who handle all their prisoner cases. The process devolves into an assembly line, with prisoner cases regularly dismissed for "failure to state a claim." The magnitude of filings by prisoners can quickly jade a person.

Mr. Kendrick's suit alleges that the prison officials intentionally failed to provide the vital, lifesaving medicines for his heart on a regular schedule, and their deliberate indifference caused him to suffer, violating his Eighth Amendment rights.

When the court received the complaint, the United States District Judge ordered Mr. Kendrick to complete a series of queries detailing his claims against all thirteen defendants. Upon receiving the questionnaire answers two years ago, the Judge dismissed the complaint as frivolous with no arguable basis in law.

Undeterred from his prison cell, Mr. Kendrick appealed the dismissal to the United States Court of Appeals for the Fifth Circuit in New Orleans, Louisiana. The Fifth Circuit vacated the District Judge's order, holding that Mr. Kendrick provided specific instances that might give rise to an Eighth Amendment claim, and that the District Court should give him an opportunity to develop the claims in his complaint.

Upon remand, the District Judge transferred the case to United States Magistrate Judge Carmen Navarro. Judge Navarro entered a scheduling order in March last year, and the case proceeded to discovery.

Discovery, at its core, allows the parties to secure documents that relate to the claims at issue. Mr. Kendrick sought documents while locked in solitary confinement, and he petitioned for documents from the State of Texas related to his medical care and the medical treatment of prisoners. Texas, however, did not cooperate fully.

Mr. Kendrick filed several motions to compel, which the court granted. Texas failed to provide the ordered documents. Mr. Kendrick filed motions to sanction the Assistant Attorney General defending the matter.

Judge Navarro agreed. She ordered the Assistant Attorney General to provide a letter explaining his failure to comply with her previous orders to produce documents. She also ordered him to attend a two-day legal education course on discovery, including a segment on attorney ethics. That order led to him being replaced.

Mr. Kendrick's tenacity piques my curiosity, and I feel proud to represent him. The prison confines him to a solitary cell for twenty-three hours a day, yet he bangs out his legal documents on a manual typewriter. Within one year, he has successfully won an appeal and sanctioned a government lawyer—unusual. Now, he has secured a trial. He is dogged and smart.

But, he might also be right.

CHAPTER
EIGHTEEN

JUNE. Dallas, Texas. Several days have passed since Dr. Abrams implanted the embryos.

Each day, excitement builds—possibility builds. Modern surgeries, as well as months of shots and tinkering—and worry—have brought us to this moment. It feels incredible. We finally have a real chance to erase the doctors and horrors in Ithaca. We can move forward with *our family*. Hannah is joyful with all the possibilities. Even Lilly chatters on about a baby sister, *or sisters*. As the days move along, peaceful and quiet, hope blossoms in all of us.

Eventually the day comes to find out. I head to work. Hannah heads to Dr. Abrams's office. The air shimmers electric as I watch her pull out of the driveway and turn left toward the hospital complex for bloodwork. On my commute, I turn on the radio and enjoy the expectancy of success and a glorious sunrise as heady rock-n-roll pours through my speakers. The light of a new day peeks through the canopy of the live oaks that line the road. I am confident in our success. I feel at peace for the first time in a very long time.

Hannah calls and tells me that Dr. Abrams sent her home

for a few hours while the lab processes the sample. In the interim, I sit at my desk at the law firm. Excitement builds. I cannot focus on my work. I find myself re-reading paragraphs because my attention falters. All I can think about are lab results.

Finally, the ringer of my phone breaks the silence, and I take a breath. Confidently, I answer the phone to hear the good news from Hannah.

"Hi, Bear. Dr. Abrams just called." A hitch mars her voice. "It didn't work . . . the embryos didn't take." Silence fills the other end of the telephone. No sobbing, no tears—just emptiness.

"I'll be right home," I say, heart racing.

I tell my secretary Ginny and run to my car.

As I leave the parking structure, the crossing guards for a commuter train drop in front of me, delaying my trip. As the train passes, heading south, each long, white car morphs into a still shot of our journey. I see Hannah telling me she is pregnant with Lilly in a national park in Ithaca. A tall, beautiful waterfall spills the heavens into her message. Other train cars carry the preterm labor struggles with Lilly—the nights in the hospital with the fetal monitor pulsing in the background. Then they slip, car by car, into a replay of the doctors letting Hannah suffer and slide away from infections, baffled by the results of their own mistakes. Finally, the train cars fade into our recent adventure. The lunch at the duck pond and the wide smile as I agree to try for a second child. Then visions of her shattered expression from the radiology department and news of the pervasive scarring appear. All the shots rush by, as the cars click along the rails. Finally, the last car rushes by and disappears into a tunnel. The vision of Hannah's smile fades as Dr. Abrams implanted the embryos. The guard rails raise, and I speed off.

When I arrive home, it's hard to catch my breath as I enter. Hannah rests in bed in the back room. Our friend Yuki sits next to her on the mattress, a compassionate smile accents her beautiful face. Her long jet-black hair cascades over her shoulders and colorful red silk dress. Pure of heart, but persistent, Yuki has a mango and a flower bobbing in a glass bowl with water.

"Mango will heal you. This will help," she insists.

"Thank you, but I really don't feel like any mango right now," Hannah says. Her kindness prevents her from saying, "I don't like it" or "I'm allergic to it."

Yuki presses. She slices the mango, oblivious. Yuki holds the fruit out expectantly in her delicate fingers. It's a cultural ritual to her, and she won't take "no" for an answer.

Hannah is eager for her friend to leave so she can tell me everything. Out of frustration, Hannah puts the mango to her lips, fakes a bite, and then sets it down.

Ceremony complete, Yuki leaves, satisfied. I hear the door click behind her as she exits.

"I'm sorry, Buzz," I say. "I wish . . ." Taking her in my arms, I feel her breathless sobs on my shoulder. Finally, they slow.

"I'd like to get out of the house. Do something with Lilly," she says in a voice marred by tears, "Let's take her someplace to play. I want to spend time with her. With you."

Lilly's current epicenter of fun is a pizza parlor and arcade palace. Not quiet, but it distracts Hannah. I sit down at a booth with our drinks and a pager ready to blink when our pizza is ready. While we wait, Hannah focuses on our toddler, chasing her through the arcade and helping her work knobs and push buttons on the games. Smiles and giggles erupt from Lilly, and Hannah follows behind her, gathering the tickets spewing from the machines. Lilly morphs into a game wizard, fascinated by all the blinking lights, movement, and digital sounds. Hannah is her entourage. The games drown out any talk or thought about the failed IVF.

Hannah smiles as Lilly plays a game with bumblebees

made from ping-pong balls. Hannah adores that little girl. I know my wife now weighs a future where Lilly is our only child. Hannah works hard to set aside disappointment and drinks in Lilly's joy, but I can see her sorrow in the dark circles under her eyes and in those moments when her smile slips.

Our pizza arrives, and we all sit down to eat. At first, I think it's a trick of the light, but then I notice that Hannah's lips are swelling. She's having an allergic reaction to the mango touching her lips.

I signal to my lips with my index finger and tell Hannah, "I'm going to run and grab some antihistamine."

Hannah nods with understanding.

I walk out of the arcade, and I see a drugstore across the street. As I wait for the light to change at the crosswalk, I tally all the money we have spent on IVF, all on credit cards. The total recently hadn't seemed so immense when success seemed imminent. Now that failure is real, the full weight of our debt crushes down. Suddenly, the hot, oppressive air envelopes me.

By the time I return, the swelling is more pronounced. Hannah scratches her ears, her telltale sign of an allergic response. Her expression latticed with concern. I give her two pills, and she swallows them. We sit and watch Lilly in silence for a while. Finally, I break the reverie.

"You want to head home?" I say above the arcade noise.

"No, I want to watch Lilly play."

Sitting in the booth, I observe Hannah encourage Lilly as our little girl scampers through the colorful tunnels of the "fun house" that crisscross the ceiling. Static has transformed Lilly's hair into something akin to a lion's mane. Tugging at my cuticles, I remain silent. Nothing I can say will fill the void in Buzz. Her expression bleeds a pervasive numbness, as we realize that a dream of four children is now gone. Lilly will have to be enough. We had only the three embryos. I don't have the heart to remind her we do not have the money to attempt IVF again; although, I suspect she knows. *That was our only shot.* Gambling is often an empty, losing game.

Later that night, Buzz and I rest in bed face-to-face. Lilly has flopped on the mattress, all sprawled out, limbs a jumble. The Teddy Bear she purchased with her arcade tickets perches in the crook of her arm. She sleeps like the dead. The pizza parlor exhausted her—she passed out before bath time, and we didn't even change her from her simple blue cotton dress.

Despair puddles in Hannah's large, beautiful eyes. The only sounds are our breathing, and Lilly's occasional snortle as she dreams about all the fun she had today.

"How are you?" I ask.

"Numb."

"Just give it some time, Buzz."

After a few moments of silence, Hannah whispers, "Want to sneak off to the couch and fool around?"

"You sure, Buzz? It's been a hell of a day."

Hannah bites her bottom lip and lays a hand on my chest, her delicate fingers gripping into my skin like a rock climber touching the face of a cliff. The moonlight reflects off the whites of her eyes. Tears perch on the rims.

"I want to feel, Bear, to feel alive. I need you." She crawls out of bed, takes my hand, and leads me to the couch. She pushes me back and crawls onto my lap. Her beautiful, long blond hair drapes over her shoulders. I place my palm over her heart and can feel it pounding. She lowers her lips to mine, and her breath is hot, the moisture from tears on her cheek. I tuck her hair behind her ears and wipe away teardrops with my thumbs. For a few minutes it's just the two of us as I feel Buzz softly, rhythmically giving up on her dream.

CHAPTER
NINETEEN

JUNE. Dallas, Texas. Eighteen weeks to trial.

Soon after returning from Teton Springs and our visit with Emmett, three banker's boxes greet me at my office. I welcome the diversion from our failed IVF attempt. My secretary, Ginny, printed off a copy of all the case briefs, exhibits, and pleadings—plus we received a copy of everything the government produced in discovery from the Texas Attorney General's Office. Ginny is as nice as they come. Nearing retirement, a lifetime of working for lawyers has taught her immense patience. She is always impeccably dressed in red, white, or blue—her favorite colors—with a coordinated silk scarf from her vast collection. Her bobbed gray hair frames a welcoming smile, and her eyes sparkle with a hint of laughter. Ginny has cheerfully and efficiently organized all the documents, boxed them, and lined them up along the wall behind my desk. The full universe of documents also includes everything Emmett submitted to the court to prove he deserved a trial. I do quick math. Each banker's box holds approximately 5,000 pages of paper. I have a lot of reading to do.

Piles of billable work crowd my desk, stacks of paper threating to flop on the floor. The omnipresent business of law takes precedence. Emmett's case will have to fit in the gaps in between. Curiosity, however, proves powerful. I set down my coffee and pull off the box lids. On top of the second box, a transmittal letter from the current Assistant Attorney General, Rose Walker, welcomes me to the case. I tell myself, only one path exists through a pile of papers like this: one page at a time. The first box includes all Emmett's grievances and appeals. The folders are a graveyard of past attempts to get his medicine sorted out.

Inside prison, an inmate fills out forms to complain. One of the wardens investigates the complaint and decides if it has merit. The wardens don't grade harshly those who keep the inmates locked up. Indeed, the wardens denied every grievance by Emmett as "unsubstantiated" or "without merit." A fat "DENIED" stamp perches in the upper right-hand corner of each form.

The inmate can then appeal, and that appeal goes to the next highest warden on the food chain who denies it. This gristmill churns, sometimes for years, with prison staff grading their own papers until an inmate gets to the final "DENIED," the end of the line, and has "exhausted all administrative remedies." Finally, that is the ticket to sue.

Emmett's bad heart has not drawn a lawyer close enough to care. The United States graduates almost forty thousand new lawyers a year. But once they make money, the new and the seasoned attorneys all become ghosts, unwilling to answer a prisoner letter. The vast majority of prisoner lawsuits lack a lawyer because no pot of gold rests at the end. The inmate's family, if it has any money at all, exhausted all spare funds on the defense at the criminal trial years ago. After years of confinement for their loved one, the family moves on. They realize their subsistence as regular folks outside the four walls of a prison requires their full care. Paying lawyers to sue over a prisoner's existence inside threatens to drain off any chance they have of staying afloat.

Then over the months and years, many forget about their incarcerated family member—except for the obligatory yearly visit.

Without a steady source of funds, lawyers will touch a case only on a contingency fee. If they win, they keep thirty-three percent of any money damages (some charge forty percent if they go all the way to trial). In the interim, they invest billable time and out-of-pocket expenses on a gamble. Gamblers don't like small bets. Generally, lawyers need to smell thick blood in the water to pique their curiosity and hunger. Prisoners who draw those kinds of money damages are one in a million with sexy facts that play well in the news —like invalids left in a wheelchair in their own excrement until the bedsores eat through to their hipbones. That kind of suffering has dollar signs attached to it. Big dollars. Lawyers will circle, hunting for a way to take their chunk.

With no lawyer, Emmett filed suit himself, no small feat from prison. If he lived in the general population, he could have used the prison law library for hours at a time. Locked in AdSeg, he must request books or papers from the library and wait until he receives them through the bean slot in his door. He uses those materials, returns them, and then requests more to arrive a few days later through the slot. Emmett moved his case forward one page at a time, one book at a time, all typed on an old typewriter.

I look at all the pages in the boxes. To get to this point, Emmett had to survive a summary judgment motion filed by the government. Essentially, the government argued that Emmett presented no fact that required a jury to decide who was right and who was wrong. Responding to such a motion requires sworn affidavits and evidence. Most prisoner suits die on this hill if they survive dismissal.

The appendix to Emmett's summary judgment motion contains the paper trail for his grievance efforts—pages and pages of prison forms with dozens of names. With multiple grievances in different phases of the appeals process, no set chronology emerges, and the cast of characters devolves into a messy web of names. The trial will include six defendants. We will need evidence of acts by each defendant, and evidence that they deliberately turned a blind eye to Emmett's plight. I map out who did what when and sort a thousand puzzle pieces. I hope some will fall in a distinct order we can spell out in simple terms to a jury. We must figure out how to present the facts in Emmett's file in a way that convinces the jury that the prison purposely mistreats Emmett.

Beyond exhibits—documents to prove his case—we need corroborating testimony. Emmett submitted nine affidavits from fellow prisoners in AdSeg. Each swore to the exact same facts. They are short on details as to each defendant. We can call each inmate at trial, but that carries risk. They will testify from the stand in their prison fatigues and manacles. Their criminal history is fair game to impeach them if it relates to truthfulness or "crimes of moral turpitude," your basic vile conduct or depravity. Mostly, because of their prison jumpsuits and chains, the jury will perceive them as liars before they even raise their hands to swear to tell the truth.

We'll lose before we ever begin.

CHAPTER
TWENTY

MID-JULY. Dallas, Texas.

Over time, the ache of the failed IVF wanes and life picks up a simple rhythm. I continue to make it a habit to arrive at the firm before sunrise and have a cup of coffee with John. I tell myself I keep this schedule because I would like to get home by 5:30 pm to have dinner with Hannah and Lilly. White lies don't count when we tell them to ourselves. Nothing in a law firm stops at 5:00. My firm is more humane than most; they don't demand that you to stay late *if* you get the work done.

Expectation and reality, however, rarely meet. In the law, there is always one more document to review, brief to write, legal principle to research. "Being done," appears as ephemeral as a mirage in the desert. I stay late many nights at the firm, watching myself work in the reflection of the office window, now a mirror from the blackness of night outside.

Saturdays remain my favorite days to work because very few others populate the office. I can "finally get something done." Occasionally I will have to jet out of the office to attend a kiddo's birthday party at a mini-gym or park. But once the kids sing and they cut the cake, it's my signal to excuse myself and run back to work. Hannah and Lilly like to sleep in on Sundays, and I find it simple to go to the office from early morning to noon, when activity heats up around the house. The grind of the office blunts the sorrow of no more children. Mostly it blunts the ache from witnessing my wife's disappointment, which tugs at her.

Shortly after the embryos failed to take, Hannah spent more and more time at home. It has more than sufficient space for the three of us and our Labrador, Porter. He is a hulking white dog, and Lilly loves to hang around his neck. Sometimes, she will sit him down and explain precisely what she is doing with her toys. Lilly spends hours playing in the backyard, often splashing in water to quell the intense Texas summer heat. Our house sits across from a school play-ground. With school out, Hannah and Lilly love to play on the monkey bars or on the slide together, mostly in the morning or at dusk, as the blistering sun makes the metal too hot to touch in the afternoon.

Hannah pours herself into Lilly, partly making up for lost time spent in Dr. Abrams's office and the regimen of tests, shots, and tension—but mostly because she adores that kid. Lilly's smile and tender nature works like a salve on the raw wound of failing to conceive. I blame the idiot doctors in Ithaca. Hannah blames them too. But I know—in those quiet moments when I see her staring off into the distance—that she also blames herself.

Without all the fertility treatment madness, Hannah reclaims hours in her day. She fills them with activities for Lilly—playdates, music, reading. They're inseparable. Lilly has her own room, but rarely disturbs the bedding. She sleeps with us in our bed, mostly curled up with her momma.

I think, "Three can be a simple, peaceful number."

We don't talk about a second round of IVF. Dr. Abrams is brilliant, but expensive, and we can't afford to try again. We could barely afford to try the first time, and juggling all the credit cards is daunting.

We're now buried in debt. All our money evaporates into paying it off. We have developed a system where, beyond our cars, mortgage, and utilities, we budget $25.00 for every day and track it religiously in the pages of a notebook. We have big loans to pay off. Spending money while chasing a dream is easy because hope exists. The excitement blinds you. Paying off debts after a failure feels like an endless ditch you fill one shovel full at a time. We agree to delay discussing any further fertility treatments until next year, which allows me to defer telling her the devastating conclusion that our finances likely cannot support another chance. We will give the summer, fall, and holidays to Lilly and our little family of three to heal. Then we can recalibrate.

In early August, we enroll Lilly in a half-day preschool at the local Methodist church. This leaves Hannah alone in the mornings. I like to check on them when Lilly returns home from school around lunch. It's a day like any other day in the office, so I grab a few documents from my secretary and head for my desk. I pick up the phone and call Hannah.

"Did you enjoy lunch?" she asks, her voice ripe with excitement.

"As much as you can enjoy an iceberg lettuce taco salad in the building's basement," I say.

"What time will you be home today, Daniel?"

"Probably not until late, Buzz. I have a ton of research to do, and they need it like yesterday. Sorry."

"I get it. I was going to wait to tell you. But. I. Can't. Wait!"

"Tell me what?" A few beats of silence pass on the telephone line.

"We're pregnant!" Her pleasure vibrates through the phone.

Confused, I almost choke on my coffee and sit quietly for

a moment. Words escape me. You hear about this happening all the time. Husbands and wives wind themselves so tight during IVF that even the greatest medical minds and talents can't force conception. Then, in the disappointment, the body relaxes. Nature takes its course and, "Bam!". . . you have a baby.

"You sure?"

"Just got back from Dr. Abrams's office," she says. "He really is quite pleased with himself. He says he painted the perfect hormonal canvas, and he says pregnancy looks good on me." I can hear her giant smile through the phone.

"I'll see if I can find some help around here. I want to come home, to see you."

I hang up the phone, and the excitement builds. My heart-beat ticks up, and I want to run a victory lap around my office floor with my arms held high. I don't, though, not sure that it would be professional.

But I'm elated. We did it! Maybe not the turkey baster way, but we *will* have another kid. Plus, it will be different this time. The doctors are different. The bilobed placenta that caused so much trouble last time was a fluke, a one-in-a-million anomaly. Besides, Dr. Abrams will watch over Hannah. He said a pregnancy, just the normal stretching of it, would likely break up any residual scaring, leaving the possibility for even more children. Hannah's dream of a big family has new life.

Our path forward has new life.

CHAPTER
TWENTY-ONE

LATE JULY. Dallas, Texas. Thirteen weeks to trial.

During our visit, Emmett told us about two nurses in the AdSeg unit who believed him: Lana Watts and Amanda Ryan. Steve rounds the corner into my office. He has evidently been thinking like me.

"Any luck finding the nurses?" he asks.

"None. I've searched all over the Internet. I've also plowed through the file twice and can't find any nugget that leads us to them."

"The cross-examination on Emmett's prisoner friends is likely to be brutal," Steve says. "Did you read the affidavits? They all say the same thing, word for word, like carbon copies."

"At least they're consistent."

"Yeah, consistent," he smirks.

"The nurses have to be somewhere in that city. I doubt they upped and moved away," I mutter in frustration.

"Not sure they'll advertise where they went. I'm pretty sure they'd like to remain hidden from any prisoners released."

"You remember anything Emmett said about why they left?"

"Only that they were gone about the time the Court said he was headed to trial."

"You don't think the prison was dumb enough to fire them?"

"Emmett said they used to fight with Nurse Hatcher. Who knows if that's true? I'm still amazed Emmett can find out any information locked away in solitary."

"Who knows how the rumor mill works in prison?"

"Maybe our law librarian can help us search the public records."

"It's worth a shot," I say.

With only prisoners for witnesses, we really need a solid citizen to testify on Emmett's behalf.

Right now, these nurses are ghosts.

CHAPTER
TWENTY-TWO

AUGUST. Dallas, Texas. Thirty weeks to a full-term baby.

Dr. Abrams hovers over Hannah. His desire to get the "mix" to his liking did not go away just because Hannah was pregnant by the natural order and not by IVF. He has restarted the weekly IVIG drips at $5,000 a pop. He also wants to keep her insides "supple and favorable." He is like Goldilocks—everything must be "just right." So, our regimen of shots does not stop. He added a new one, Heparin, an anti-coagulant, to help with smooth blood flow.

Luckily, the needle for Heparin is tiny, and we use a small diabetic's syringe. One night, on the way to visit Yuki I give Hannah the Heparin shot while we wait for the burger joint to finish our order in the drive-thru overflow. Another, we attend a birthday party at a giant Renaissance Fair under one roof with knights, serving wenches, and jesters juggling in the aisles. They don't believe in silverware. So in between scarfing down roast chicken and half a potato with my hands, I slip Hannah a quick Heparin shot under the table.

This go-round, however, the shots have even more purpose. Rather than hope for a child, we already care for one in utero. So night after night, exactly at 7:00 pm, I give

Hannah estrogen, progesterone, or both. Dr. Abrams drills into our heads the need to remain diligent about these two shots. Hannah gives herself the Heparin during the day (a tiny stab to a pinch of skin on her stomach), and I do it and the progesterone or estrogen at night. I make sure I'm home from work by 7:00 pm to deliver the shot. I then work from our kitchen table into the night.

The problem with regimens is that they become regimented. You end up planning your life around them or you adjust. We can't always be at home at shot time—life intercedes. The tiny Heparin needles fit easily into our schedule wherever we might be, but the estrogen and progesterone need the "big" needles, and those we must do at home. I won't do them in the bathroom of a 7-11 on a pit stop before a movie. We remain disciplined, and the system works well—until my firm sends me to Houston overnight for a client meeting.

"Hey, Buzz, I can't be home for the shots tomorrow, I have to fly to Houston for the firm."

"Don't worry," she says confidently. "I can go to the clinic on the corner. They can do it."

The next morning. I fly to Houston, counting on the clinic to take care of it.

That night, I am in the restaurant bathroom in a stall when my wife calls.

"Hey, Bear," she says. I know it the moment I hear it, her tone. . . . Something is wrong.

"What's up?" I press.

"Well . . ." she says, "I stopped by the clinic, . . . but they were closed. I didn't get my progesterone shot." She pauses a beat and then says, "It's okay though, I'll go back tomorrow morning."

"Whoa . . . ," I say. "It's 7 pm, you gotta have that shot. Tonight. . . . Now."

"But I told you they're closed."

Even though I am indisposed and in a different city, I start working the problem until I come up with the obvious solution. "You gotta give the shot to yourself."

"Daniel!" she protests. "I'm not sticking that needle into my butt."

The gentleman in the stall next to me flushes the toilet.

"Are you in a bathroom?"

"Let's focus on the mission at hand. What about your dad?" I ask. "Is he there?"

"I am not dropping my pants for my dad to give me a shot."

"He changed your diapers."

"Thirty years ago!" she says. "Things have changed."

"Just put your dad on the phone."

I can hear Lilly in the background, "Mom's in a mood!"

My father-in-law, Adam, gets on the speakerphone.

"Adam, you have to give her the shot. It's easy. The nurse drew a circle on her hip with marker. You just slide it in and push the plunger. Pull it out."

Silence.

"Adam?" I nudge. "You there?"

"I gotta practice," he blurts out.

"Practice? . . . Adam, this ain't exactly a practice sort of activity."

"You want that shot, I gotta practice."

I devise a way to help Adam rehearse.

"You in the kitchen?" I ask.

"Yes"

"Is the fruit bowl behind you?"

"Yes."

"Grab an orange. Practice on that."

After a few beats I can hear him. "Stick. . . . Push. . . . Pull. . . . Stick. . . . Push. . . . Pull."

Finally, I ask, "Adam . . . we good?"

"We're as good as we're gonna get," he says.

"Okay, well here we go . . . I'll count to three. . . . One . . . two . . ."

"Wait!"

"What?"

Adam asks, "Are we going, one, two, three then stick . . . ? Or one, two, stick on three?"

"Adam . . . I'm on a toilet in Houston . . . I'll go with whatever you decide."

"Okay. Let's go."

I count, "One . . . two . . ."

He goes on three. I know because I hear Hannah breathe in sharply.

"I don't like this . . . I don't like this . . . I don't like this!" Adam yells. Then, "Clear!"

Hannah shouts, "Good God!"

A few moments later, she comes back on the phone.

"How's Grandpa?" I inquire.

"He's chugging a beer, but we're all good here. . . . Thanks, Bear."

CHAPTER
TWENTY-THREE

AUGUST. Dallas, Texas. Ten weeks to trial.

Steve and I chat over lunch in the basement of our office building. We have a mess of a record and no corroborating civilian witnesses. The nurses have disappeared, vanished.

Steve toys with his lunch, worried. "We have no medical expert, no nurses, no civilian witnesses." Steve says. "The holes in our case are like Swiss cheese."

In a medical malpractice case, you must have one doctor testify that the defendant failed to operate within the standard of care for accepted medical practice. Here, we were not accusing the staff of malpractice, but we were accusing them of failing to acknowledge the severity of their indifference to Emmett's health.

Our only witness is Emmett, a career criminal and an inmate. All he can offer is what he understands as a patient about his heart condition and its treatment. He's not exactly a medical professional.

"It's too late to hire an outside medical expert now. We missed that window," I say. "I was counting on finding those nurses."

"Damn!" Steve swears.

On the defendants' side will be the prison physician and several nurses, all able to weave a complicated tapestry of his condition in medical jargon, leaving Steve and me at a disadvantage. They will try to convince the jury we are seeing ghosts in the shadows, that Emmett's complaints are overblown. I expect they will tear him down, beating the drum that Emmett is in prison for robbing a bank and can't be trusted.

Steve tosses his napkin on top of his half-finished lunch.

"We have no expert, no witnesses, and a maze of documents," Steve says. "All we really have is Emmett."

There's no way we can win.

CHAPTER
TWENTY-FOUR

SEPTEMBER. Wichita Falls, Texas. Eight weeks to trial.

The courthouse in Wichita Falls is conducting another prisoner's trial. The local newspaper, *The Times Record*, runs stories daily about it. Another prisoner from Teton Springs has made it to a jury. He is a gay black man in the general population of the prison. He alleges several gangs prostitute him out to other prisoners, force him to endure rape after rape for their profit. The lurid details of the claims draw big guns. The American Civil Liberties Union took his case and geared up for war. I drive up to see jury selection and the jury pool. I also want to see how the Judge runs it. I need to understand the logistics. I'd like to avoid making rookie mistakes in our trial and looking like a fool.

When I arrive, cars pack the parking lot. Overflow lines the street. News crews perch on the courthouse steps. I walk inside and wait my turn in the security line.

The United States Post Office and Court House is a gray granite building on the corner of 10th and Lamar in downtown Wichita Falls, Texas. It looks much like any other government building built by Franklin D. Roosevelt during the Great Depression—ornate and solid, but solemn. The post office resides on the first floor, appointed with brass fittings around the windows and other fixtures of a bygone era.

The courtroom rests on the top floor, a bell in the elevator dings as it passes each level. I walk in and take a seat on a pew in the back to observe. The courtroom has thirty-foot ceilings and oak paneling everywhere. Heavy maroon velvet curtains drape both walls of floor-to-ceiling windows. It radiates the power of the Federal government.

During jury selection in Federal court, the Judge goes first and asks most of the questions. The exercise seeks to find hardships, conflicts, and unbendable biases in the jury panel. Next go the lawyers for the litigants. From the entire panel from which the jury is drawn (known as the venire), they will select twelve jurors and two alternates to hear their case. Depending on the issues in the lawsuit and the publicity in the community, the jury pool will vary in size. Sometimes it takes many jurors to find twelve impartial ones. For this case, the Judge has requested one hundred potential jurors. I have arrived in time for the final question by the Judge.

"How many of you work for or have someone in your family who works for the prison system?" More than half the hands go up in the pews. The Judge instructs, "Keep your hands up so counsel can get a count. I imagine they may have some questions about that later."

After the Judge finishes, counsel for the plaintiff questions the panel. The ACLU assigned three lawyers from New York City to try the case. They sound and look very East Coast, an oddity in what many would consider middle-of-nowhere, backwater Texas. Attuned to the potential problem, the ACLU hired local counsel from Lubbock to do most of the talking. He is tall and all Texan. His deep drawl falls out from under a cowboy handlebar mustache as he probes the panel for bias.

"Juror Number Twenty, Mr. Stewart. You indicated someone in your family works for the prison system. Can you tell me more about that, sir?" asks the Cowboy Lawyer, "Tex."

"Well, my daughter works over in Vernon at the jail there. She's a guard. She's tough and all, but some of those inmates say the most god-awful things to her, her being a woman and all. Some of them are just outright animals." An unsettling number of heads nod in agreement. Tex draws similar answers from several other potential jurors who raised their hands.

"How many of you agree with the statement, 'prisoners deserve what they get in prison?'" Tex quizzes.

Hands shoot up all over the jury panel.

"Juror Number Twelve, Ms. Anderson is it? Ms. Anderson, can you tell me what about that statement you agree with?"

"Well. They did something to end up where they are. If they didn't want to have a rough go of it, they should've thought about what they were doing before they did it. Their crime, I mean. Say they're in prison for shooting a person. They didn't think about how that was gonna hurt that family before they pulled the trigger, did they? Not sure they should be crying for sympathy now. They did it, and they deserve whatever they get. Fair is fair."

Heads nod in agreement throughout the panel. The East Coast lawyers from the ACLU scribble notes furiously. Question after question teases out the pervasive anti-prisoner sentiment.

Tex probes, "Does anybody here believe that it's impossible for a man to get raped?"

More hands.

"Juror Number 34, Mr. Foster? Mr. Foster can you tell us your view on whether a man can get raped."

"Well sir, and I'm just being honest here because you told me to, but, no . . . unlessen he's dead, no man can get raped. He'd have to fight 'till he was good and dead before any *man* would let that happen to him. That's just how I feel."

I stand up quietly and head back down to my car. After a

few moments, I merge onto the highway and start the long drive back to Dallas. I mull over our potential jury pool. For our trial, the court will summon jurors from the same counties, from the same people.

People who will tell me "fair is fair."

CHAPTER
TWENTY-FIVE

MID-SEPTEMBER. Dallas, Texas. Twenty-four weeks to a full-term baby.

The summer temperatures start to break. Hannah glows with pregnancy. Fall rolls along. Football is well underway in Texas; we hear whistles from the morning practices at the local high school. Dr. Abrams's chemistry experiment is working wonders. We hit all the regular markers. One evening, Hannah and I decide to head to a college football game in town. We walk into the stadium. The crisp fall air feels great, and the game is exciting. We enjoy being out, the normalcy of it all. After bedrest and preterm labor with Lilly, we have welcomed the simplicity of this second pregnancy.

As we wrap up the evening and head up the bleachers, Hannah turns to me. "Something's not right," she whispers, her jaw tight. "I'm bleeding."

"How much?"

"I don't think much. Maybe just spotting. I don't know."

We rush home to figure out what is going on. She calls Dr. Abrams and explains what happened. The magnitude. He calmly reassures her. He tells her to lie down and take it easy.

If something gets worse, he tells us to call him and come see him in the morning.

That night, as I fall asleep, a storm of worry roils through me. I push away the memories of preterm labor and the full cascade of life-threatening events in Ithaca.

When we arrive the next morning at Dr. Abrams's office, his nurse whisks us back immediately to the examination room. Dr. Abrams sings while he runs the sonogram, a tuft of gray hair flopping over his ear as he plays with dials and the sonogram wand. He sings during all procedures, and he claims it relieves any stress in the room. He checks the baby. The heartbeat is pounding away, and the little kiddo seems calm and peaceful growing inside Hannah. Dr. Abrams explains everything he sees as he sees it, pronouncing it excellent, pronouncing the baby healthy.

"Do we have a name?" He asks.

"Bailey McKenna," Hannah says.

"Family name?"

"No, we just like it."

"Lilly and Bailey. Beautiful names for beautiful girls." He goes back to evaluating the sonogram screen. His singing never once stops, but something changes, and he suddenly looks serious. The tone of his voice tenses, his jawline set with concern.

"Let me guess," I say, "a bilobed placenta."

"Oh no. No, no. Not bilobed at all. It has attached well and seems to be just the one lobe."

"That's good," Hannah reassures herself.

"We will want to watch it, though," he says, concern in his voice. "The location of the placenta caused the spotting. We will want to keep a keen eye on it."

"What's wrong with it?" Hannah asks, her voice tight with apprehension.

"Nothing is wrong. It just attached low. We will want to watch it. It's a previa."

"A previa?" My throat tightens; my mouth suddenly dry.

"Yes. Placenta previa. Also known as a low-lying placenta. It has attached low in the uterus near the cervical opening. But it's early. It could migrate. As Bailey grows, the uterus grows, and the previa may move away from the opening. All could turn out fine. It's too early to tell. Too early to worry."

"Can we fix it?" I say.

"No. We wait. This one we just have to watch and wait."

Hannah's palms rest in her lap as we drive home, slouched in the passenger seat. I think, *We are batting a thousand for pernicious placentas.*

Over the next few weeks Hannah takes it easy. She visits Dr. Abrams regularly. He seems relatively unconcerned but places her on a mild regimen of bed rest. She must lie down when she can and not pick up anything over 10 pounds.

How does that work with a toddler running around the house a million miles a minute? Hannah keeps off her feet as much as possible. She and Lilly watch movies and take naps together.

Lilly enjoys playing with Grandpa. Hannah's dad works on an engineering job in Oklahoma City helping rebuild the main Interstate through downtown. The job site is straight up I-35. He stays in Dallas on the weekends or when he can and works in Oklahoma City during the weeks. Some days, he commutes up and down—about three hours each way. But I can see the dark circles under his brown eyes and graying hair.

All is happy and going well. It's hard, though, not to drag concern and doubt forward from what happened when Hannah was pregnant with Lilly. The Ithaca doctors also put Hannah on bedrest for risk of preterm labor. An uneasy familiarity exists with the bedrest we now follow with Bailey.

In Ithaca, we spent several winter nights at the hospital for preterm labor pains. Hannah would sleep, and I would read law school books while listening to the fetal monitor. I remember one particular dirty look from a nurse who noticed

I was reading books on divorce. I guess she figured I had had enough, but I was just studying for the legal clinic at law school.

Juggling it all proves difficult. Life at the firm is busy. William Paul Moore III needs his billable hours. No matter what time I arrive or leave, I have more work than I can complete. It overflows into the weekends.

But now, on top of the normal career pressures, Steve and I are rocketing toward a trial in a matter of weeks. No matter what, I'll have to leave town for a week or more. The long, black hole of sleeping two hundred miles away from Hannah terrifies me. All of us juggle hard to keep balls in the air, but that is not the hardest part. The most difficult times come watching Hannah worry. I can't control how angst plays within her. Sure, she keeps a cheerful face around Lilly and others; she enjoys life, and takes it in, but I know she frets. When she thinks no one is watching, maybe when she washes a dish, folds a blanket, or picks up a few toys, I glimpse her large, beautiful hazel eyes puddled with concern. Her smile tightens, her gaze a little distant.

But I also know she is the stronger of the two of us.

CHAPTER
TWENTY-SIX

OCTOBER. Wichita Falls, Texas. One week before trial.

The Mexican restaurant in Wichita Falls hums with the lunch crowd. Noise bounces off all the hard surfaces and mixes with the piped-in music. We have not ordered yet, waiting for former nurses from the Teton Springs Prison.

Aside from the prisoners Emmett suggested as witnesses, he listed two nurses: Lana Watts and Amanda Ryan. Emmett told us they would back up his claims as to the spotty supply of Isosorbide and Nitroglycerin, and that the head nurse, Nurse Hatcher, had ignored his difficulties. They both had worked in the medical unit in AdSeg. It had taken us some time to find them—folks who work in prisons try to make their addresses and phones as inaccessible as possible, so prisoners can't look them up after release. Fortunately, on a fluke, I tracked down a relative and left a message to call me. Ms. Watts did call, and said they would both meet with us when we arrived in Wichita Falls. Buying them lunch seemed as good a plan as any.

Steve and I have also enlisted another associate, Ashley Carmichael, to help us research and prepare pretrial materials. Ashley has become invaluable. Good things come in small packages—she's just five feet tall but smart as a whip with her clever brown eyes framed by attractive designer glasses that rest on her aristocratic Roman nose. She believes Emmett and works excitedly with us. But . . . she has also adopted the role as Devil's advocate, punching holes in all our arguments. To our amusement and dismay, she takes great joy in that part.

The waitress brings chips and salsa. The minute hand on the clock is well past the agreed meeting time.

"What'll it be?" the waitress barks, ready to take our order.

"We're waiting for two more," I say, and she leaves with a slight huff.

"They're late," Steve says. "Think they will show?" He chews on his fingernails, the usual habit when he's stressed.

"They better. Or we don't have a case," I say.

"They're not coming," Ashley says, pushing her long brown hair back behind her ear. "Why should they help a prisoner? They've got nothing to gain and everything to lose —their jobs, friends, reputation, and time."

"Do you *always* have to play Devil's advocate?" I sigh.

"That's my job," Ashley says defensively.

"There's a time and a place," I say.

"She's right," Steve says, coming to Ashley's defense.

"And do you *always* have to play the knight in shining armor?" I chide Steve. I wonder if I should tell him not to flirt with Ashley—she's off limits to any prowling during our trial.

"I don't need a knight in shining armor or in a fancy suit," Ashley snaps, pushing her designer glasses up the bridge of her nose.

"Glad you like it," Steve retorts and brushes the lapels of his pricey suit. As usual, his attire is more expensive than mine. I prefer to dress more modestly—I want to be more approachable—and besides, let's be honest, I'm on a strict budget.

A waiter carries a hot iron plate of fajitas covered in steaming, smoking butter by our table, filling the air with the heavy scent of delicious food. We're hungry and on edge. I change the topic. "Let's give them a few more minutes. I'd hate to be eating when they get here, make them wait for their lunch."

"They're not coming," Ashley predicts again under her breath with a sigh, and silence breaks out between us.

Steve gestures to the waitress for more chips and salsa. "I'll bet they got a call or two from 'friends' at the prison, and they decided to skip lunch. Why bother for a convict, you know?"

As the waitress sets down a fresh bowl of chips, I offer, "How would anyone know we found them?"

"Small town," Steve says.

We fill up on chips and salsa as we wait for thirty minutes. Just as I'm about to give up, two women walk in the front door. One is a tall pale-skinned redhead with freckles, the other a shorter brunette with an olive complexion. They match the descriptions Emmett gave us. Each of them scans the room as if looking for people they might know.

Bingo! Flooded with relief, I meet them by the hostess stand. Without these witnesses, we don't have a case. With them, we might have a case—*if they will testify.*

"Ms. Watts, Ms. Ryan?" They nod. "I'm Daniel Simmons, we're sitting over here." I guide them to our table. Steve and Ashley introduce themselves, and we finally order lunch.

Steve asks questions about Emmett's case. Ashley and I scratch out notes. Each time the door opens, Watts and Ryan glance at who enters, as if on watch.

"Did you both work in the AdSeg Unit?" Steve asks.

"Yes. We were both nurses doing the medical rounds. Amanda also worked in the pill room, where all the medicine comes in. It gets shipped in bulk. She would put together the pill packets to hand out to the prisoners."

Steve asks them about how they ended up at the Teton Springs Prison and gets a few more background facts. We will need those to make them relatable on the stand, . . . *if they agree to testify*. Once those details are covered, we get to Emmett.

Nurse Watts bites her lip for a moment. "I liked Mr. Kendrick," she says, pushing her brunette hair away from her face, a wistful gaze from her caring brown eyes. "I don't think he was ever lying about his meds. He wasn't trying to game the system and get something he shouldn't or more than he needed. When he said he was missing his meds, he was missing his meds pure and simple. We'd tell Nurse Hatcher, but she didn't much want to listen." They describe several times how they asked Nurse Hatcher about the problem getting no answers.

"Why did you leave?" Steve pries.

Nurse Watts sighs, "AdSeg got to be stressful, exhausting. Plus, you can only fight about things so long. They just didn't care about getting the prisoners their meds. We didn't want to fight against that day in and day out."

"I'm going to use a legal term," I say. "You tell me if you disagree. Would you say they were 'deliberately indifferent' to supplying Mr. Kendrick his medicines."

"Yeah. You could say that," Nurse Ryan, jumps in and agrees. Her fire-red hair frames her hazel eyes and long eyelashes, and her expression flashes a moment of relief, as if confessing a burden.

Nurse Watts chimes in, her gaze now fierce. "They went *well beyond* deliberately indifferent. They went out of their way *to not give a damn*."

"Do you mind testifying at trial?"

"No," they both say at the same time. Nurse Ryan clears

her throat and continues, "Someone should say something and make them do what they should."

Steve and I look at each other. Until now, the case seemed impossible. We have Emmett; that is all. The prisoner witnesses may very well be useless, and we have no expert medical testimony. Now, though, we have insiders, two of their own who will call them to account.

The waitress drops the check, and I'm ecstatic to pick it up. I ask the nurses, "Either of you want some desert?"

—

CHAPTER
TWENTY-SEVEN

OCTOBER. Wichita Falls, Texas. Five days before trial.

Steve and I pull out of the hotel parking lot. My hotel room serves as the main war room where we can strategize. It's jammed with the case file, the equipment we will need at trial and empty fast-food to-go boxes. Over the previous weeks, we have worked carefully to streamline the evidence and Emmett's case into a series of events that the jury might believe—a simple story. Our banker's boxes contain organized folders and copies of exhibits. They also contain legal cases and articles from prestigious medical journals researching Isosorbide, Nitroglycerin, and many heart ailments.

Steve and I drive to the prison to interview Emmett's inmate witnesses who might support the claims of poor medical care. If we have time, we may visit with Emmett briefly today. We have communicated with him by mail over the past few weeks. Tomorrow morning we have a pretrial hearing with the Judge. In the afternoon, we will go over Emmett's testimony with him and lay out the overall final trial strategy. Today's mission is to see if we can salvage a prisoner witness or two.

We arrive at the prison and go through the metal detector like before. Officer Larkin walks us into the center of the facility to the same waiting room where we first met Emmett. She gives us a wry smile and sticks her thumbs in the straps of the protective vest she is wearing.

"It's gonna be awhile. They started late serving lunch to the cellblocks where we house your inmates. Once they're done, we'll find the ones you want to visit with and get you to a visitor's station."

"How long does lunch take?" Steve asks, flashing a smile at Larkin.

A hint of mischief creeps into Larkin's expression. "Not long . . . no more than an hour usually, if there's no trouble" she says. She stares at us, then shakes her head and struts out of the visitor room, shutting the door behind her.

Steve and I take in our surroundings. We are two solitary figures in the room. The lights are off, solely dull gray light spills through the windows, and the only sound is the compressor cooling cans of soda in the vending machine. Steve gets up and pulls on the door handle.

"Locked," he says. "You know they could have told us when we got here." Exasperation invades his voice. "We could have gone and picked up some lunch while we waited, right?"

"I'm pretty sure we are exactly where they want us," I say. I pull out the binder that holds Emmett's witness outline, and flip it open. I work through the questions I will ask Emmett from the stand, double-checking the exhibits. Those I want to work from sit behind the correct tab in the binder, and they are cross-referenced to the witness outline. After a few minutes, I pick up the only other sound in the room: a large round clock sits high on the wall behind a wire cage, and the secondhand ticks loudly as it creeps around the large white face.

Two dreary hours later, Steve and I finally hear a key turn

the lock in the door to the visitor's room. The beautiful Officer Larkin stands in the doorway, looking ready to pounce.

"You two, come on. They're done with chow."

Steve and I police up all our papers, stuff them in our briefcases, and follow Larkin. Evidently, she will take us to the prisoners rather than bring them here. Larkin snakes us through a series of hallways and past gate after gate of thick bars. The smell of germicide and institutional food grows thicker as she takes us deeper and deeper into the prison. We come to a large steel door.

"This is the inside of the AdSeg unit," she says. "They might be moving some of the inmates around because it's shower day for some. Don't talk to them. Don't make eye contact. If they have to pass, we'll press up close to one of the walls and let the CO's take them by. Some of these boys would break you for sport, just to have something to do. They have nothing to lose. So pay attention and do what I say—or I won't be responsible for your safety."

She opens the door and holds it while Steve and I walk through. I'm surprised by what I see. I had expected to see long rows of cells with bars. Mostly, I had expected to see every jail scene from the movies where prisoners rattle their cages with metal coffee cups. Instead, a long white hallway with shining tile floors extends out in front of us. A couple of Corrections Officers walk the halls shuffling to their next task. She leads us to a door with a small square window, the view partially obscured by wire mesh in the glass. She opens it.

"This is one of the lawyer rooms. We'll bring the inmate in soon. That phone by the window is to talk to the prisoner," she says. "That phone on the wall by the door is to call a guard to come get you." She shuts the door behind us, and we hear a key turn.

Again, Steve and I wait; no clock on the wall this time. We are in a room separated down the middle with a half wall below and then glass to the ceiling. One bulb illuminates each side, casting downward shadows on everything. Finally, we hear chains clinking. The door opens, and the inmate performs the same ritual we saw when we first met Emmett. The guards remove the leg restraints, and then inmate Carter steps inside. After the door closes, he places his hands back through the slot to have the restraints on his wrists unlocked by a guard. Then the slot slams shut. The prisoner sits down and picks up the phone. The volume on the handset speaker is loud enough for Steve and me to both hear him.

"You two Emmett's lawyers?" Carter asks.

"Yes. I'm Daniel Simmons and this is Steve Davis."

"I'm Darby Carter. I know why you're here. Hell, the whole jail knows why you're here. Emmett is a downright celebrity with his fancy lawyers and all. What do you want with me?"

"Well, Mr. Carter, Emmett says you can tell us about the medical care here and if it's shoddy."

"You bet it's shoddy. They're supposed to come around once a day and check each of the prisoners through the slot, talk to you. If you're sick, they supposed to do something about it."

"And that's not what they do?" Steve asks.

"Hell no. Nurse comes on the block and yells out medical. If they have your pills, they pass it through the slot. If not, they pass you by; never pay you much mind. Last fall, I had some kind of awful bug or flu. It was days before any nurse checked on me. One guard finally took notice because I was hacking up a lung in the shower. That landed me in medical for a week."

"You know anything about how they treat Emmett?"

"He tells me about it in the yard, in the dog runs once in a while. Although we're not supposed to talk. I don't see him much. We're on different schedules. He's on A-Block, I'm further in on C-Block. I'm closer to the crazies in the back."

Steve follows up, "Mr. Carter, what do you mean, crazies?"

"AdSeg has five cell blocks, son. A-Block houses your regular guys, the ones that don't give much trouble to the CO's. As you go back, they house the troublemakers. E-Block is full of the nut jobs, and guys that are hard to control. I spent a year back on E-Block—real wackos."

"You ever file a grievance on the medical staff?" I ask.

"I used to file grievances pretty regular. No point, though. Each warden stamps it 'unsubstantiated' and they all have each other's backs as it goes up the chain."

"Can you see the doctor if you're sick?"

"He's worthless. Nice guy, but worthless. Let's just say it this way, not many folks go to medical school to end up a prison doc in the middle of nowhere. Most of them done something to land here. Career not going too great you might say."

"And you're still willing to testify for Emmett, right?" I say.

"Yep. I'd be happy to sit in that chair and tell anybody about the lousy medical staff in here."

I finish jotting down some notes. This prisoner is shaved and clean. He looks somewhat credible. His testimony matches Emmett's. A jury might believe him if we keep it simple. I look at Steve and nod at the door.

Steve says, "Just a couple more questions. What did you do to end up in here?"

Mr. Carter takes a long look at Steve.

"Few years ago, I forged a bunch of checks. Was living good on that money. They busted my girlfriend with drugs, and she ratted me out to get probation. Cute bitch, but still a bitch."

"You're in AdSeg for writing bad checks?" Steve says incredulously.

"No. Once I was in the system, they matched me to a few

rapes in Dallas. I was all over the news at one point. Those rapes are what landed me here. Fighting with the guards landed me in E-Block for six months. Good behavior got me transferred to C-Block."

I watch his expression as he tells us about forging checks, raping women, and getting in fights. Not a stitch of remorse crosses his face. In fact, when he tells me about the news covering his rapes, he seems proud. Chances are he is itching to tell stories about his past from the stand on cross-examination. Steve and I thank him and use the prison phone to call the guard. They take him out the same way they brought him in.

Then Larkin appears, opens the door, and barks, "Come." We step into the passageway, as a prisoner approaches.

"Stand against the wall there," she points. "We're gonna let this one pass."

Steve and I watch as the prisoner shuffles down the hall, hands chained to his waist, another chain between his ankles. He is coming back from the shower, and he stands tall and muscled, a towel wrapped around his waist. Tattoos cover his body; the black outline of eagle talons are drawn across his bald head. A guard walks several feet in front of him, two walk on either side. Behind him several feet strides another guard. The prisoner looks at us like we are odd animals in a zoo. They pass after several moments, the prisoner's chained gait takes time.

"Four guards to move one inmate?" Steve asks Larkin.

"The one in front looks for anyone coming down another hall. Two on the side control the prisoner. The one in the back will drop him with a stun gun if he does something stupid. Come on . . . your next one is in High Security."

She guides us through another series of halls. As we pass from AdSeg to High Security, the walls change from white to gray. She leads us to another visitor booth and locks us in. We wait. After a few minutes, a bald head pops up in the door's window on the prisoner's side. He stares at us for a moment, looks nervous and fidgety. His head pops up and down like a prairie dog. Finally, the guards place him in the box, and take off his cuffs. No leg chains—must be a perk of High Security. The prisoner sits down at the table on his side. No glass separates us, just a steel grate. We don't need telephones here. He introduces himself as Charlie and walks us through how awful the medical care is and what a "bitch" the head nurse can be. He backs up what Emmett says. He looks rough and tells us he's Emmett's nephew, but an obvious meth problem has made him look like he's the uncle. The meth has also robbed him of any calm, as he constantly shifts in his chair and looks over his shoulder while he tells us about his testimony. He is less presentable than the other prisoner, but what he says dovetails exactly with Emmett's claims. Maybe we can get him up and off the stand quickly. As we wrap up, Steve asks what he did to land in prison.

"Meth. I got a meth problem and that got me in some bigger trouble."

"And what trouble would that be?" Steve nudges, I can tell he senses something.

"They arrested me for bedding my girlfriend's daughter," he blurts out, a flash of energy in his gaze. "That's what they say, anyway. I was high as a kite for a week before she claimed it happened. Don't remember nothing. She might have been thirteen, maybe fourteen but I think they both made it up as some kind of revenge."

I'm repulsed, and I signal to the guard we are done.

As Charlie stands up, he says, "Hey, don't tell Emmett about the daughter. He wouldn't understand. He's real old school about crimes, and he'd kill me for shit like this."

Officer Larkin meets us at the door. Steve flirts with her, and she raises an eyebrow archly. But she's beautiful, so she expects the flattering attention. She escorts us back to the visitor room where we first met Emmett. Then she walks to the other side of the room to give us the illusion of privacy.

We hear Emmett's chains jingling before we see him. The door opens, the guard unlocks Emmett's chains, and then locks him in the booth. Emmett greets us with a giant smile and a glint in his ice-blue eyes. Trial starts in a few days, but he looks calm, peaceful—even happy.

I pull out a three-ring binder.

"Emmett, this is the outline for your testimony. I need you to study it, go over it in your cell over the next few days." I motion to Larkin. "I need to get this to Mr. Kendrick. Do I give it to you?"

"He can't have that," Larkin says and points to my binder.

"Wait. This is legal paperwork, I'm his attorney, and I need him to have it for the trial next week," I argue.

"He can have the papers, just not the binder. Not saying Mr. Kendrick would do it, but those metal rings will end up jabbed in someone around here. They make shanks out of anything—toothbrushes, sticks, combs. Those rings are prime, sharp."

Emmett nods. "I can read the papers without the binder."

I take the documents out and give them to Larkin. She flips through them.

Emmett explains, "She's checking for paper clips."

Larkin finishes scanning for contraband and walks out the door. In a few moments, the slot opens up, and the papers appear. Emmett grabs them. He flips through the outline and some exhibits. Then he grins.

"I'll study all weekend."

"Well, we have a pretrial hearing tomorrow morning, and then we'll come back. We can tell you then what some of the Judge's rulings are. Emmett, we need to talk about your prisoner witnesses. We want to cancel their trial subpoenas. They might help you on the medical, but they got problems. Drug problems, forging, rape." I don't mention Charlie specifically.

"The government is likely to tear them up on cross-examination, and that could kill your case."

Emmett thumbs through the outline, gathers his thoughts, and then looks inquiringly at Steve and then me.

"If they have to go, then they go. You're the lawyers, I'll follow your lead—I trust you," he decides, releasing the many months of hard work he spent gathering those witnesses, typing up their testimony, and preparing his case.

"We found Nurse Watts and Nurse Ryan," I say.

Emmett's eyes widen, a pulse of energy flashes through them.

"Did they say I was telling the truth?"

"They said you were a model prisoner, not a complainer. That you didn't get your meds when you should. They told us you'd tried to get the staff to fix it, and you weren't very successful. I'll tell you, neither Watts nor Ryan like Nurse Hatcher. They don't think she cared much to fix the problem. We asked specifically if they would testify that the prison officials were "deliberately indifferent," the words in the jury charge. Both Watts and Ryan agreed with that term."

"That's a breakthrough!" Emmett says. "Nurses trump prisoners any day of the week. Do you think we can win?"

"Well, we are better off today than we were, that's for sure. We still face an uphill climb. We'll know more once the jury is in the box," I say, managing his expectations.

Steve and I finish up and say goodbye to Emmett. We still have a ton of work to accomplish. As we walk out to my car, the sun begins to set, splashing oranges and pinks across the cloudy sky as if to celebrate our day of progress. Fall days now shrink, and the light is already fading. The prison sits out in the middle of a wide-open field. There are no trees for cover. The guards could see any prisoner trying to escape for a mile in any direction. I glance up and see the sharpshooter in the tower. A slight wind blows. Emmett's words reverberate in my mind: "I trust you."

CHAPTER
TWENTY-EIGHT

FRIDAY; Wichita Falls, three days before trial.

"All rise. The court in and for the Northern District of Texas is now in session, the Honorable Carmen Navarro presiding."

Steve and I watch the Judge come out on the bench in her long, black robe. Her short, professional haircut frames an expression of authority and intelligence. Trial starts Monday. Before any trial, however, the Judge holds a pretrial hearing to finalize the general logistics of the proceeding: how many days, how jury selection will work. We tell her we no longer will call the prisoner witnesses, so she can cancel the trial subpoenas to the prison. Most of the hearing is not contentious until I make one final important request.

"Your Honor, we'd like to request that Mr. Kendrick be given the opportunity to appear in court in a suit rather than his prison fatigues," I say.

Rose Walker, trial counsel for the State of Texas opposes. "You're Honor, it's hard enough to transport these prisoners from AdSeg around safely without making the guards keep track of a pinstriped suit. I mean, where's he going to keep it .

. . in his cell?" Rose is the epitome of a hard-scrabble professional, complete with a practiced resting bitch face. Dark, smoky makeup accentuates her piercing hazel eyes that bore into anyone catching her gaze. Her short auburn hair perches in an all-business cut, with a slight flourish over her right cheek. A chain made of thick silver links adorns her neck, complete with a prominent cross. *Is she a devout Christian or will it all be a ploy to curry favor with the salt-of-the-earth jurors in this county?* A tight, merciless navy-blue skirt and blazer stress her athletic frame. She is all business, and in it to win it. A statement from Hitch pops into my mind, *"Trial law is a full contact sport. If you don't like it leave your uniform in the locker room."* Her full lips form a slight, skeptical frown to everything I say. *Intimidating*.

Clearing my throat and my mind from its novice panic of facing a seasoned Rose, I turn back to the Judge. "Your Honor, we just feel that if Mr. Kendrick is forced to testify in his prison fatigues, the jury is going to discount immediately everything he has to say, even before he opens his mouth. We're just asking for a fair, impartial shot to present him on the stand."

"Mr. Simmons," the Judge says, "Mr. Kendrick has been incarcerated a long time, does he even have a suit?" she quizzes.

"Yes, Your Honor, if you allow him to wear one in court, he'll have one by Monday." I say not knowing how I'll get one.

"Ms. Walker, I don't see a reason why Mr. Kendrick can't change here at the courthouse in the holding cell. We'll lock it up at night. He can leave the suit here. Mr. Simmons, you have your suit. Anything else?" Rose's brow furrows with determination. I know I will pay for this.

"No, Your Honor," I say.

"Well then. We'll see you Monday at 8:30 am."

I glance at Steve, triumph glinting in my eyes. If Emmett appears dressed in a suit, he has a chance at a fair trial. Maybe we could win.

CHAPTER
TWENTY-NINE

FRIDAY. Noon. Teton Springs, Texas. Later that same day.

Officer Larkin leads Steve and me through the labyrinth of the prison toward the visitor room, her tight, perfect braid tucked in her body armor, and the light glints off the handcuffs on her duty belt. We don't have to wait this time. Emmett shows up promptly. Steve and I cover the pretrial, and explain what will happen in court on Monday. Then we get to the suit.

"I get to wear a suit?" Emmett asks, incredulous. It might as well have been Christmas.

"What size are you?" Steve asks.

"I do not know. It's been so long since I've worn a suit. And I'm not the man I used to be. I've shrunk."

"How are we going to get your measurements?" Steve mutters, pulling at his shirt cuffs. He glances at Officer Larkin, "Could you help?"

She frowns and shakes her head. "What do you think I am —a tailor?"

We can't get near Emmett to measure him, and the guards will not help. But appearing in an ill-fitting suit might do as much damage as appearing in prison fatigues. Somehow, we must get the right measurements. But how?

Suddenly, I have an idea. I tell Steve, "Tear off some sheets from your yellow pad."

I grab a sheet of paper from Steve and tear it into half-inch coils. Then another one. We tear pages until we have a dozen coils. I pull out a large envelope and place the coils inside. We ask Larkin to give the envelope with the shredded paper and a pencil to Emmett.

"You better make sure he gives you that full pencil back when you're done," Larkin says curtly. She delivers the envelope as requested.

"Emmett, I need you to take that first coil of paper and wrap it around your neck—not too tight." He does. "Now tear it off and mark it with your pencil, 'Neck.'" Emmett complies, and I note how easily he follows commands—an institutional habit. A tailor recently measured me for a tux for a wedding, and I remember all the measurements he took. We measure Emmett's chest, waist, arms, and inseam, tearing each spiral of paper and marking it with the body part. He tells us he takes a size seven shoe. He places all the coils in a manila envelope, holding the full pencil clearly in front of the glass for Larkin to see, then he drops it into the envelope, too. Emmett knocks on the door and signals the guard. Officer Larkin walks to the back hallway and retrieves the envelope. She checks for the pencil and then hands me the envelope with his measurements.

"I'll study," he says.

Steve and I take our leave.

He dons his shackles to head back to his cell.

As we exit the prison, Steve says, "Is it just me or does Officer Larkin really fill out those prison fatigues?" I roll my eyes, but also somewhat agree.

Later, Steve and I head to a department store for a suit. We run into the Menswear Manager. He is short and stout, with graying blonde hair combed over to hide his severe receding hairline.

"What can I get you?" he asks, tugging on a worn burgundy tie, flashing his best sales floor smile.

"We need a suit."

He looks me up and down appraisingly, then inspects Steve's much taller frame.

"Which one of you wants to go first?"

"It's not for us. I need to get a suit that fits this." I dump the paper coils out on his counter.

His eyebrows shoot up in surprise. I guess he's never had to fit a suit this way before. "What's this?"

"Those are his measurements. See, this one's the neck. This one's the inseam," Steve explains, showing him the pencil marks on the coils of torn yellow legal pad.

"We're lawyers, our client is locked in solitary confinement. We need a suit for him for trial on Monday," I say.

"I see." The Menswear Manager turns suddenly frosty, pulling a measuring tape from around his neck. "What color?"

"Blue suit, white shirt, blue tie," I say. "Women prefer a blue tie."

The salesman walks us to a rack of suits.

"You doin' one of those prisoner trials downtown?"

"Yes. The Court appointed us," Steve says.

"Well . . . good luck with that. People around here like their prisons. You want pinstripes or no pinstripes?"

"No pinstripes," I say. "I think he'd prefer not to wear stripes for a while."

CHAPTER
THIRTY

LATE NIGHT FRIDAY. Dallas, Texas. Three days before trial. Eighteen weeks before our baby is due.

After purchasing Emmett's suit, I drove back to Dallas to see my pregnant wife and toddler. I have not seen them for days, and I'd like to visit them before the trial consumes all my waking hours next week. I'm thrilled—yet nervous—to have my first "at bat" as first chair on a trial, but it won't be easy to win. It won't be easy to pull it off without embarrassing myself, my team, and my firm as a rookie. But I am determined to do a brilliant job. For my future—for Emmett—and for my family.

It's a long drive. Hannah and Lilly are asleep in our big bed by the time I get home, so I take off my suit and crawl into bed. Fatigue and the even, reassuring sound of their breathing lulls me to sleep.

"Daniel!" Hannah's voice jolts me awake. "I'm bleeding. Oh God! There is blood everywhere." Hannah is back-lit, standing framed in the bathroom door.

It's the middle of the night. The monster we both dread shows up as a blood-soaked stain on her pajamas.

Our contagious fear infects our daughter, who jerks awake beside me and cries. "Mommy?"

"Grab a towel! Quickly. We're getting in the van," I say.

"Should we call 911?" Hannah's large eyes ablaze with panic.

"No time. We have to go *now*." In a matter of seconds, I'm helping my wife into the passenger seat, buckling our daughter into a child seat in the back. I look down at my jeans and sneakers—I don't remember putting them on. The hospital is just a few miles away. Some streetlights blink amber with the early hour. I flick on the hazards and speed toward the hospital. I'll explain to the police—if they show up—later at the ER. Hannah calls Dr. Abrams's service.

"Yes. We're headed there now," she says, a frantic pulse just under her tone. "No, I can't tell if it stopped. It's a lot. My clothes are soaked. I don't know. Let me check." She peers out the window looking for street signs. "We're at Forest and Preston. Go where? In the back?" She clicks off.

"They said to drive to the Women's Center in the back. Double doors at the bottom of Building D. They will be waiting for us."

The bottom of the minivan scrapes the asphalt as I speed through another intersection. Speed limits are optional under the circumstances. In the car seat in the back, Lilly is torn between fear and excitement. She knows something is wrong with her mother, but the roller coaster ride fascinates her. Even though I am gunning the accelerator, it feels as though we're creeping along as if driving through mud.

Time is not my friend. Finally, the top of the tallest building at the hospital appears over the treetops. I flip through my mind, working to remember where Building D is, and which side street gets me there. We snake our way around, and I pull up. Two obstetric nurses stand just outside the doors with a wheelchair. When we stop, neither of them moves as urgently as I would like. They calmly place Hannah in the chair and tell me they will see me on the fourth floor. I follow.

"You can't leave that van there," the gray-haired nurse scolds.

"There should be some parking over there," the redheaded nurse says compassionately. She points to a dark lot to the right.

I want to scream at them both because I want them focused on Hannah, not where I should park my car. It's hard not to let the Ithaca baggage contaminate my view of all nurses and doctors. But I don't want my parked van to block the next husband arriving with a panicked wife.

"Come here, little one. You can come with Mama," the redhead says as she picks up Lilly. The severe, gray-haired nurse pushes Hannah inside.

"The fourth floor," she directs over her shoulder.

I drop the van into gear and head for the parking lot. I wait for the impossibly slow machine to spit out a ticket, and I select a space and ease in the van. A few moments ago, the inside of the minivan was chaos—fear bleeding from all of us. Now, silence. The middle of the night in a hospital emergency room parking lot morphs into the loneliest place on earth. I turn the van off and sit for a moment to compose myself for Hannah. I know she is scared, and I know I am scared. Me freaking out won't help her. For the first time in a long time— since her fever topped 106 degrees in Ithaca, I scream into the steering wheel and then say a prayer.

God and I have a rocky relationship. He took my mother when I was six years old. When we left the church that morning after the eulogy, my father left the Church for good. Religion at the dinner table was mostly the target of derision. But being angry at something does not mean it does not exist. It mostly means you have cut yourself off. Alone in the lot under a clear October sky, I say the prayer I told Lilly when Hannah was in surgery in Ithaca, "You will always be safe, and I will always love you." And I say a simple prayer for my wife and unborn daughter. "Please protect them."

When I get to the fourth floor, a chubby nurse in purple scrubs hands me a clipboard with paperwork and a pen. I can't go back and see my wife until I finish "checking her in." I want to yell in frustration, but this is not my first rodeo. Adrenalin makes it hard to fit letters into the small boxes. Once the dreaded paperwork is done, the portly nurse takes me to Hannah and Lilly.

I'm startled and frantic to see that Hannah is in bed *in a delivery room*. It's too soon! Our baby can't come now. Bailey needs eighteen more weeks to be safe, to reach full term.

Our toddler dozes, nestled in the protective curl of Hannah's arm.

"How do you feel, Buzz?" I ask.

"They say she might come tonight. That she can't come tonight."

The fear in her voice knocks me back. "Has the doctor been in?"

"A minute ago. She's coming back."

I look around the room. Bailey's soft heartbeat streams from the fetal monitor. I recognize all the machines—comforting and horrifying. The door opens.

"You must be the husband," the doctor says, her ebony skin framed by a mass of elegant blonde braids.

"Yes. I'm Daniel."

"Glad you're here. I just spoke with Drs. Abrams and Phillips, and here's where we are."

She turns to Hannah, places her hand on hers, her elegant eyes projecting calm. "You have to keep that baby girl inside, alright. That's our mission. Your baby is close to twenty-two weeks. That is a dangerous time to come early. Most babies that make it twenty-eight weeks have few if any problems. After twenty-four, you are in for a long stay in the NICU with her. But before twenty-four weeks gets really dicey. Some babies born that early make it, most honestly don't. So keep her inside, alright mom?" She rubs Hannah's hand between her palms in a relaxing rhythm.

"NICU?" I ask. This is a new hospital adventure.

"Neonatal Intensive Care Unit."

"That's it, just 'keep her inside,'" I say, frustration shading my voice with anger. "Isn't there some procedure, something you can do to stop it?"

The doctor turns her piercing, dark brown eyes on me, as if giving me a gentle but forceful reprimand. "We are giving her all the medicines we can. But there is nothing physically to do but rest and try to remain calm. Keep that baby inside. One more significant bleed from that previa, and we may have to take the baby. We don't want that. Or your baby may just decide to come. Maybe she is stubborn. We have no say over if she decides to come. If she comes, we'll do what we can. But right now, and I know it's not a great answer, we wait and see. Say a few prayers." She pats Hannah's hand. "You okay?"

Hannah nods, as a nurse spreads out another warm blanket on top of her. As they leave the room, the nurse dims the lights "so we can relax." The door shuts.

"It's really awful if she comes early, Bear," Hannah says in a voice soft enough that Lilly's eyes stay closed, but panic vibrates in the tone.

"Let's just take it minute by minute, then hour by hour, Buzz," I say. "We're here. They have incredible doctors in Dallas. Dr. Abrams is watching over you. Dr. Phillips is watching over you. God is watching over you. If she comes early, I'm sure the NICU doctors are amazing."

"I just want her safe," she says as if whispering a prayer.

"We're all here, Buzz. We're all safe. I promise. I'll call Steve and the Judge; we can continue the trial. I don't have to go back up for a while."

Hannah closes her eyes. I know she is not sleeping. Her

jaw set firm, she focuses on willing her body to behave, begging our baby daughter to stay inside where she is safe.

"Bear, you have to go," she whispers. Quiet fills the gap between us for a moment. "I'll be safe," she says. "Grandpa's here. The doctors are here. There is nothing you can do here. You can't stop the trial. But you can make me proud of your first time as first chair."

In the background, Bailey's heartbeat resonates from the monitor, psh, psh, psh.

CHAPTER
THIRTY-ONE

MONDAY MORNING. Wichita Falls, Texas. Zero days to trial, seventeen weeks before our baby is due.

I arrived back from Dallas yesterday morning. As I drove away from home in the first rays of sunrise, the ache of leaving Hannah in the hospital took my thoughts into an endless loop of horrible possibilities. The three-hour drive provided ample opportunity to ruminate. Somewhere near Decatur, Texas, my thoughts spiraled around all the holes in Emmett's case. The chances all seemed bleak. I needed to show up fresh, centered, and clear—but I was exhausted, anxious, and foggy. I had to get my act together—somehow. No matter what happens in the hospital, I am responsible for what happens in the courtroom.

Steve and I arrive early at the courthouse, where we meet up with Ashley, our colleague and Devil's advocate. Her long brown hair is perfectly straightened and ready for court. Last night, I barely slept, and I feel like I look a bit of a mess. The Marshal lets us in the courtroom. The oak walls and heavy fabric curtains leach a smell of authority and time-honored traditions. I hand Emmett's new navy-blue suit (without pinstripes) to the Marshal.

"Prisoner is already here. They transferred him at seven. I'll give him this. Give him a few minutes to change, then if you want to visit, the holding cell is down the hall. Black steel door on your left."

Steve, Ashley and I lay out files, folders, and yellow pads, hoping organization and preparation can overcome inexperience. Then we sit and wait.

"Which one of you is Mr. Simmons?" the Marshal asks a few minutes later.

"Me."

"Well, he's ready if you're wantin' to visit."

I follow the Marshal down the hall, through the black steel door into a room. Bright white light blasts off the whitewashed walls and industrial tiles. The holding cell is ten by twenty feet—twice the size of Emmett's cell in solitary confinement. I wonder if this larger cage is freeing, less claustrophobic. The cell has no glass between Emmett and me. One stark chair sits in front of a large span of expanded steel—the diamond shaped grate of metal with holes too tiny to get a finger through. But even with all the steel, I can see Emmett clearly.

He looks handsome in his new navy-blue suit. Emmett reminds me of an old man headed to church on Sunday. The suit fits well, considering our makeshift haberdashery. When he hears the door close, he turns and looks at me, his ice-blue eyes alight under the bright fluorescent bulbs. He is centered, together, and calm. I am not. I shove my hands into my pockets, afraid they will betray me by shaking. My gut roils.

A Marshal hands me the belt we bought and Emmett's shoelaces.

"He can't have those . . . suicide risk."

I glance at Emmett, and he shrugs. Seems silly to me; he has had three heart attacks. Emmett's heart could give out any moment, and he has fought for years to take these folks to trial; nonetheless, the Marshal is worried about suicide risk.

Emmett would never choose to bail before his long-awaited day in trial.

"How do I look?" Emmett asks, slapping the suit flat on his shoulders with his palms.

"Very dapper, Emmett. You look dressed to the nines like you're going somewhere. What do you have planned today?" I joke.

"I'm going to have the time of my life, I think. Just sit back and watch my excellent attorneys go to work."

In my mind, I flash back over my very thin résumé, "We'll do the best we can to get after them."

"I have no doubt."

"Did you have time to study your testimony?"

"I read it all weekend. They tossed my cell on Saturday . . . and Sunday. Dumped those papers all over the floor both times. But I think I got them back in order. We'll see. If not, my testimony may be backward. I'm sure you'll manage."

The back of my neck warms, anger flushes my cheeks. Tossing his cell both days before trial was a threat.

"You mind if I take a seat. Let's visit some about today," I say.

"Please. I'd like to hear."

Over the next few minutes, I cover the basic schedule for the day.

"I suspect since you're a prisoner—and everyone around this town seems to be a guard or related to a guard—that it will take most if not all of today to pick a jury. We'll work to knock out potential jurors who will never see things your way. We want jurors who have an open mind and empathy for your heart ailment and stage of life."

"You mean old codger on death's door," Emmett says.

"Senior citizen," I respond. "After we get the jury picked today, we can finish up our openings and such tonight. We'll get after them full bore tomorrow." Emmett nods at the information, soaking it all in. "You'll go first on the stand. We'll get your story out first. Take whatever time you need to do it."

"Okay. I'll be ready."

A bit of silence passes between Emmett and me, and I look down at my shoes, laces and all. Pressure comes in all strengths. Hannah is fighting to keep Bailey safe inside her. . . . I'm about to try a case with *no* courtroom experience. I doubt that I have sufficient skill to keep Ashley, Steve, and me from embarrassing ourselves.

Soon fifty people will fill the pews of the courtroom answering my questions, me probing them for bias and any hint that they will rule against Emmett no matter what. Steve, Ashley, and I have come up with a list of questions to encourage the jurors to talk. Ashley did a masterful job of cataloging facts and concepts we might want to elicit. Nobody enjoys talking in public, least of all in front of a large group. Now we will ask some personal questions for them to answer in front of the Judge, lawyers, and their peers. I must keep all my personal worries hidden and present a mask of confidence and strength.

Turns out the jury selection I attended earlier went on for several days before they found twelve jurors both sides were comfortable seating. I don't think it will take days to find jurors for Emmett, but I am sure it will take most of this day because who knows how people really feel about prisoner complaints. Then there is the ever-present problem that the Judge and Jury may figure out that I don't know what I am doing.

"Emmett, we'll give it our best shot," I say and let out a sigh I did not intend.

He rubs his hands over his freshly shaven head—no nicks, so they must have given him a new razor this morning when he showered. "Did I ever tell you how my dad taught me to drive a tractor?"

"No. I don't think I've heard about the tractor," I say, wondering if he's just killing time.

"Dad needed some help in the field. My brother, who was older than me, was down workin' at the feed store, and my mother was in town. I was the only one around. Dad tossed me the keys and told me to hop on the tractor and drive it out behind him in his truck. I'd never driven it before, would ride it all the time, but never drive. I got up there; my feet barely touched the pedals. Dad watched as I fired up the diesel engine and dropped it in gear. I let go of the clutch and that tractor started wobblin' out into the field. Dad just got in the truck and pulled out in front. That was it. No instructions, no nothin', just the keys and permission. First few hundred feet I was all over the place gettin' used to it, trying to figure out how to steer that tractor. But it came pretty quick, and before long I was a real pro." Emmett pauses, then continued, "Life is full of uneasy moments, but most things just take patience and time, and a little bit of brass, but they're all learnable."

"Judge wants to see y'all in the courtroom," the Marshal announces.

Emmett smiles, his ice-blue eyes piercing into me. "You got brass." He stands and straightens his jacket. "See you in there."

CHAPTER
THIRTY-TWO

A FEW MINUTES LATER. Wichita Falls.

Quiet descends throughout the courtroom. Occasionally the click of the Court Reporter's stenographic machine echoes in the silence. The potential jurors mumble whispers as they find their seats. For jury selection, the Judge has turned around the chairs in the well of the courtroom. Rather than facing her at the bench, we're now turned around looking out into the pews in the gallery. Fifty potential jurors stare back at us. Some dressed up; most are in their everyday work clothes, waiting for the court to release them from jury duty so they can go back to their lives. Jury duty is a pain to most folks. The government pays them forty dollars a day—or less—and in exchange, they need to find childcare, tell their boss they won't make it to work, and folks paid by the hour give up their living wage. Everyone one of them seeks an excuse that will spare them the hassle of sitting in the jury box for the next week.

The Judge goes first. As I listen, my insides continue to toss, and I hear Steve tap a pen against his knee in a nervous rhythm. She explains the main gist of the case, why we are here, and the importance of the jury to our system of government. Then she probes hardship excuses. Some folks explain how they won't get paid if they have to sit on the jury. She probes whether anyone has a health condition that makes it impossible to sit for long periods. She assures one diabetic she will have the ability to eat something in the courtroom if needed to keep her blood sugar normal. A juror mentions prepaid cruise tickets that will go unrefunded on a long-planned trip with her husband if they can't leave by Wednesday.

Once she finishes with the general probing of the jury panel, the Judge turns it over to the lawyers. While jury selection can go on for most of the day, if not days, sometimes the Judge limits the amount of time to select a jury. Judge Navarro has informed us this morning that she will give each side forty-five minutes to question them—less than a minute each to figure out who will give Emmett a fair shake. With so little time, strategy comes into play. Each side has seven peremptory strikes, meaning we can dismiss a juror for any reason not based on race, religion, or other protected status. These peremptory strikes are submitted separately; each side has a confidential strike sheet. Neither side knows which jurors the other will dismiss. If both sides strike different jurors, that means fourteen will leave. The jury will ultimately be twelve plus one alternate in case someone gets sick. So, fourteen strikes, plus twelve, plus a spare totals twenty-seven. If the Judge strikes a few for cause (meaning they have biases they can't set aside), we could end up around thirty. Thus, potential jurors thirty-one through fifty might as well be ignored, as they have little chance of making it on the jury. If they raise their hand to one of our questions, we'll have to remain polite, but each second talking to them bleeds time from probing the ones who matter—the first two dozen. One lawyer from each side can examine the panel, so I start as the plaintiff's attorney.

"If you will, please raise your hand if you or a family

member or close friend works for a prison here in the area." A sea of hands juts into the air. I quiz a few jurors in the front row. With so many folks tied to the prison system the only strategy is to inoculate them against prejudices. So, my questions turn to whether they could set aside any preconceived notions, follow the Judge's instructions, and give Emmett a fair shake. Most agree. Two jurors in the first few rows work at a prison. They confess they have no way to trust anything a prisoner says and won't be able to set that thinking aside. I can strike them for cause. My time has almost run out when I ask one last question.

"Is there any reason that you have not told us so far why you think you could not sit on this jury and give Mr. Kendrick a fair shake?" A hand in the front row goes up. "Juror Number Four; Mr. Jackson, is it? Why did you raise your hand?"

"It's my religion, mostly. Human beings are not to sit in judgment of others. Our church teaches that judgment rests with God, and no one else. So I can sit in the trial and listen, but I don't think I'll be able to sign a verdict. That's not my place."

My time runs out.

My adversary, Ms. Walker, is a formidable opponent. Rose has years of experience with cases just like this one. And her ramrod posture suggests that she always wins.

Ms. Walker then stands up for the defendants and begins her inquiries. Her patent-leather black stiletto heels push up her demure height and elongate her calves adorned in black hose. The chalk-stripes in her jacket and skirt accentuate all her curves and angles. I'm sure the potential male jurors' dream of buying her a drink in the local watering hole. The women may very well want to be Rose, able to draw the gaze of an entire bar by simply walking through the door. Her flinty look drives home her competitive nature. The long,

French-tip manicure on her nails looks like talons. She is all predator.

"How many of you have heard stories about the violence in prisons and how dangerous it's working there?" She's designed this question (and every other one out of her mouth) to get the jury to judge Emmett through guilt by association before he ever gets to the witness stand.

After twenty-five minutes of painting prison work as Hell on Earth and the staff as saints, she sits down. The Judge asks the jurors to wait in the hall while the lawyers make their strikes. The final selection process goes quickly, and the Judge tells us she wants the jury empaneled before a very late lunch. Steve, Ashley, and I figure once the Judge swears in the jury she'll give them the last few hours of the day to take care of personal business before they have to come back and sit four days in trial. We could use the extra time to finalize the opening statement. Steve has been working on it, but I know he wants more time to polish the words. The Judge calls the jury panel back. She reads off the names of those selected to sit. We hear a few muttered grunts and several sighs of relief. The Marshal directs them to chairs in the jury box. The Judge thanks everyone else for their patience. She swears in the jury, an equal mix of men and women. They are relatively young and look upwardly mobile. Not much of a jury of peers to a sixty-seven-year-old inmate with severe heart trouble and a few blemishes on his record. But we have a jury, and Steve, Ashley, and I ready ourselves to prepare for tomorrow, gathering our pads and pens. We are about to stand up to finish packing when the Judge says, "It's late and we've already pushed lunch a little past 1:00 o'clock." The Judge looks directly at the portly juror who indicated her blood sugar would require her to eat regularly, "Ms. Parker can you push on a little further, or should we stop to eat?"

Ms. Parker nods, and the Judge continues, "Okay, good. So this is what we'll do. We will have opening statements now and then give you forty-five minutes to get lunch. Then we'll come back and get started with our first witness." She looks at Steve, Ashley, and me. "Mr. Simmons, your side may give your opening statement."

"So much for opening in the morning," Steve whispers to me, forcing the panic out of his voice. He thumbs through the files on our table to find the one with his statement. Ashley hands him a manila file folder with his notes. She straightens her glasses and leans back in the chair trying not to look concerned.

"No worries. You have most of it written anyway, right?"

"Let's see what we think after I give it." Steve smooths his tie, buttons his coat, and moves to the lectern facing the jury. After tugging on his French cuffs, he begins.

"Your Honor, will the Court allow me to move around the courtroom during opening."

"Yes Mr. Davis, just don't encroach on the Jury box."

Steve nods, takes a deep breath, and begins.

"May it please the Court, counsel for the defendants, ladies and gentlemen of the jury. This is a simple case, with one unanswered question: Why? Why is it after five years of requests by Mr. Kendrick these defendants still can't provide him his prescribed cardiac medicines and common-sense care consistently? Mr. Kendrick is sixty-seven years old and sentenced to prison for fifty-five years. He lives in Administrative Segregation, which is solitary confinement because the State alleges he tried to escape one time many years ago. He freely admits he deserves to be in jail. Nonetheless, Mr. Kendrick has serious medical conditions. He has congestive heart failure, hypertension, chronic obstructive pulmonary disease, and angina. While in prison, he's had three heart attacks, two bypass surgeries, and two angioplasties. And the prison doctors have prescribed essential medicines to care for these conditions.

"But a problem exists. Mr. Kendrick does not receive these

critical prescribed medicines regularly. The care that he receives disregards his medical condition. For five years!" Steve moves away from the lectern and holds up five fingers for the Jury. "For five long years, Mr. Kendrick has consistently made the problems known to anyone and everyone. But no one has fixed the problems. You don't have to be a doctor to know something is seriously wrong at Teton Springs. No medical degrees needed. You need only common sense.

"We are here today because everything has failed. This is an Eighth Amendment cruel and unusual punishment case. Under the Eighth Amendment of the United States Constitution, prisoners like Mr. Kendrick still have rights and can't be subject to cruel and unusual punishment. The defendants are prison officials and medical staff who had the ability and the opportunity to fix Mr. Kendrick's issues. But no one did. I do not know what reason they are going to give you. I suspect they will point to policies, point fingers at others, and say 'I'm too far up or too far down the chain of command to do anything.' Or, they will throw up their hands and say, 'We do the best we can.' These excuses are red herrings. Why can't they do something as simple as provide prescribed medicine and appropriate medical care for Mr. Kendrick's needs on a regular schedule?

"With all this finger-pointing going on, most everyone will point fingers at Mr. Kendrick, who ironically, is the one person who can do the least to fix the problem. For over five years, he has done the one thing he can do. He has filed grievance form after grievance form, making the same requests. But the problem is still not fixed. Why?

"We are not here for some multimillion-dollar, jackpot-justice verdict. We are here to ask you, the Jurors, to force the defendants *to do what they are supposed to do*: give Mr. Kendrick the medicine and care the Eight Amendment and common sense require, and to compensate him for the indifference that damages his heart, the anxiety of being trapped in a cell during an angina attack, the physical and mental injury, and to punish the defendants so this never happens again.

"Three things to remember as the trial unfolds. First, the evidence will show that for five years, Emmett Kendrick has made the defendants aware of the problems, using the grievance system. Second, after five years, the defendants have still not fixed the problem. And third, the continued reckless disregard for Mr. Kendrick's requests aggravates his health condition, making it more likely he will suffer a fatal heart attack. And, why? See if the defendants ever really answer *why* this problem is still not fixed."

Steve stands in the well of the court for a moment surveying the Jurors, then he sits down. Emmett leans over and whispers in his ear.

"Ms. Walker, the State's opening please," the Judge says. Rose stands, working all her curves. She straightens her dark blazer and gathers her notes at the lectern. Her fierce gaze surveys the jury as she lets a hush fall over the courtroom. She steps away from the lectern and struts to the well of the court. With no notes in front of her, she digs into Emmett from memory.

"Ladies and gentlemen of the Jury, medical care is important to any healthcare worker. The defendants will tell you they treat the prisoners under their care the same as they would any person out in the free world. But . . . in a prison you must be mindful of security. No matter how good a nurse's intentions, they are worthless if a prisoner attacks her. And the risk grows as you get closer and closer to more dangerous prisoners. Treating a prisoner in the general population is different from treating those in AdSeg.

"What is AdSeg—Administrative Segregation—you might ask? You know it as solitary confinement. Prisoners find themselves in solitary confinement because of their own actions. They deserve to live there, and they are dangerous and a risk to others and themselves. They have proven themselves violent and untrustworthy. So much so that the State is forced to confine them by themselves twenty-four hours a day. Ask yourself how difficult would your job be if you constantly feared for your safety. At any moment, the people you try to care for can stab a shank in your ribs or choke the life from you. Or, if instead of a thank you, they rewarded you by spitting in your face or chucking urine out the bars of their cells. These professionals on trial today want to help; that is why they became doctors or nurses. They are caregivers. And the wardens on trial want to provide a safe environment for that care. During this trial, you will hear about the dangers of working in a prison, and how security, which is paramount, can make it more difficult to render care to violent offenders like Mr. Kendrick.

"Mr. Kendrick has a heart condition, and we wish him good health. But his past acts have landed him in solitary like other violent inmates. He must now understand that when he landed in jail, he gave up the right to get what he wants, when he wants, on the terms he wants. He is not a free citizen, and he will have to learn patience because he lost the right to make any demands when he robbed a bank with a gun, stood trial, and heard the court impose a fifty-five-year sentence.

"The evidence will show that Mr. Kendrick never once suffered harm because of some alleged failure to provide him medicine. That is simply a fantasy dreamed up by the big-city lawyers that he conned into trying his case. In fact, you will learn that Mr. Kendrick has turned complaining and suing prison officials into his job—that's all he does. But I can also tell you that you won't see one shred of evidence that these defendants saw something dangerous happening to Mr. Kendrick and failed to act. In fact, they did the best they could within the confines of a demanding job. Unfortunately, because his behavior landed him in solitary confinement,

Mr. Kendrick has twenty-four hours a day alone to plot and scheme about how to make their jobs harder. Now, he seeks to make these fine folks come out of pocket and pay him damages direct from their own paychecks. Make no mistake, I believe he is enjoying every minute of this. This is his ticket to the carnival. Indeed, suing prison officials is the best job Mr. Kendrick ever had. The evidence will show that no defendant turned a blind eye to Mr. Kendrick's alleged suffering. Rather, it will show they provided excellent care. And, at the end of the trial, we will ask you to fire Mr. Kendrick from this newfound job of harassing prison officials, and allow the defendants to get back to the important work of doing theirs." Rose squares her shoulders as if victory is already hers.

"Thank you, Ms. Walker," the Judge says. "We'll take forty-five minutes to grab something to eat. See you all back in your seats shortly. We'll start with Mr. Kendrick's first witness."

Emmett's time has come.

CHAPTER
THIRTY-THREE

MOMENTS LATER. Wichita Falls. Courtroom.

"All rise," the Marshal calls, and we all stand while the Jury leaves the courtroom, then the Judge and her staff. When they're gone, the Marshals come and shackle Emmett.

"You do what you need to do," Emmett says, his blue eyes calming. "I'll study in the back with my sandwich."

Steve, Ashley, and I head out of the courtroom. We pass a few Jurors, and politely ignore them as the Court admonished all of us to do until after trial; we wait for another elevator.

At the burger joint across the street, we sit down at a corner booth.

"Not sure how much of Emmett you'll get through today, Daniel," Steve says.

"Probably a good idea to end on a dramatic note. No way you should pass Emmett and let them get to cross-examination today," Ashley adds, nudging her glasses up the bridge of her nose.

"I bet the Judge calls it at about 5:00 pm," I say, "Although, all my guesses have missed the mark so far in this trial."

"She'll ask if you're getting to a good stopping point. Don't you think? I mean, I think that's what she'll do. Can't imagine she'd just stop you mid-sentence," Steve says.

"Let's hope. I'd hate for the ending of our first day to disappear like a fart in the wind."

It takes much longer than expected to reassemble the Jury, pushing further into the afternoon. After a soft warning from the Judge, the Jurors takes their seats. Emmett takes his seat on the witness stand. "Mr. Kendrick, place your right hand on the Bible. Do you swear that the testimony you are about to give in this courtroom will be the truth, the whole truth, and nothing but the truth, so help you God?"

"I do."

"Mr. Kendrick you may be seated," the Judge says. "Mr. Simmons, begin your examination." Emmett straightens the lapels on his suit and sits.

"Emmett, please introduce yourself to the jury."

Emmett turns to face them—just like I instructed him to do. He looks each juror straight in the eye with a kind smile and then starts.

"My name is Emmett Kendrick. I'm currently a prisoner at Teton Springs, just outside of Wichita Falls."

"Emmett, tell the jury how you ended up in prison."

"Over twenty years ago, I robbed a bank in Tarrant County. I'd grown up in towns outside of Fort Worth, and back then my family was poor, dirt poor. I made the decision to rob that bank. I chose to use a gun. Make no mistake, I'm guilty of that offense. I did it. I accept responsibility for it. I actually agree with the fifty-five-year sentence the jury gave me after they convicted me at trial. I broke the rules, and the good folks of Texas had a right to put me behind bars."

"Objection," Ms. Walker says. "Your Honor, if we could proceed by question and answer that would be better than Mr. Kendrick telling his life story."

The Judge looks at me. "Your Honor, I'm just trying to move efficiently through the background."

"I'll overrule the objection. Mr. Simmons, I'll give you some leeway, proceed."

"Thank you, Judge."

"Mr. Simmons, you do not have to thank the Court when you win an objection," the Judge chides. "Move along."

Ms. Walker smirks at the small reprimand, her dark eyeliner accentuating the laughter in her eyes. A slight flush crosses my cheeks at looking like a rookie. A chuckle spills out of the jury box.

"Emmett, did you start serving your sentence at Teton Springs?"

"No, I started at a place in Huntsville. That's the prison capital of the world. I've never been to it, but they tell me it has a great prison museum, complete with the original electric chair they used for executions. But that's neither here nor there. At Huntsville, they tossed my cell and claimed they found civilian clothing. The warden called it escape contraband and took away my good time credits. At that point, I had served quietly for nineteen years and had 7,528 good credit days. That's almost twenty years off my sentence. The warden at Huntsville took all those good behavior days away after they tossed my cell. Then they sent me to Teton Springs and placed me in AdSeg. They claimed I was an escape risk."

"Emmett, now, you developed several health conditions while serving your time?"

"Yes. I have a family history of heart disease. The prison doctors diagnosed me with congestive heart failure, hypertension, COPD, and angina."

"They're serious?"

"Serious as a heart attack. I've had several. Plus, I've had two bypass surgeries. My heart keeps trying to give out and they keep putting it back together. They've cracked my chest and had to wire it back together twice. My sternum, this part here . . . ." Emmett points to his chest, right at his tie. "This here is just a mess of wires these days, stitching that rib cage closed."

"And, these *serious* medical conditions require medicine, I imagine. Emmett, tell the jury about the drugs you have to take."

"I have several I have to take daily. Isosorbide, that's the big one, keeps my heart from going crazy, Clonidine is for the hypertension. They give me a diuretic to help keep fluid off my heart and lungs. And, I'm supposed to have a supply of Nitroglycerin with me at all times to calm down any angina attacks."

"These have been prescribed for years, I suspect."

"Yes, I started all these medicines down in Huntsville. They were good about getting them to me. But Teton Springs? Well, they've had their problems with providing those medicines to me when they are supposed to."

"These drugs are all critical for your care?"

"They keep me alive."

"And if you don't get them, if the delivery stops abruptly?"

"Then, as I understand it, I'm not alive for long."

"You said, Teton Springs has had trouble providing some of these drugs regularly. Which ones?"

"The Isosorbide and Nitroglycerin."

"Mr. Simmons," the Judge says, "let me know when you are at a good stopping point, and we'll knock off for the day."

"Yes, your Honor. We're close."

"Emmett, do you have the Nitroglycerin with you now?"

"In my shirt pocket." Emmett takes out a small bottle, shakes it, and shows it to the jury. "I'm supposed to have some with me all the time. The angina acts up, and I can place a pill under my tongue to calm it down."

"So, you can always get to it?"

"No, not always. If it's not there, I can't. I can't take it if they don't provide it to me. And if they shackle me for transport, I can't. The shackling is difficult. Not moving around in the building, but on transport, say like driving me to the hospital. Sometimes, they have to drive me out to Abilene, to the Robertson Unit that's close to the hospital out there. The Hendrix Medical Center has the prison contract. That drive takes three or four hours. To transport us, they shackle our hands to our waist, connected by chain to another set around our ankles. Once in the van, they lock the chains, sometimes tighter than others, to the floor, as well. The way the chains fit, they pull on my sternum, pull on those wires. After a while, with the vibration of the road through the tires, that pain wears on me and sometimes the pain pushes me over into an angina attack."

"And the Nitroglycerin is with you."

"If I have it, it's in my shirt pocket."

"Out of reach."

"Yes. No way to reach it. I'll tell you, it's a crazy frustration to have your heart pounding and pain fills your chest, with a tiny pill just a few inches away that can stop it. But you can't reach."

"Can a guard get it for you?"

"No sir. Policies don't allow them to stop mid-transport to get in the back to help a prisoner. Not unless there's some disturbance, like a fight. Or maybe if I had a full-blown heart attack they could stop."

"Your Honor, may I have Mr. Kendrick step down into the well of the court for a moment. I have something the jury ought to see."

The Judge removes her half-moon reading glasses, a curious gaze focused on me. "You may."

"Emmett, step down here a minute and face the jury." One

of the Corrections Officers from Teton Springs sits in the first row of chairs right behind our table. He is a large, muscular, black guard. His six-foot-three frame dwarfs Emmett, and his form-fitting uniform accentuates his power and strength "Officer Anderson, you have the restraints with you?"

"Yes sir."

"Please shackle Mr. Kendrick exactly like you do before you place him in the van, so the jury can see the process, how he's transported?"

Officer Anderson pulls a set of shackles from the floor, and they jangle like a sinister wind chime. Four cuffs connected by a thick, tarnished chain attach to a belt in the center. Anderson steps forward, the gear on his duty belt jangling, and he walks toward Emmett. Almost as if a Pavlovian reflex to the clink of the chain links, Emmett places his hands behind his back. With a precision built from repetition, Officer Anderson straps the belt around Emmett's waist and clicks one cuff on the right wrist. Then the left. The steel restraints pin his wrists low and tight near his belly, slightly to the back. Then, without command, Emmett kneels in front of the jury, head bowed. The chains rattle as they hit the floor. Officer Anderson, his face void of emotion from shackling thousands of prisoners over the years, slides the next two cuffs around his ankles. Emmett stays there, frozen until the next command.

"Officer Anderson, can you pull that chair over to Emmett?"

Officer Anderson nods at me and politely complies. He sets a heavy oak padded chair behind Emmett.

"Emmett, can you sit in the chair please?" I ask.

"No." His refusal causes a slight stir. Seconds tick by. "But, if CO Anderson helps, I can get there."

Officer Anderson slides a large, meaty hand under Emmett's arm, and steadies him as he lifts Emmett's aged body, chains jingling, unable to move his hands or arms for balance. Anderson helps Emmett lower himself into the chair, his arms slightly behind him. The chain from his wrists runs between his legs to his ankles and dangles toward the floor. The cuffs on his wrists have pulled his shoulders back, and the lapel of his navy suit spreads wide. His blue tie juts at a jagged angle, amplifying the pull on his chest and sternum. The normal glow of his ice-blue eyes blunted by the pain I know he feels.

"Emmett, you say they hook the chains to the van floor?"

"Yes," he sputters.

"Officer Anderson, could you please put your foot on the chains where they would lock to the van floor?" Officer Anderson lips pucker as he looks at the chains, calculating the exact spot. Satisfied, he steps down on the long dangling chain with a steel-toed boot, pinning it to the floor. The boot yanks Emmett's head and shoulders downward. He stoops, as if in some contorted, suffering prayer. A quiet gasp escapes from a juror.

I let this vision of Emmett burn into the jury's mind. Some may see a convict; but I suspect most see a frail old man completely immobile under the State's leather, steel, and boot.

"Emmett, can you move your hands?' I ask.

"No, sir." His breath labored, I worry about the distresses my demonstration causes him. "They're pinned down here around my waist."

"Emmett, remind the jury where you keep your Nitro-glycerin."

"In my shirt pocket," a hoarse whisper all he can muster by now.

"Thank you," I say. Not a soul speaks as Officer Anderson helps Emmett to his feet and removes the shackles. I hear several jurors shift in their seats with discomfort. Emmett's labored breathing obvious in the silence, Anderson holds him under the arm for a moment as Emmett catches his breath and steadies himself on his feet. The light in his ice-blue eyes sparks, as his breathing quiets. After a moment, he straightens his tie and the lapels on his blue suit.

I glance at the Judge, her lips pursed with concern for Emmett. "Your Honor, I think we are at a good stopping point for the day."

The Judge admonishes the Jury not to speak about the trial to anyone and then dismisses them. After they exit, she and her staff leave the courtroom.

The Marshals shuffle Emmett back to the holding cell. It will take time for him to change and for the Corrections Officers to transport him back to the prison—time to travel, check him back in, strip search him. I wonder if they tossed his cell again while he was in court. Chances are high he will have to clean up his belongings when he gets home. That's a funny way to think about prison, a cell: "home." But that is Emmett's reality. Except for a shower or an hour three times a week in a chain-link dog run, he has not stepped out of his small concrete box for years. Most of what he needs slides through the bean slot in his door. A simple conversation with another human a luxury, if it happens at all. Tonight, he will sit alone on the bunk and diligently study the materials I gave him until lights out. Then he will restart the process in the morning. Emmett told me that to get to court by his 7:00 am arrival time, they come to his cell at 4:00 am. Prison time breeds waiting.

Steve, Ashley, and I head for the hotel. Emmett's shackling has lit a fire in me. We have plenty of work to do for the next day. I must finish Emmett's direct examination. Then we will put the two nurses on the stand. I review their testimony in my mind, what they both told us at the restaurant. I scribble notes and then distill the scratched words into a witness outline. A charge of excitement courses through me. We have no depositions or witness statements in the case to alert Ms. Walker. All the State knows is that we placed Nurses Ryan and Watts on our witness list. They admitted that the prison staff deliberately ignored Emmett's medical needs, that Nurse Hatcher and others did in fact violate his Eight Amendment rights. These words will come as quite a shock to the defense. The most potent witness in a trial points to the defendants and says, "they did it."

We have two of them.

CHAPTER
THIRTY-FOUR

LATE NIGHT. Wichita Falls, Texas. Seventeen weeks before our baby is due.

After hours of trial prep, I call Hannah before I crawl into bed. I long to wrap her beautiful hair in my fingers, to feel the heat of her golden skin next to me. A pang of guilt flashes through me, knowing I delayed calling her until late night. The heater in my hotel groans out a monotonous squeak. I pace in a T-shirt and shorts as I listen to the phone. After several rings, she finally picks up.

"Hi, Bear," she whispers. Through the phone, the sound of the fetal monitor pounds out its soft rhythm in the background. Her greeting wrenches me between the joy of listening to her sweet voice and the remorse of not being with my family.

"How did trial go today?" she asks quietly.

"It's going," I say. "How are you?"

"We're okay. Bailey's heartbeat raced a couple of times. False alarms, though. Everyone's calm right now." A twinge of exhaustion laces her words.

"Lilly there?" I miss presenting her with a special chocolate every night. Her beautiful smile flashes through my thoughts as I imagine the patter of her pudgy feet down the hallway.

"In the covers with me. Grandpa is asleep in a chair in the corner. I think he's going to have a sore neck in the morning. He can't be comfortable."

"Buzz, I should be there," I confess.

"You're right where you're supposed to be." Her voice drops into a determined tone.

In the background, the fetal monitor's beat picks up—way too fast. An alarm pings, and suddenly I hear a nurse's voice.

"Buzz, is everything okay?" I ask.

In the background, I hear Grandpa's groggy, baritone voice. He sounds stressed.

"I got to go, Bear. Probably just another false alarm. But they're grabbing the phone from me." Then silence.

The line disconnects before I can I tell her I love her. I flop in bed and my mind focuses on the incessant warble from the heater, making it impossible for me to rest from the dual worries of court and home.

What if it's not a false alarm?

CHAPTER
THIRTY-FIVE

THE NEXT MORNING. Wichita Falls, Texas.

The Judge ascends the bench in the courtroom.

"All rise," the Marshal calls in his loud, commanding voice.

The Judge picks up her half-moon reading glasses, scans a piece a paper and then says, "Counsel, anything we need to take up before we summon the Jury?"

"We have one item, Judge."

"Mr. Simmons."

"Your Honor, the Court was kind enough to allow Mr. Kendrick to appear in a suit to avoid any undue prejudice. So the Jurors wouldn't automatically discount everything he said because of his prison fatigues. But the prison officials insist that an armed Corrections Officer sit right behind Mr. Kendrick when he is at counsel table. I'm afraid that is just as, or maybe more, damaging than the fatigues. It sends the message that Mr. Kendrick is a constant risk. But nothing in his recent prison profile suggests such danger. I believe it's an intentional trial tactic."

The Judge purses her lips as she considers my accusation.

After a moment, she asks, "Ms. Walker, why the extra security?"

Rose straightens her severe black skirt as she stands. "Your Honor, Mr. Kendrick is in prison for aggravated robbery with a deadly weapon, and he lives in solitary confinement because of his violent tendencies."

"Over two decades ago," I interject, directing my comment at Ms. Walker.

"Counsel," the Judge barks, "You will direct all comments to the bench not opposing counsel."

"Yes, Your Honor," I concede.

Ms. Walker huffs and continues with a controlled contempt in her eyes. "That prison guard is behind Mr. Simmons and the others for *their* safety. Who knows what Mr. Kendrick is capable of at any given moment? The State cannot have an inmate shank his counsel with a pencil during a trial."

I turn to Emmett, a smirk on my face. "Emmett, you have any present plan to stab me with a pencil or beat me to death with a three-ring binder?"

"None," Emmett says and smiles, a slight gleam from his ice-blue eyes. He's enjoying this confrontation.

"You're not going to bludgeon me with a legal pad?" I jest. The Judge coughs to hide a chuckle.

My sarcasm irritates Ms. Walker as she chimes in—my first blood drawn on an adversary, "Your Honor, Mr. Kendrick is also a flight risk, and prison procedure requires that a Corrections Officer be within reach of the offender in case he tries to flee."

"Your Honor," Emmett says. He stands, his voice calm and respectful. The Judge taps her glasses on her bottom lip when Emmett addresses her. "Ma'am . . . my heart would give out on me before I could get to the door if I tried to sprint anywhere." His voice quiet, but honest.

Interlacing her fingers at the bench, the Judge considers

Emmett's statement. Finally she says, "Ms. Walker, I don't think Mr. Kendrick will make a break for it. And if Mr. Simmons wishes to take the risk at counsel table, that is *his* risk. Please have the Corrections Officer sit in the benches in the gallery." She pauses a moment, and then turns a schoolmarm's stare on Emmett, her voice drops an octave with authority. "Mr. Kendrick, just so we understand, and I want you to promise me, there will be no craziness in my courtroom. The Corrections Officers are here, and the Marshals are in the courtroom as well. Any shenanigans and I'll bring the full force of this Court down on you. Do you understand me?" Her final words announced one by one with command.

"Yes, ma'am," Emmett responds in a long-learned voice of obedience.

She nods at his answer, slides her reading glasses on and says, "You may get back on the stand. You're still under oath Mr. Kendrick. Let's bring in the Jury."

Emmett steps back on the stand. Same blue suit, same tie. The Jurors are no longer in casual clothes. Most of them have come as if dressed for church, what Emmett would later tell me his uncle would call "Sunday Go to Meetin' Duds." We resume his direct examination.

"Emmett, yesterday we discussed your health problems. We talked about the Nitroglycerin, and how sometimes you don't have it, or can't reach it. We talked about the Isosorbide and how they fail to give it to you regularly. Did you ever speak up, try to get them to fix it?"

"All the time. Shortly after I got to Teton Springs, the medicine stopped coming regular. I'd talk to the nurse on medical rounds. Whoever it was that day said they would talk to Nurse Hatcher and get it fixed."

"And remind the jury who Nurse Hatcher is."

"She runs the clinic in AdSeg. The main infirmary sits over in building twelve. That's where you would find Doctor Ralston. The AdSeg clinic deals with the inmates over in solitary. It has its own pharmacy, and that is Nurse Hatcher's realm. She's the one in charge of ensuring the AdSeg prisoners have all the medicines they need."

"And is she a defendant in this case?"

"Yes sir. That is Nurse Hatcher over there in the blue blouse and sweater." Emmett points to Nurse Hatcher: a stern, plump, matronly woman with graying hair, a wry, condescending curl to her smile, as if she's untouchable.

"Did you ever talk to Nurse Hatcher directly?"

"Yes. Sometimes she comes on the unit to do medical herself. I'd tell her then. I'd also tell her whenever I was in the AdSeg infirmary for visit or checkup."

"Did she say she would get your medicines sorted out?"

"She said they were sorted out. She didn't seem to think there was a problem. She blamed it on the system, said she could not control the deliveries from Huntsville. That's where all our medicines come from."

"If Nurse Hatcher did not listen, did you have a way to make the issue known to others, say Doctor Ralston or the wardens?"

"They have a grievance system. You fill out the form and send it in. A Step One grievance goes to Doctor Ralston. He didn't see any problem either. So then you appeal to the Deputy Warden with a Step Two grievance. That gets denied. Then you appeal up to the next warden. No warden will say a fellow warden screwed something up. So you keep appealing until you get to the Head Warden, who will deny it. After that, you file a lawsuit and hope."

"Is that what you did in this case?"

"Yes. The appeals in the prison took months and months to run their course. But finally, I had run out of appeals. My only shot was to file a lawsuit. And that is how we came to be here today."

"All these months of appeals, did you have a regular supply of Isosorbide and Nitroglycerin?"

"No. The Isosorbide would come in fits. Sometimes it would be there steady. Sometimes I missed it for days in a row. And the Nitro? Well, I would get a vial when they had it. But sometimes there were weeks without it."

"How did failing to provide these medicines regularly affect your heart?"

"Angina. And without the Nitro, I had no way to stop the Angina attacks."

"How often do you suffer Angina attacks?"

"Sometimes once a week. Sometimes more."

"Emmett, I want you to tell the jury about what it's like to suffer an angina attack in your cell."

Emmett turns so his shoulders are square to the jury. He pauses. His blue eyes survey them.

"Sometimes I get a short warning that an attack is coming. My neck and arms burn, and then my jaw aches like I've got a tooth rotting. I get dizzy and must lie down on my bed. My breath doesn't come easy, and I sweat all over. Then it comes in waves, like a vice clamping down or an elephant sitting on my chest. I can barely whisper, and if I try to move around much, the dizziness drives me to where I feel like I might throw up. So, I try to lay real still on my bed and count breaths. The deepest breaths I can get, but my body feels like it doesn't want the air, like it's forcing it out."

"Can you call for help?"

"I have to get the attention of a guard. I can yell out the slot in my door when they open it at mealtime, or maybe wave a hand. But if the guard doesn't notice, then it's just me in the cell. I count and slow down my breath. I wait for someone to come around for medical and check on me. Most of the time, when the nurse comes on the unit, they just call out 'Medical!' from down by the guards. But you can't call back, so they don't come check. They're supposed to check, look at you through the bean slot to see if you're okay. But they don't. Nurse Watts and Nurse Ryan did, but the rest just do a quick yell and then move to the next block."

"Emmett, does this ever scare you?"

"Every time. I've already had heart attacks. The doctors tell me it would be a miracle for me to survive another. The worst part? Is the buzz from the lights in my cell. When you rest there on the bunk, on your mattress, it's like someone reaches down in your chest and squeezes your heart. Maybe other parts ache . . . your jaw . . . an arm. Every new twinge sends a new wave of panic through you because you don't know if the angina attack will ebb or if it's just gearing up to grab you again. Or . . . maybe it will grow into a full-blown heart attack. You notice any twitch in your body. Your heartbeat pounds in your ears. Your ability to scream vanishes because the angina robs you of breath. And those lights. The ballasts in them buzz. Most days you don't notice them. But I curl on the bed, with my eyes closed. I pray for the angina to recede. The buzz bores into my mind like a hellish ring. And I wait. Sometimes for hours with that infernal hum."

"And with the regular medication, none of this has to happen."

"It does not when my medications come on a regular schedule," Emmett says.

"And the defendants know this."

"I made them know it. But nothing changes."

"Emmett, have you had a heart attack while housed at Teton Springs?"

"Yes, when I first arrived, the doctor, a Dr. Patel, not Dr. Ralston, took me off my Isosorbide. He didn't think I needed it. I had a heart attack a few days later. The emergency room doc called it a widow-maker, which is ironic because I'm not married."

"What did he mean by widow-maker?"

"It's a heart attack that normally kills a man. I was dead

on the table for over five minutes before they brought me back."

I let that hang in the air for a moment, then say, "Your Honor. We pass the witness."

Ms. Walker stands at the lectern to cross-examine Emmett; the angles of her posture sharp and aggressive. As she organizes her pen and pad, her motions mirror a raptor homing in on a rabbit.

"Mr. Kendrick, you're a bank robber, correct?"

"Yes, I admit to that. That is why I'm in prison."

"You used a gun in that robbery, right? It was an aggravated robbery?"

"Yes, ma'am. I robbed a bank with a gun. But that was more than two decades ago."

"You tried to escape prison?"

"The warden said I had civilian clothes in my cell when they tossed it. So, they claimed I was an escape risk."

"You disagree you had civilian clothes?"

"Let's just say I'd never seen them. Plus, they were several sizes too big."

"You complain about a lot, don't you Mr. Kendrick? For example, here's another grievance for foot cream."

"Yes, ma'am, I put in for foot cream. The showers in a prison are not the cleanest place you've ever seen. Everyone has athlete's foot. I got a real bad case. They were all cracked and bleedin'. I thought one of my toes was going to fall off. After a month, without medicine to treat it . . . and I'd been asking regularly, real polite, at the medical check . . . I did file a grievance. I have no idea why Nurse Hatcher was not willing to give me a cream to treat it."

"So, you are a violent, convicted bank robber, who tried to escape, and who complains all the time."

"I wouldn't sum it up like that. I only complain when someone ignores their job and when I need my medicines. I can't go to a drugstore and buy them myself. I'm in solitary confinement."

"Well . . . let's talk about what it's like to work in a prison, in solitary confinement. Do you know what a shank is, Mr. Kendrick?"

"Yes. I try to avoid them."

"Mr. Kendrick, describe a shank for the Jury."

"Well, the boys inside will make a stabbing device out of just about anything. Some rub a toothbrush against the concrete until it has a razor-sharp point. There are gangs and tempers in prison. Some folks try to get even."

"So these nurses have to watch out for shanks while they try to deliver medicines."

"The guards are always with them, near them."

"You say they don't check on the prisoners. They don't talk to them through the, what did you call it, the 'bean slot.'"

"Not like they're supposed to. I've read the regulations. They are supposed to get a visual on each prisoner every day, not just call out 'Medical!' down by the door to the unit."

"You ever heard of 'chunking'?"

"Yes. Some of the crazier inmates, the angrier ones will chunk. They toss urine or semen or worse out the bean slot. They try to hit a guard."

"Or a nurse?"

"Some of the more vile prisoners will try to hit a nurse."

"If you were a female nurse, would you want prisoners to throw semen on you if you were just trying to do your job?"

"Nobody wants that. I don't do that. Just because some wild inmate does vile acts doesn't mean the medical staff shouldn't follow protocol."

"Well Mr. Kendrick, you've done some vile things, haven't you?"

"No ma'am. I'm not like that."

"Well, isn't it true that you once threatened to cut off another inmate's head and roll it down the hallway?"

Emmett looks from Ms. Walker, to me, to the jury.

"Yes. That is true. Years ago, at Huntsville, an inmate was all over me. In my face every day. Talking bull. He told me he planned to kick me around the place. I'm not a very big fella, and he'd have beat me to a pulp. I said it to get him to stop. And it worked. He stopped."

"A violent bank robber who uses threats to get his way. Sounds like you deserve to live in AdSeg. Nothing further."

"Mr. Simmons, any redirect?" the Judge nudges.

"Yes, your honor." I stand and straighten my suit coat. "Emmett. You ever shank anyone?"

"No."

"You ever chunk bodily fluids at a guard or a nurse?"

"Never."

"How do you address the nurses?"

"Yes, ma'am and no, ma'am."

"You ever have a nurse tell you they were afraid of you, or file any sort of paperwork saying you'd mistreated them?"

"No."

"Nothing further," I say.

The Judge removes her reading glasses and nods to the court reporter, who can finally remove her fingers from her stenographic machine. "Mr. Kendrick, you may step down. Members of the Jury, we'll take a fifteen-minute break and reconvene for more testimony."

Since the Judge has called a brief recess in the case, Steve, Ashley, and I stand while the Jury and Judge retire. The Marshals remove Emmett to his holding cell. Nurses Ryan and Watts are our next two witnesses. I spy Nurse Watts. She sits alone in the furthest most pew in the courtroom, over in the corner. She pulls at the tips of her long brown hair flowing over her shoulder. I make my way to her. Steve follows my lead.

"I'm sorry," Nurse Watts says, as I approach, but before I can sit down. Her brown eyes fill with regret.

"Sorry for what?"

"Amanda, Nurse Ryan . . . she's not coming. I talked to her this morning. I tried to convince her to come. She wouldn't do it. Said she thought it best if she stayed home."

"She give any reason why?" Steve asks.

"Not at first. Then later she said she received a few anonymous phone calls. Bumped into some old friends at the grocery store. She thinks it's best not to come. She doesn't want to cause any trouble."

"But you'll still testify?" I nudge.

"I'm here, aren't I? But you best get me up and off that witness stand before I change my mind." Nurse Watts says. Panic flashes through her gaze as she surveys the courtroom.

Steve and I rejoin Ashley at the counsel table, and share what just happened.

Ashley says, "We should subpoena her."

"Can't," Steve says. "Deadline for trial subpoenas has long passed. Passed well before we learned what they had to say last week."

"Let's get Watts on quickly before we lose her, too," I say.

The Judge and Jury return.

"Counsel call your next witness."

"Your Honor, Mr. Kendrick calls Nurse Lana Watts."

"Ms. Watts, come forward and be sworn."

Nurse Watts walks toward the witness stand, sits, and places her hands in her lap. She tries not to look at the defendants, but their accusing gaze drill into her. They are her former colleagues. They're neighbors in her community here in Wichita Falls. Nurse Hatcher glares at her.

Emmett touches the cuff of my shirt meaningfully. We've told him that Nurses Watts corroborated his story. Electricity pulses through Ashley, Emmett, Steve, and me. The defendants likely do not know what the nurses told us over enchiladas. Nurse Ryan had disappeared. Nurse Watts is it. The make-it-or-break it moment has arrived.

I straighten the lapels on my suit as I stand at the lectern. "Ms. Watts, please introduce yourself to the Jury."

"My name is Lana Watts. I was a nurse at Teton Springs for several years. I worked in the AdSeg Unit under Nurse Hatcher." Her voice catches as she forces out the words.

"Did you have occasion to care for Mr. Kendrick?"

"Yes. I often did the medical call on his cell block."

"Was he a difficult prisoner to deal with?"

"No, he was always polite. Always, 'yes ma'am, no ma'am.' He kept to himself. I didn't ever see him make any trouble when I was at Teton Springs."

"Do you know much about his condition?"

"Mr. Kendrick has a significant heart condition. I know he's had heart attacks, and he is on several medications to prevent another."

"Those medicines he needed, did he receive them regularly?"

"*No.*" Her voice suddenly forceful.

The Judge looks up and taps her reading glasses against her bottom lip. Ms. Watts's clear and startling "*No*" hangs in the courtroom, electrifying the moment.

Nurse Watts continues, "There were many times when either his Isosorbide or his Nitroglycerin were not on the drug cart. Often, we would run out. He'd ask us to get more."

"Did you tell Nurse Hatcher."

"I did, regularly." Nurse Watts says, avoiding Nurse Hatcher's nasty gaze.

"And how did she react? I mean, did she fix the problem, so Mr. Kendrick's medicines would arrive in a regular and timely fashion?"

"No."

"Did you ever ask her about this issue?"

"Yes. She blamed it on Huntsville—that's where the main prison pharmacy is—not shipping on time. She always said she would check into it, but nothing seemed to change. Most times I would do the medical call Mr. Kendrick would remind me he was out of one or both of those medicines."

"You knew, actually the entire medical staff knew, those medicines were essential to care for Mr. Kendrick's condition."

"Yes." Her bluntness reverberates in the courtroom "The issue of Mr. Kendrick's meds was commonly known among the nurses."

"Including Nurse Hatcher?"

"*Especially* Nurse Hatcher. She was in charge of the prescriptions. She was supposed to get it fixed. But it never got fixed."

I can feel the surrounding hush in the courtroom as I pause.

"Ms. Watts, do you think Nurse Hatcher turned a blind eye to this problem, do you think she deliberately *ignored* the fact that Mr. Kendrick was not receiving his critical medicines on time. Was she *deliberately indifferent*?"

Her lips tighten into a grimace as if the words are dangerous to her. Seconds tick by. Nurse Watts looks to her lap, then to the Jury. She tugs on her sleeves. Finally, she looks at Mr. Kendrick and then the defendants, including Nurse Hatcher, who all glare at her. She lifts her gaze to the back of the courtroom, staring into space.

Nurse Watts finally closes her large brown eyes. "No."

Her answer stuns me, as I exhale a long slow breath. Sweat beads in the small of my back, and my heartbeat speeds up. In the words of Hitch, "I'm porked." Without a sworn statement or deposition, it's impossible to impeach her testimony. I have no physical evidence to prove she has recanted what she told us in the restaurant. I possess no leverage to make her tell the truth. I clear my throat and scribble on my yellow pad, scrambling to decide my next question.

"Ms. Watts, did we talk over the weekend?"

Nurse Watts looks past me at the courtroom doors, greedily eyeing the exits. "We did."

"And didn't you tell me emphatically that the defendants, in particular Nurse Hatcher, were *deliberately indifferent* to Mr. Kendrick receiving his medications on time?"

She takes a long time to answer. The silence uncomfortable. Finally, staring into the distance, she says, "I believe I may have been confused if I said that." She takes a deep, remorseful breath. "Trying to get medicines to prisoners can be complicated. It's not always easy to control. Nurse Hatcher could have been trying to do her best. I just don't know."

I pause and then decide to risk it.

"Ms. Watts, did any lawyer for the defendants speak with you recently?"

"Yes, Ms. Walker called me last night to talk." Rose shifts uncomfortably in her chair at counsel table.

"What did you talk about?"

"I'd rather not say."

"Your Honor, I'd request that the Court direct the witness to answer."

The Judge points her half-moon glasses at the witness. "If you can answer the question, please do so."

Nurse Watts pauses a moment. "I don't remember. It was a brief call."

Her last words hang in the courtroom for a moment. Adrenaline floods my bloodstream. Our case has collapsed around me—the silence pronounced and awkward, all eyes of the jurors intent on me.

The Judge coughs to draw me from my daze. "Mr. Simmons, do you have any further questions for this witness?"

I rub the back of my neck, all focus on me. Then I concede, "No your Honor." I avoid Emmett's gaze as I capitulate.

"Very well. Ms. Watts," the Judge says. "You are free to go."

Nurse Ryan has not shown. Bile roils my stomach. With

only Emmett and Nurse Watts testifying for our side, we must rest our case. They are all we have. The Judge excuses the Jury a little early for its morning break.

"Your Honor," Ms. Walker says as she stands up triumphantly.

"Yes."

"The State moves for a directed verdict on all of Mr. Kendrick's claims. Mr. Kendrick has failed to submit sufficient evidence on any of his claims that warrant these issues making it to a jury."

"Mr. Simmons, what says the plaintiff?"

"Your Honor, we would ask the Court to deny the State's motion. On Mr. Kendrick's testimony alone—which can't be discounted simply because he is a prisoner—we have produced sufficient evidence that the Defendants have intentionally turned a blind eye to securing proper medicines to treat his serious heart condition. I believe we have also shown that the way Teton Springs transports Mr. Kendrick causes him significant pain sufficient to violate his Constitutional rights to be secure from cruel treatment. You saw it with your eyes."

The Judge flips through a few pages of her notes on the bench, then says, "Counsel, after hearing the testimony and reviewing the law on point, I am going to grant the motion for directed verdict."

Ms. Walker stands tall, smiles, and straightens the cruel pleats of her skirt in victory.

"But only as to the transportation claim," the Judge continues. I hold my breath. Mr. Walker's lips purse in disgust. The Judge continues. "I don't find sufficient evidence to move that claim forward and submit it to the Jury. There is insufficient evidence that the prison transports him any differently than other prisoners or that transport as done is cruel and inhumane. However, Mr. Kendrick submitted sufficient evidence on the medicine claim that it's best a Jury decide." Ms. Walker's smile morphs more into a sneer. She's not free and clear, *yet*.

The Judge turns a frosty gaze on Ms. Walker. "Is the defense ready?"

"Yes, Your Honor."

"Then you will call your first witness when the Jury comes back from its break."

We have a few minutes to gird against the onslaught.

CHAPTER
THIRTY-SIX

TWENTY MINUTES LATER. Wichita Falls.

My stomach starts to ache as Emmett and I watch Ms. Walker stand. Steve nervously clicks a pen next to me. Ashley straightens her glasses, bites her lip and passes me a note, "Here we go," it says.

"The defense calls Doctor Ralston."

A middle-height, scrawny man wearing thick bifocal glasses and dark gray suit that looks like it hasn't been worn in years shuffles to the stand and takes the oath.

"Dr. Ralston," Ms. Walker says, "are you the head physician in charge at Teton Springs?"

"Yes. I have been the head physician for almost five years now."

"And you've had the responsibility to oversee Mr. Kendrick's care?"

"Yes."

"Will you please describe his care and condition to the Jury?"

"Mr. Kendrick suffers from several severe heart ailments that require monitoring and a regular regimen of medicines to keep under control."

"And do you oversee that regimen?"

"Well, I oversee the care *at the physician level*. I see Mr. Kendrick in the infirmary if necessary, but most of the time I simply review the data provided to me by the staff that works in the AdSeg Unit. Nurse Hatcher, actually, as the Chronic Care Nurse, would be the one most directly in line with Mr. Kendrick's care. She would see that the staff carried out my medical orders in the chart. And, she would oversee the delivery of any prescribed medications."

"Did you ever have occasion to learn that Mr. Kendrick was complaining about his care."

"Yes. I had seen notes in the file. Once, one of the wardens asked me about the supply of Mr. Kendrick's medicines. As far as I know, the supply was as consistent as possible."

"How so?"

"Well, medicine inside a prison is much different than outside a prison. As a prison physician, you don't write a prescription, and the patient runs down to the corner drugstore to get it filled that day. Rather, the prescriptions come up from Huntsville. If they don't arrive, that is not the fault of the staff at Teton Springs. Of course we contact Huntsville, and try to get it corrected. But we are at the mercy of what drugs they send us because all drugs have to be tracked. We must account for in the system. You can't have drugs wander off in a prison."

"Do you believe at any time, Mr. Kendrick's care was compromised by the few hiccups in delivery of his medicines?"

"No."

"At any time did you purposely ignore Mr. Kendrick's complaints about his medicines?"

"Certainly not."

"And he complained all the time?"

"Yes. Mr. Kendrick always complained."

"Pass the witness."

"Dr. Ralston," I begin from the lectern. "Mr. Kendrick has a significant heart condition, right?"

"Yes. He has had previous heart attacks and a number of surgeries. He also suffers from regular bouts of angina. So it's fair to call that significant."

"You have been his primary doctor over the past few years?"

"Yes."

"Isosorbide and Nitroglycerin are critical medicines to treat his significant heart conditions?"

"Yes. They are."

"And it's dangerous to stop those medicines abruptly, right?"

"Well. Many factors go into whether it could be dangerous if one stopped the medications abruptly. Many other variables could also lead to a heart attack."

"So, it wouldn't be dangerous to stop them abruptly?"

Dr. Ralston adjusts his thick glasses. The wheels turning behind his stare. "Maybe, but I doubt it. Many circumstances could play into the cause of a heart attack. My experience suggests that it would not result from stopping Isosorbide."

"Dr. Ralston, have you always been Mr. Kendrick's physician at Teton Springs?"

"No. I arrived after Mr. Kendrick. Dr. Patel was his initial treating physician at Teton Springs."

"Did Dr. Patel ever stop the Isosorbide for Mr. Kendrick?"

Dr. Ralston takes a beat, calculating his words. "Yes. When I arrived, I noted in the chart that Dr. Patel had stopped the Isosorbide."

"What happened after he stopped the medicine?"

"Mr. Kendrick suffered a heart attack."

I pause for a moment to let the answer reverberate around the courtroom.

"You're a licensed physician?"

"Yes."

"Practicing for over three decades, right?"

"Yes."

"Would you recognize the British Medical Journal and the American Medical Journal as authorities in the medical literature?"

"Yes. Both journals are peer reviewed, and they publish articles on the best in medicine."

"So if these journals published articles that state that discontinuing Isosorbide abruptly is dangerous and could lead to an immediate onset of a heart attack, would you have any reason to disagree?"

"No, I would like to think the way I practice medicine is consistent with what those two journals publish."

"Let's look at a passage together," I start.

"Objection," Ms. Walker states as she stands up.

"What's your objection, counselor?" the Judge presses.

"Hearsay, your honor. Mr. Simmons is simply reading information into the record from outside sources. It does not bear on this matter."

"Mr. Simmons, what say you?"

"Your honor, Dr. Ralston has already qualified these journals as 'authorities' in the medical literature. To the extent his opinion on the stand disagrees with leading authorities on medicine, the jury should be able to consider that."

"I'll sustain the objection. Mr. Simmons, I will not allow you to read outside published statements into the record. Find a different way to ask the question or move on."

I pause for a moment and try another approach. "Dr. Ralston, I'd like to hand you a copy of an article of the British Medical Journal. Please read—to yourself—the highlighted passage."

Dr. Ralston peers through his bifocals and reviews the journal. Then he looks at me, then Ms. Walker, then the Judge.

"Dr. Ralston, does reading that passage from the British Medical Journal, which you have already told the jury is a recognized authority in the medical field, lead you to change any part of your previous answer that discontinuing Isosorbide likely would *not* lead to a heart attack."

A slight flash of anger on his face, Dr. Ralston answers. "It would appear that some physicians have concluded that it's an almost certain risk."

"Physicians in the British Medical Journal?"

"Yes."

"You also testified earlier that Mr. Kendrick complained all the time. Was that your testimony?

"Yes."

I take a beat. "And, indeed, Dr. Patel stopped the Isosorbide, and a heart attack followed immediately."

"I don't know if it was immediate."

"Did Dr. Patel stop the Isosorbide?"

"Yes."

"Did Mr. Kendrick have a heart attack?"

"Yes."

"Did he complain about angina and not having the Nitroglycerin?"

"Yes."

"Have you ever had an angina attack, doctor?" I press, relentless.

"No."

"Never felt the pain?"

"No."

"You have no idea what it's like to have a crushing pain in your chest, isolated in a cell, with no one caring about your 'complaints'?"

"No."

"Yet to be certain, you were the physician in charge of Mr. Kendrick's medicines?"

"Yes."

"No further questions."

"Ms. Walker, anything further?" The Judge asks.

Finally, Ms. Walker states, "Nothing further."

"If Dr. Ralston is through, then please call your next witness," the Judge says.

"Defendants call Nurse Iris Hatcher," Ms. Walker says as Dr. Ralston exits.

Nurse Hatcher stands up from the defense table. She is short and stocky, wrapped in a professional dark blue pantsuit and comfortable nurse dress shoes. She struts to the witness chair and takes the oath—the whole truth and nothing but the truth.

"Nurse Hatcher. Please introduce yourself to the jury and tell them your current job position."

"My name is Idris Hatcher. I'm the Chronic Care Nurse at Teton Springs."

"Let's step back for a moment. Have you always worked at Teton Springs?" asks Ms. Walker.

"No. I graduated from the women's college down in Denton with a Bachelor of Science in Nursing. After that, the local hospital here in Wichita Falls hired me as a nurse in the intensive care unit. I worked there for ten years. The hours in intensive care are long, and the schedule can prove difficult. I wanted more predictable work hours. So, when I saw an advertisement in the paper for the Choric Care Nurse at Teton Springs, I applied for the job."

"How long have you been in that position at the Teton Springs Unit?"

"Next July will be ten years."

"Please tell the jury what you do as the Chronic Care Nurse at Teton Springs."

"Well, I oversee the day-to-day care of the prisoners in solitary confinement—Administrative Segregation—and see to their general medical care. I have about a half dozen nurses that work under my charge. We review the treatment plans for all the prisoners we treat regularly, and I ensure we carry out those treatment plans. We also make medical rounds to check on the health and wellbeing of every inmate at least once a day. If a virus is going around, say like the flu, we may round twice a day, but usually it's just the once."

"Do you oversee the storage and dispensing of medicines at the AdSeg Unit?"

"Yes. That falls under my duties. When we receive the drugs into the AdSeg Unit, we inventory them and then store them in the drug room to dispense to the inmates," says Nurse Hatcher.

"And, they get dispensed?"

"Yes, according to the treatment plans."

"So, ten years in intensive care at a local hospital and ten years in leadership as the Chronic Care Nurse in the AdSeg Unit at Teton Springs—is it safe to say that you have had significant experience with patients that have chronic cardiac conditions?"

"Yes. Just by the nature of the conditions, cardiac care is one focus of intensive care at any hospital. And, at the prison, several older inmates have issues with their heart."

"You are well versed in the drugs needed to treat such conditions?"

"Yes, you have to be. The doctors, of course, prescribe the medicines, and we have to follow their orders. But once they write those orders, we are responsible to carry them out."

"And, would you say that you do the best you can to implement those orders?"

"We do. We do all we can within the prison system to make sure we follow those orders."

"You said, 'within the prison system,' what did you mean by that?" prompts Ms. Walker.

"Well, practicing medicine inside a prison is not the same as inside a hospital. You see, in a hospital, there is a pharmacy right there, just a couple of floors down from the ICU. If a doctor prescribes a medicine, it's a matter of minutes or hours until the pharmacy provides it. And, the pharmacists monitor those medicines. They make sure that the patients in ICU have the medicines that they need, when they need it. That's not the same in a prison. We have no pharmacy at Teton Springs. The pharmacy is actually in Huntsville, Texas, hundreds of miles away. They fill the orders and deliver them to us. Sometimes it can take days to get a drug. Some drugs weeks. It depends on the urgency and the supply Huntsville has on hand."

"So you rely on Huntsville to get it right?"

"Yes. And if they don't, we push as hard as we can to make them get it right. These medicines, some like those Mr. Kendrick takes, are critical. So, when Huntsville has a hiccup, we call and work to get it fixed."

"Did Huntsville ever have a hiccup with Mr. Kendrick's medicines?"

"Yes. Sometimes they would not send the full supply of Isosorbide or Nitro. And when we realized it, we would work to fix it. Sometimes we'd have to raise holy heck to get them to pay attention. But we did it because caring for patients, like Mr. Kendrick, is our responsibility."

"Did you ever allow Mr. Kendrick's drug supply to run out?"

"Not to my memory, no. I can't think of a time that Mr. Kendrick was without his medicine. The supply may have been low, but I believe at all times we pushed Huntsville hard enough to make sure Mr. Kendrick had his medicine when he needed it."

"But how can that be true? Mr. Kendrick has testified to this jury that he sometimes went days without Isosorbide, or that he suffered on his bunk with crushing angina because he had no Nitroglycerin and no one would pay attention to his cries for help."

"It can't be true. First, we would have noticed if he was in trouble. The regulations require that a nurse go on the unit and call out 'medical' loud enough for all the inmates to hear.

Then a nurse, accompanied by a Corrections officer, goes past each cell and visually checks on each inmate to make sure they are mobile and that if they have medical issues, we address those issues. We take pride in the care of our patients even if they are in prison."

"So you are confident a nurse would have noticed if Mr. Kendrick was suffering from an angina attack."

"Absolutely. Sometimes I would walk the units myself to make sure."

"Is that the only reason you have to doubt Mr. Kendrick's testimony?"

"No. The Corrections Officers on the block keep a watch as well. They stay mostly in the picket, but they also walk their unit at regular intervals. So if Mr. Kendrick had an angina attack, he could have flagged down one of the COs."

"You said a 'picket.' Tell the Jury what a picket is."

"Oh sorry. A picket, well a picket is the guards' office on the block. The Administrative Segregation at Teton Springs has several cellblocks—I believe they are 'A' through 'E'—and on each cellblock the guards have an office with big glass windows. They monitor the cellblock and take care of their administrative duties from there. That's a picket."

"So there are eyes on these prisoners all day. Nurses make rounds. Guards stand watch and monitor from the 'picket.' Is that correct?"

"Yes. That is correct. As you told the jury, Administrative Segregation is another name for solitary confinement. AdSeg holds the problematic prisoners, so they must have a higher level of supervision."

"Problematic prisoners?"

"I use that word to be polite. AdSeg holds those prisoners who can't *and won't* follow the rules. They pose a danger to others or the staff. So they are locked down—mostly because of their own behavior."

"You said they are dangerous."

"Yes. All of my nurses have to watch themselves in AdSeg. We've treated some horrific wounds on a couple nurses that let down their guard. They trusted too much. One prisoner stuck a shank made from a filed-down toothbrush through a nurse's cheek. That left an ugly red scar."

"Is it just the threat of physical violence that could unnerve a nurse on AdSeg?"

"No. These prisoners can say and do, vile things. All they see all day are mostly men. We have a few female Corrections Officers. My nurses are typically the only women these men see. They say horrible sexual statements to them—lewd perverted comments. They call them cruel names. Some inmates masturbate in their cells and then throw the semen at my nurses. I think the guards call it 'chunking.' Hurling deep bodily fluids like that puts my nurses at risk."

"Have you been a victim of chunking?"

"Yes. I have."

"And is it safe to assume that, for your own safety, you approach Mr. Kendrick with the same level of caution you do the other inmates."

"We do. I presume that any inmate in AdSeg poses a risk to my nurses. Those prisoners are on that cellblock for a reason. And, it did not surprise me the other day, when you made Mr. Kendrick admit on the stand that he threatened to rip off another inmate's head and roll it down the hallway."

"You're here on trial because Mr. Kendrick accuses you of failing to provide him his medicines. Indeed, he accuses you of purposely denying him those medications. What do you say to those accusations?"

"His accusations are false—and hurtful. I have worked as a nurse for twenty years. Never in my career have I purposely withheld medicine for a patient, prisoner or otherwise. That is ludicrous."

"Well, in your experience, why would a prisoner make such an accusation?"

"I don't know. Boredom, I guess."

"Boredom?"

"Yes. Solitary confinement is lonely … and dull. You're alone twenty-four hours a day, every day, for years. Eventually, I think it gets the best of any prisoner. So they look for activities to pass their time. Mr. Kendrick has made an art of complaining and filing grievances. It seems like a new one each week. And, the longer a prisoner stays in AdSeg, it seems, the more they look for someone to blame for whatever they are complaining about, real or imagined. Mr. Kendrick appears to have selected me as his target, and he claims I have mistreated him, withheld medicines from him."

"Would you categorize him as a model prisoner?"

"I would not."

"Why?"

"As I understand it, Mr. Kendrick is in prison for bank robbery. He is in AdSeg for an escape attempt. He has turned complaints and grievances into sport. He enjoys this. Look around. Look at all the defendants, the court. He has pulled all these Jurors away from their families and jobs, so he can have a little fun to break up his day. A model prisoner? No. A model prisoner does their time and thinks about why they are in prison in the first place. They don't spend all their waking hours harassing the staff and dreaming up complaints."

"Nurse Hatcher, I have one last question. Did you ever purposely withhold medicine from Mr. Kendrick to harm him?"

"No."

"Pass the witness."

Emmett pats the sleeve of my suit jacket. Steve gathers a few documents and heads to the lectern. He tugs on his French cuffs, flips over a sheet on his legal pad and begins.

"Ms. Hatcher," Steve says, "Just so we are clear, you are in charge of the pharmacy in the AdSeg Unit, correct?"

"Yes."

"So you control what medicines the nurses deliver to Mr. Kendrick and those they don't, right?"

"Well, I don't *control* the medicines."

"But just a moment ago, you testified to this Jury that you receive the drugs, inventory the drugs, and dispense the drugs, correct?"

"That is correct."

"Do any medicines leave the drug room without your sign off?"

"No," she says smugly. "They should not. I know what drugs come in, and what drugs go out."

"So, if Mr. Kendrick complains he was often without his heart medicine that would fall on your shoulders?"

"It's not true."

"Ms. Hatcher, we'll let the jury figure out what is true and not true. All I'm asking, and it's a simple question: if Mr. Kendrick's medicines did not make it out of the drug room that would be something that falls under your charge, right?"

"If they did not make it out of the drug room, yes." She retreats briefly in her seat and then juts out her chin. "But they did."

"And it's your testimony that whenever the drugs were there, you provided them to to Mr. Kendrick."

"Yes. That is my testimony."

"Always?"

"Always." Nurse Hatcher says flatly.

"Earlier you testified that any, I believe 'hiccup' was the word you used."

"Yes."

"Any hiccup in the supply of Mr. Kendrick's critical heart medications resulted from the pharmacy in Huntsville failing to send the medicines. Do you remember that?"

"Yes. That is correct."

"So there was never an occasion when Huntsville

provided the medicines to you, and you failed to provide them to Mr. Kendrick."

"Never. If we had the medication, we provided it to Mr. Kendrick, any inmate, really, that had prescriptions in the drug room."

"So you would have this Jury believe that it's all Huntsville's fault."

"If they don't send the medicines, we can't dispense them to the prisoners."

"It's true, however, that Mr. Kendrick went without his medicines correct?"

"I can't remember a time."

"But it's possible?"

"Possibly. I can't remember any. But it's possible, yes. Mr. Kendrick may have had to go without certain medicines for a short period."

"You were here during Dr. Ralston's testimony?"

"I was."

"You heard him indicate that stopping Isosorbide abruptly could actually trigger a heart attack?"

"I heard him agree that whoever wrote that article Mr. Simmons made him read suggested that could occur. But I have not seen the article. And it seemed to me, Dr. Ralston was of a different view."

"But you heard him admit that researchers in the British Journal of Medicine had come to that conclusion."

"That appeared to be what the article said. But again, I have not seen it."

"You were at Teton Springs when Dr. Patel was the prison physician?"

"I was."

"And Dr. Patel stopped Mr. Kendrick's Isosorbide when he arrived from Huntsville."

"I believe that is correct."

"Mr. Kendrick then had a heart attack."

"He did. But there is no certainty that stopping the Isosorbide caused it."

"I'm just trying to establish the timeline. Mr. Kendrick arrived at Teton Springs from Huntsville. Dr. Patel stopped the Isosorbide. Mr. Kendrick had a heart attack. Those three facts, in that exact order are correct."

"Yes," she concedes. She shifts in the chair and squares her shoulders, "But I'm not sure I blame Dr. Patel."

"You are saying the facts are wrong?"

"No, I'm saying that sometimes when they transfer a prisoner from Huntsville, their medical records take a few days to arrive. Dr. Patel may not have known."

"So he was ignorant of Mr. Kendrick's condition?"

"I'm saying the records might have shown up late." Her voice ticks up an octave.

"Let's talk about rounds. You testified that you and your nurses made regular medical rounds."

"I did, and we do."

"On those rounds, you—or whomever the nurse is—calls out 'medical' and then gets a visual on each prisoner?"

"That's the policy from the Texas Department of Corrections, and we follow that policy."

"Ever deviate?"

"No."

"Ever say to yourself, I'm just too tired today and don't want to do rounds, don't want to get a visual on each prisoner?"

"That would be against policy. So, no."

"Never? Not once?"

"No. We do our job professionally, Mr. Davis."

"You testified earlier about shanking and chunking, remember that?"

"Yes."

"You describe a pretty horrific environment with nurses

stabbed by shanks and male inmates flinging semen on them."

"Yes."

"Do you know of any report of Mr. Kendrick stabbing anyone?"

"No."

"Ever heard of, or read a report of, him tossing semen on a nurse?"

"No. I described that conduct to demonstrate how dangerous and difficult this job is. It's not for the faint of heart. We do this job because we love nursing. We do it despite the physical risk to ourselves and the horrible things the inmates say to us."

"Has Mr. Kendrick ever said one harsh word to you?"

"He complains. He files grievances on me all the time."

"He does that within the policy allowed to him by the Texas Department of Corrections, does he not?"

"Well, yes. There is a policy for grievances."

"You're not suggesting that he shouldn't follow policy and exercise what limited rights he has, are you?"

"No, I'm not saying that. I'm saying he complains a lot."

"You just told us how important policy is."

"Yes, but—"

"Mr. Kendrick strictly follows policy."

"Yes."

"So that brings me back to my original, simple, question. Has Mr. Kendrick ever said one harsh word to you?"

"No."

"Ever hear of him say one harsh word to any of your nurses?"

"No," Nurse Hatcher admits grudgingly.

"Pass the witness," concludes Steve.

"Ms. Walker," the Judge inquires. "Anything further with Nurse Hatcher?"

"Nothing further, Your Honor."

"Ms. Walker, who is your next witness?"

"Your Honor, may I have a few moments to confer with my co-counsel. We may be done."

"Let's go ahead and take lunch a little early." The Judge twirls her reading glasses in her hand. "Members of the Jury, please return in one hour, and we'll see if the State is done with its case."

A sixty-minute reprieve.

CHAPTER
THIRTY-SEVEN

MINUTES LATER. Wichita Falls.

Steve and I make our way over to the burger joint across the street. Ashley waits for us in a booth. Her blazer rests over her lap, and her cream linen blouse looks wrinkled as if she's been canvassing the entire town. She has been hunting our missing key witness: Nurse Ryan, the tall redhead.

"Did you find Nurse Ryan?" I prod.

Ashley pushes her designer glasses up the bridge of her nose. "Wasn't easy. She kept dodging my calls. Then I called her mother, who I found in the directory, and a few minutes later, I got a call."

"What did she say?"

"They've been all over her." Ashley says in a huff. "Phone calls. Bumping into her at the grocery store. One guy even showed up while she was pumping gas. Can you imagine? These creeps."

"Did she say what they told her?"

"No, she wouldn't tell me anything, just that they were everywhere." Ashley pauses and sweeps her long, brown hair away from her face. "But . . . I just got off the phone with her." A sly smile accentuates her lip. She pauses, and then says,

"*She's thinking about it*. Says she's driving around downtown. She'll let me know in twenty minutes."

Silence envelops our little table. A small whisper of hope passes between all of us.

"As long as we're waiting, let's eat," Steve says. He winks at the waitress and asks for a menu.

As we wait for our food to arrive, I step out on the sidewalk and call Hitch. He can be a harsh mentor, but I'm floundering. He might know what to do.

"Denise," I say into the phone. "Is Hitch running around?"

"Honey, he's had four wives. He's always runnin' around." She chuckles at her own joke.

"I mean is he there? Can I talk to him? I'm on a break in trial. I have no time, and I need to ask him a question."

"Hang on. I'll go find him." I picture Denise jetting down a hallway, her severe braids trailing behind her, hunting Hitch like a bird dog.

The phone fills with dead air for what seems like forever. Finally, Hitch comes on the line.

"Now what in the world is so shit fire important that Denise had to come pull me off the toilet?"

"Hitch, I'm in trial. I have two key witnesses and the other side is jacking with them." I pace in front of the diner window as I talk, my arms flailing with anxiety.

"Who are they?"

I still my voice. "Two nurses who used to work at the prison. It's a prisoner trial. Our prisoner, Emmett, claims they withhold his heart meds and leave him at risk for a heart attack. A couple of days ago, two nurses told us we were right, that the head nurse doesn't give a hoot about getting Emmett his meds. She even delays it on purpose. They're the lynchpin, without them we're screwed. But, the first one recanted her statement when we put her on the stand. She tells us she received calls. The other one has disappeared, apparently too scared to testify. We're tracking her down."

Hitch lets out a whistle. Moments tick by. "You said 'former.' They no longer work there?" The concern in his voice obvious.

"That's right."

"Well son, they're free game for anyone to talk to, unless they're threatening them. Are they telling your nurses what to say?"

"I have no proof of what they're telling them. I think they are mostly reminding them how small this town is." I push my fingers through my thinning hair in frustration. "All I know is the nurses are saying something completely different today than they said before."

My heartbeat pounds in my ears as I wait for Hitch's response. Finally, he breaks the silence. "Well, let's think this over." A jolt of adrenaline shoots through me.

Hitch rattles off a strategy. Through the window I see my lunch arrive, and I know it's going to go cold and uneaten as Hitch runs through a game plan.

I hope it's enough.

CHAPTER
THIRTY-EIGHT

AFTER LUNCH, the recess over. Wichita Falls.

We wait at counsel table for court to restart. I look over my shoulder and see Ashley finally sprint into the courtroom, her long brown hair slightly mussed from running to court. We exchange a knowing glance, and she nods as she catches her breath.

"All rise," the Marshal calls. The Judge takes the bench and the Jury shuffles into the box.

"Ms. Walker?" the Judge presses.

"Your Honor, the defense rests," says Ms. Walker with a smug smile, her rapacious eyes telegraphing confidence.

"Mr. Simmons. Anything further?"

"Your Honor, we have one rebuttal witness." A slight jolt of electricity flashes through the courtroom.

"Proceed."

"We call Amanda Ryan." Murmurs wash through the defense table.

The large doors to the courtroom open, and Nurse Ryan appears. The sun from a window highlights her fiery red hair, the pale skin on her neck splotchy with nerves. She could be an angel appearing in our hour of need.

"Ms. Ryan please come forward and be sworn," the Judge says.

Through the quiet of the courtroom, Ms. Ryan walks to the witness stand, lays her hand on the Bible, and swears to tell the whole truth and nothing but the truth. As if a schoolgirl in the principal's office, she tucks her dress underneath her as she sits. I step to the lectern.

"Ms. Ryan. Please state your name for the record and give the Jury a brief introduction as to who you are and why you are here."

"My name is Amanda Ryan, and I am here, I believe, because I worked as a nurse in the AdSeg Unit at Teton Springs."

"Did you say you *worked*, as in you no longer work there?"

"Yes. I left Teton Springs just this past summer."

"Why?"

"The job was stressful. When I first started there, I used to look forward to my work. But by the end, I couldn't wait to clock out and head home."

"What made it so stressful, the prisoners?"

"Well somewhat. It's a prison. So you have to keep your wits about you. But with the COs always with us, and guarding us, most of the prisoners behaved. So, no, I did not leave the prison because the prisoners made it stressful."

"Why did you leave then?"

"I ultimately left because it was difficult to do my job."

"How so?"

Ms. Ryan takes a deep breath. She peers at Emmett with her hazel eyes. He looks innocent, like someone's grandfather dressed for church. His ice-blue eyes flash a knowing twinkle back at Nurse Ryan. She then glances at all the Defendants lined up behind Ms. Walker, including the glowering Idris Hatcher.

Nurse Ryan confesses, "Nurse Hatcher." A moment of silence passes in the courtroom.

"What about Nurse Hatcher made your job difficult?" I nudge.

Nurse Ryan nervously clears her throat and then says, "She would ride me all the time because I would advocate for the inmates. If an inmate needed something medically, I would often go to bat for them. Nurse Hatcher didn't like that."

"When you say she didn't like '*that*,' help the jury understand what you mean."

Ms. Ryan turns in the chair and talks directly to the jury, as if blocking out the stares from the defense table. "I'll give you an example." I do not know where her story will lead, but I'm desperate enough to follow. She continues, "One of the prisoners, Inmate Parker, suffered from migraines. He always told us the lights hurt his eyes and that his head was pounding. I mean, it's a fact that some of the ultraviolet bulbs can flicker or buzz and trigger migraines in sensitive people. When we called, 'medical,' on the unit, Mr. Parker would frequently sit at the meal slot telling us it felt like a vice was crushing his head. The guards would tell us, he was always complaining that his head hurt. He'd tell Dr. Ralston, but that led to an order for an occasional aspirin or other over-the-counter pain pill. They told him to relax, breathe deeply in his cell, and the headaches would likely resolve. But he kept talking about the lights. So, one day I brought in a sleep mask for him. I researched it online, and I thought maybe if he could rest in darkness his migraines would go away. I gave the mask to him on rounds one day. And it worked. The pain subsided, and he complained less about his head hurting. The migraines disappeared."

"What happened next?"

"Well, one day, a rumor went through that a few prisoners in AdSeg had shanks in their cells, so the COs tossed each cell in the whole cellblock—one by one. The COs found the sleep mask and grilled him about it. Mr. Parker finally confessed that I had given it to him. Nurse Hatcher was mad as a hornet. She yelled at me that 'it didn't come from Huntsville, it wasn't a direct order from a physician.' Then she threatened to write me up for smuggling in contraband if I ever did something like this again." Nurse Ryan takes a breath and looks down at her hands folded in her lap. He voice proceeds with a twinge of remorse. "It was just a simple sleep mask. And it *was working*. For that *she* threatened to fire me." Her pale skin on her chest and neck were now ruddy.

"Did incidents like this affect your daily job?"

"Yes. Nurse Hatcher stayed mad about that sleep mask. From then on, she criticized anything I did for a prisoner. She rode me. Double-checked me on everything. Always making a snide comment when I saw her."

"Do you have any idea why the sleep mask or these other things you did for prisoners upset her?"

Nurse Ryan's voice falters with exasperation. "She called me 'soft.'"

"Soft?"

"Yes. She used to brag that she was a law-and-order type of person. That these prisoners deserved to be in prison, and prison was not supposed to be easy. It wasn't a country club. She wore her disdain for prisoners as a badge of honor." I rifle through my notes, buying time so her last statement can hang in the courtroom.

"Let's turn to Mr. Kendrick. Did you ever interact with Mr. Kendrick?"

"Regularly. Mr. Kendrick, because of his heart condition, was someone that the nursing staff was well aware of." Her face washes with compassion and a smile. "Emmett, I mean Mr. Kendrick, was someone of concern."

"Concern?"

Nurse Ryan straightens in the witness chair and continues in a more clinical tone. "Well, Mr. Kendrick had already had heart attacks. We all knew his heart condition was serious, advanced. He'd had another heart attack while at Teton Springs."

"Did he ever tell you he was out of his Isosorbide or Nitroglycerin?"

"Yes, frequently. When he'd come to the meal slot, he'd tell me he was running low. Sometimes he'd tell me he was out—had been out for days."

"Did he ever mention angina attacks?"

"Yes, frequently."

"What would you do?"

"I'd tell Nurse Hatcher."

"How did she react?"

"She'd say something like, 'that one . . . he's always complaining. His medicine is on the way.' Then she'd tell us to relax, that angina is no worse than a dull ache, like if you'd left a rubber band tight around your finger too long."

"Did you ever check to see if Mr. Kendrick was correct? That he was indeed out of his medicines."

Nurse Ryan sighs. "I did. A few times, I'd go back in the drug room and look him up. His drug pouch would be empty."

"So it's true, then, that several times his supply of Isosorbide stopped abruptly."

"That is true. I can't say how many times. But Mr. Kendrick was good about telling us when he was out. And, he said it often."

"Also true for his Nitroglycerin?"

"Also true, mostly."

"Why do you say, mostly?"

"Well, a couple of times, when Mr. Kendrick's drug pouch was missing Nitroglycerin—he'd mentioned his angina—I checked the drug cabinet. We had the Nitroglycerin, but someone had not dispensed it to Mr. Kendrick. I asked about it. Nurse Hatcher said it was an oversight."

"Nurse Hatcher tells us that can't be true. That she immediately dispensed medicine when she received it. That if a problem existed, then the problem was with Huntsville."

"I don't believe her." A hush permeates the courtroom. The Judge removes her reading glasses and focuses on Nurse Ryan. She continues, "We receive two shipments a week from Huntsville. Monday and Thursday. And, Mr. Kendrick's condition was chronic. It was ongoing. The prescriptions were something he needed, always. They were on a regular refill and shipped on a regular schedule."

"Do you have any idea why the supply of Mr. Kendrick's drugs became spotty?"

Nurse Ryan tugs at the cuticles on her nails. "Never could figure it out."

She pauses and shifts in the chair. "Huntsville is good about the ongoing prescriptions, and good about sending out shipments. And, for something serious like Mr. Kendrick's heart medicines, if there was a break in treatment, we could get a special overnight shipment."

"Do you know if Nurse Hatcher ever requested an overnight shipment of Isosorbide and Nitroglycerin for Mr. Kendrick?"

"I don't. Whenever I brought it up, she seemed upset, frustrated with Mr. Kendrick. She'd bark at me to drop it, and then she'd turn back to what she was doing. I just assumed she would take care of the order. Now, looking around at all this, I doubt she ever did."

"Did the spotty delivery of Mr. Kendrick's medicine ever get corrected?"

"*Obviously not,*" she says with disdain as her eyes bore into Nurse Hatcher.

"Did you ever see Nurse Hatcher interact with prisoners on the cellblocks?"

"No. I wasn't there every day she was, but I never saw her go out and do rounds."

"Did she ever say she had done rounds?"

"Just the opposite. She said that was *our* job, the nursing staff. She enjoyed being the boss, enjoyed being in charge as the Chronic Care Nurse, and she would come to work and retreat to her office. She'd stay there all day and clock out to go home. In her office, she was always busy.

"How about Dr. Ralston, did you ever see him on the cellblocks?"

Nurse Ryan scoffs. "Dr. Ralston? Not in AdSeg. He stayed over in the infirmary in another building. If an inmate wanted to see him, the inmate would have to beg for a visit, or if he complained of being sick, he'd have to have symptoms that warranted a transfer to the infirmary. For an AdSeg prisoner, that can be hard, because of the extra security around them."

"What about this policy Nurse Hatcher told the jury about, that a nurse would call 'medical' and then look into each cell to check on each prisoner, actually lay eyes upon them to check on them?"

"That's the policy. That's the way it should be done."

"Was it?"

"*No*," she says and flinches. "I'm ashamed to say it wasn't. Not always," Nurse Ryan's confession causes her to blush.

"How so?"

"Well, AdSeg at Teton Springs houses a lot of inmates. There were several cellblocks, and rounds happened twice a day. Plus, all the other things a nurse is supposed to do—charting and such. Nurse Hatcher would say, 'she runs a tight ship.' She wanted us out by 5 o'clock each day. The State gets unhappy about paying overtime. We were supposed to complete those two rounds and get out. A lot of days, there simply wasn't enough time to do it according to policy."

"So on those days, how did it go?"

"On most days, we go out on the cell block and say 'medical,' and we'd wait for a prisoner to bang on the meal slot. If no one knocked, we assumed they didn't need to talk to a nurse. We'd visit with those that flagged us down. The others, we assumed they were fine because the guards were there all day. If there had been a problem, the prisoners would have told a guard."

"Do the guards walk the floor regularly?"

"They are supposed to. But I think most of them stay in their observational picket for most of the day."

"Don't the wardens inspect the cellblocks; check up on the guards?"

"They do. But the guards flick the lights on and off if a warden is on his way. By the time the warden gets there, a CO is walking the floor."

"Nurse Hatcher describes AdSeg as a place full of shanks and prisoners chunking semen or other body waste on nurses."

Nurse Ryan looks at me and cocks her head to the side. "She's right to some extent. Prisoners on AdSeg, most of them are there for a reason. There have been problems with shanks. And some of the crazies chunk. But you figure out who those prisoners are pretty quick. Most of the time the guards warn you. So, you up your carefulness around them."

"Was Mr. Kendrick one of those you had to be careful with?"

"No. . . . *Never.*" Her voice firm as if insulted by the question.

"Why not?"

"Emmett was always polite. He kept to himself mostly. He didn't bother the nurses. He'd tell us he was out of his medicines. Sometimes he'd ask if we have any Nitroglycerin in the drug room, that his chest was hurting. Mostly, he just let us know about his medicines. The rest of the time, he was quiet. He didn't cause any trouble that I saw."

"Nurse Ryan, as you look back over the treatment of Mr. Kendrick, do you think it has been done correctly?"

Nurse Ryan considers for a moment. People in the courtroom lean forward, eager to hear her answer. She tucks strands of her red hair behind her ears and then closes her eyes for a moment, as if weighing her answer.

"*No.*" Her answer balloons into the courtroom. "They should have fixed the supply in his medicines. Nurse Hatcher should have fixed the problem. I do not know why she couldn't . . . or *wouldn't.*" Nurse Ryan casts an accusing glance at Hatcher.

"As you sit here today, do you think that Nurse Hatcher ignored the problem . . . was she deliberately turning a blind eye to Mr. Kendrick's complaints?"

"Possibly. I don't know what is in her head. By the time I left, she hated me and hated hearing about Emmett's, I mean, Mr. Kendrick's medicines. She was tired of his complaints. She was frustrated by how often he complained, and she was very vocal about it."

"I'll ask it a different way."

"Was Nurse Hatcher *deliberately indifferent* to ensuring Mr. Kendrick received his critical heart medicines on time and on a regular basis?"

"I have my suspicions."

"Objection," Ms. Walker calls out. "Speculation."

"Sustained," the Judge says. "The witness won't testify as to speculation or suspicion."

Cowed, Nurse Ryan answers, "I can't say. I have no direct knowledge of what was in her head."

"Nurse Ryan, you met with me, Mr. Davis, and Ms. Carmichael at a restaurant, did you not?"

"I did."

"And you are under oath today, you understand."

"I do."

"At our meeting you agreed that Nurse Hatcher's treatment, Teton Springs's treatment of Mr. Kendrick was *deliberately indifferent.*"

His gaze shifts, as if leaking an apology. "I may have said that then. But I've had time to think."

"And now?" A sinking feeling fills my gut.

Silence fills the courtroom as her gaze shifts from Emmett to the defendants as if weighing something internally on a scale. Her freckles highlight a tinge of innocence in her expression. She takes a deep breath.

"I can't say."

I think back on my call with Hitch. "Can't or *won't*, Ms. Ryan?"

She pauses and looks directly at the defendants. Nurse Hatcher flashes that tight, condescending smile, and her gaze bores into Nurse Ryan. Seconds tick by on the clock. Finally, Nurse Ryan whispers into the microphone, "I won't."

I take a breath, defeat permeates my entire body. I don't really know the answer to any of the questions I'm about to ask, but I have to risk it.

"Let me ask this. Between when we met over the weekend and your testimony today, have you been contacted by any lawyer or one of the Defendants?"

"Yes."

"Who contacted you, Ms. Ryan?"

"I bumped into Nurse Hatcher at the grocery."

"What, if anything, did she say to you?"

Ms. Walker shoots to her feet and calls out, "Objection, hearsay." The Judge gazes at me over her half-moon glasses for a response.

"Your Honor, Ms. Hatcher is a defendant. Anything she said to Ms. Ryan at the grocery store is an admission of a party. It's a non-hearsay statement."

"Overruled, continue Mr. Simmons." The Judge and everyone in the courtroom now focus on Nurse Ryan.

Thanks Hitch.

"Ms. Ryan what did Nurse Hatcher say to you?"

She clears her throat. "Nurse Hatcher told me she couldn't believe I'd risk everything to help a prisoner."

"What did you understand her to mean by '*risk everything*'?"

"She said once it got out that I'd helped Mr. Kendrick, I'd be lucky to find a job anywhere in the County."

"Did you take it as a threat?" Several jurors shift in their chairs.

Nurse Ryan continues, "Nurse Hatcher's face was almost purple. I could tell she was furious at me in the grocery store."

A juror, in the corner of the box shakes her head slightly. I look down at the notes on my legal pad, to see if I have any further questions. Silence floods the courtroom.

Nurse Ryan suddenly volunteers, "There was one other odd thing about it." A jolt pulses through the court.

"What was odd?"

"Nurse Hatcher and I live on opposite sides of town. I've *never* once seen her in that grocery in ten years. She had no reason to be on that side of town."

I pause long enough to let Nurse Ryan's statement echo in the courtroom. "Your Honor, no further questions."

I sit down and say a prayer.

I hope it's enough.

CHAPTER
THIRTY-NINE

LATE NIGHT. Wichita Falls, Texas. Seventeen weeks to a full-term baby.

One small lamp illuminates the hotel room, and the heater's squeak has evolved into a whine that flicks on and off in an irregular rhythm. A half-eaten pizza rests in a box on the dresser, the digital clock illuminates the early morning hour. On the other side of the line, the phone rings a few times. Hannah's delay in picking up fills me with angst. Finally, Hannah answers. I exhale, suddenly aware I've been holding my breath.

"How did Court go today?" she asks, groggy, as if I've awakened her.

"We may be sunk, Buzz," a slight catch in my voice. "Both nurses recanted what they told me at the restaurant."

Always the cheerleader, Hannah says, "You can pull it out with your closing. I have faith." My guilt of being away and concern for failure for Emmett make me brush away her comment.

"I'm not thinking about that." A vision of Hannah explodes in my mind. A simpler time. Her smile flashes as she twirls on a beach under a crimson sunset sky while on our honeymoon. Sand and the ocean are her secret, naughty plea-sure. I hold my hand out as if I can touch her golden hair and sun-kissed skin. Her electric energy buffers me against any storm. Suddenly, the whine from the heater in my messy hotel room clicks back on and snaps me into reality. Against the silence on the phone I say, "Buzz, I want to be with you . . . in the hospital. I *want* to be back in Dallas."

With firmness and resolves, she says, "You know that can't happen. There's nothing you can do in Dallas. Here? We just wait and pray. Emmett needs you there. You know that."

"That doesn't mean I shouldn't be in Dallas."

"Look, we made it another day. That's what matters." Her ramrod courage flows through the phone. "You'll come home soon."

Moments tick away. Finally I confess, "I don't think I can pull this off," I say. "I'm sure I have failed Emmett."

"Get your mind right. You knew it was a long shot," she says firmly.

"It may be an impossible shot . . . even if Emmett is right."

She gives me no quarter, no escape with sympathy. "I have faith in you. Someone will listen. *You* can do it."

Wrapped in my self-doubt, I ask a tiny favor. "Buzz. Can you set the phone down on the fetal monitor? I just want to hear her. I need Bailey's heartbeat."

Soon the sound pulses through the phone, a saving grace. I rest my head back on the pillow and soak in the rhythm of our baby, Bailey, as my eyelids close with sweet relief.

One day at a time.

CHAPTER
FORTY

EARLY THE NEXT MORNING. Wichita Falls.

Sleep did not come easy, and dawn came too soon. I'm worried my bloodshot eyes reveal my exhaustion. Recurring dreams of Hannah, Lilly, and Bailey plagued my dreams. The clock bangs out the seconds in the room where Emmett sits in his holding cell at the courthouse. After testimony yesterday, the Judge dismissed the jury for the day, and the lawyers stayed behind to finalize any objections to the jury charge: the set of questions the Jury will answer to render a verdict. Now, this morning, closing arguments come next. Emmett smiles at me warmly through the expansion steel grate of the holding cell.

"Emmett," I say, my voice pensive. "I'm sorry about Nurse Watts and Nurse Ryan."

"It's a prison town, a small town. I don't blame them." Compassion flashes through his ice-blue eyes. "They have a family to feed. They have jobs to tend. I'm a prisoner. I understand." He picks a piece of lint from his trousers.

"They were solid at the restaurant. They just waffled on the stand."

"I don't know," Emmett says, with a wide, forgiving grin.

"They might have said enough. Folks have a way of looking through a fog and seeing what is really there." For a moment we both meditate to the second hand ticking away seconds on the government clock. He breaks the reverie. "You ready for your closing argument?"

I sit up straight in my chair. "Yes. Steve, Ashley, and I worked on it last night."

"I'm looking forward to it," his eagerness apparent.

"Emmett. Just so it doesn't surprise you. At some point in the closing, I'll likely stand behind you. I'll rest my hand on your shoulders. If I can . . . if the Jury has any liking for me . . . I want them to see us together. I want them to see us as a team, you sitting there in your suit asking for help."

"What if they don't like you?"

I laugh. "Well then, we're sunk."

A few moments pass before Emmett breaks me away from my thoughts and worry. "You know, I'm going to miss this suit. It may be, today is the last day I'll ever wear a suit. If I ever get my good time credits restored, and get outside, I think that may be the first thing I do is buy a suit. That, and have a giant, double cheeseburger."

"You hungry?"

"No. The COs sent along a Johnny for me in a paper bag. We started at 4:00 this morning. So I already ate it. Good, though. I like bologna sandwiches. But I do love a good cheeseburger. All that grease and some fries."

"Better watch out for your heart."

"If a cheeseburger puts me under, I'd be a happy man." Emmett's mouth turns into an amused smile, his eyes calm and playful. "You know, that's how we count time in prison. Hamburgers."

"Hamburgers?"

"Yeah. Every Wednesday we get a hamburger. There are fifty-two hamburgers in a year. Five hundred and twenty in a decade."

The Marshal comes into the room. "You ready, Mr. Simmons?"

"Yes. I'll be right out."

Emmett looks at me a moment in silence.

"I'd better get out there. I guess it's 'go' time." The Marshal leads me to the door. I look back at Emmett, and he says one word.

"Brass."

CHAPTER
FORTY-ONE

MOMENTS LATER. The courtroom.

The Judge finishes reading the jury charge to the Jury and looks at me. "Mr. Simmons, if you're ready for closing arguments, the floor is yours." For closings, the Judge allows us to step away from the lectern, out into the well of the courtroom and address the jury directly—head on.

I begin. "At the start of this week, during opening statements, Mr. Davis said this case was about, 'why?' Why is it that after five years of requests all these defendants still fail to manage to consistently deliver Mr. Kendrick, Emmett's, critical prescribed medicines for what they all agree is a serious heart condition? That question has gone unanswered by the defendants. Unbelievable.

"This has turned into a five-year saga for Emmett. It starts —and we all know because we've seen the documents—at the time Texas transferred Emmett from Huntsville to Teton Springs and into Administrative Segregation, AdSeg. We all know that a doctor there, Dr. Patel, discontinued the Isosorbide, and Emmett's heart condition worsened. It deteriorated so far, so quickly, that Emmett had a heart attack. From that day forward, every prudent medical provider and prison official was on notice that discontinuing these critical medications meant a steep decline to a heart attack. That stopping the medicines can, and does, have a devastating effect on Emmett.

"From the witness stand, you heard Emmett tell you about this struggle to get the basic medicines he needs. He has tried every way that he can to solve the problem. He's called out from his eight-foot by ten-foot cell, told nurses at the clinic, filled out sick call requests. He filled out Step One grievances, Step Two grievances and sent letter after letter. Finally, with the road blocked in every direction, Emmett filed this lawsuit, and made it all the way to here, today, to trial to tell you. You are his last hope.

"The record shows that Emmett made every one of the defendants aware of his problem. He documented that this is a chronic, pervasive issue. In addition to Emmett's extraordinary efforts to try to rectify this situation through the administrative process in the prison, we have also heard testimony and seen documents that prove the following:

"Emmett has a serious heart condition. It was obvious to all around him. Delivering critical medicines was essential. Failing to deliver them posed an obvious and substantial risk. How do we know? Because when they stopped, his heart stopped.

"Yet despite that knowledge, each defendant has failed to solve the problem. They didn't fail to see the obvious. No. These nurses and wardens refused either to verify the facts or to confirm the risk. But most importantly, they failed to act. How do we know this? Because these critical medications? The supply? It was regularly interrupted. Indeed, just last month, just before trial, Emmett wrote Dr. Ralston that he was out of his heart medicines. No fix. They simply can't answer that one simple question, 'why?'

"Yes, we've heard about them trying their best at every turn. But the best evidence of their level of effort would be if the problem—a repeat problem—stopped. But it hasn't. That open and obvious issue, this open and obvious substantial risk has not stopped. And that, ladies and gentlemen of the jury, is reckless. It's deliberate indifference.

"This failure has serious, real-world consequences for Emmett. He is totally dependent on the prison to deliver these vital medicines. Dr. Ralston, Nurse Ryan, Nurse Watts, even Nurse Hatcher, they all admit that Emmett has a genuine, life-threatening heart condition. And you have heard testimony that if the medicine stops, his heart worsens.

"Emmett testified that failing to get his medicines leads to increased angina attacks, sometimes so debilitating that they steal his breath. All Emmett can do is rest on his bunk and wait for the crushing pain to pass. He waits on the edge of a heart attack to see if it will go away. That happens frequently. Nurse Ryan testified it happened while Nitroglycerin was in the pharmacy but not dispensed. But, and this is crazy, it doesn't have to happen at all.

"It's interesting to note, that after a few days of testimony, that the State has offered no real answers to Mr. Davis's question, 'why?' Sure, they've had a few things to say. But if you take those words apart, turn them around and examine them, what you see, really, is nothing but a bunch of finger-pointing, a basket of distractions.

"What have we heard? We heard it was the other doctor's fault. Kendrick was transferred, so it took them awhile to find his medical records, get his medicines all straightened out. They blamed it on Huntsville. They even tried, at one point, to say the angina pain was no worse than putting a rubber band around your little finger—a painful ache. We heard about the worst of the worst. They talked about abusive inmates, sexually inappropriate inmates, inmates that fling semen all over the place. They told stories of prisoners shanking nurses, and the fears that female guards and nurses fight against when walking the cellblock. But all those stories had nothing to do with Mr. Kendrick, with Emmett. Nurses Watts and Ryan testified that Emmett was nothing like that. He's quiet, keeps to himself. He's respectful.

"You may ask what Emmett wants. He's not asked for much in this lawsuit. He simply wants the problem fixed. It's hard to calculate an amount that would compensate Emmett for this ordeal. But even a symbolic award of damages and a simple verdict in his favor would provide the power to fix this problem and provide Emmett the relief he seeks. For punitive damages, we ask that you award a modest sum against each defendant individually to deter their behavior in the future. We ask that you award one dollar each. A small sum? Yes. But they would have earned a rebuke from you, from a jury of their peers, from the community. That sting will go a long way to making them think twice about turning a blind eye again."

I let my last words settle into the quiet in the courtroom and then sit down.

"That was excellent," Emmett whispers.

"Hold on. It's their turn now. And they're coming for you."

"Ms. Walker. Are you ready to close?" the Judge presses.

"Yes, Your Honor." Rose steps into the well, flattening the harsh pleats in her black skirt. After a pause, she levels a determined gaze on the jurors, as if daring them to disbelieve her.

"There is no doubt that Mr. Kendrick has a serious cardiac condition. No doubt that he has had heart attacks while incarcerated. No doubt that occasionally his medicines were delayed in delivery from Huntsville. But there is also no evidence that any of these defendants did anything but their level best to deliver quality medical care under the most trying of circumstances. Let me take you to Teton Springs. It houses over three thousand inmates. It's a large, complex enterprise not unlike a machine with thousands of working parts. Even under the best of circumstances, it's difficult to make all those parts work perfectly one hundred percent of the time. But Teton Springs is also a prison, charged with housing men who decided, on their own, to break the simple rules that our society provides: Don't steal. Don't murder. Don't rob banks. Don't commit violence against others. Every one of those men has done something that a jury like you decided was wrong or dangerous, and that they deserve to sit in a cell and think about the harm they caused. But also at Teton Springs is the Administrative Segregation Unit. Some call it solitary confinement. It houses the worst of the worst, men who oftentimes are beyond the pale. Not only do they fail to live by the simple rules society has provided, but they choose to break the rules in prison. Punishment has not, and won't, change their behavior. Many have killed or injured other prisoners—maybe with a shank or their bare hands. Many have tried to escape, thumbing their nose at the juries that told them they deserve punishment for hurting their fellow citizens. They choose to live by their own rules, rules they make up. They truly think only about themselves. No one else. And somehow, we are supposed to just go along with their every whim.

"Mr. Kendrick is one of those inmates. He chose to rob a bank in Tarrant County at gunpoint. He chose to try to escape. He chose a path that led him to AdSeg. Did prison change him? Rehabilitate him? No. Your heard him admit from the stand that he threatened another inmate—threatened to cut off his head and roll it down the hallway.

"It's true that a prisoner in AdSeg is isolated. They have to be. They spend twenty-three hours in their cell, and one hour in a specially designed yard—fenced-in solitary pens. They have to be penned because they are a constant threat to all those around them. Indeed, you heard about one nurse that let down her guard and paid for it with a horrific wound to the face.

"Mr. Kendrick would have you believe he is harmless. That he is old and frail. But even though some of these inmates may look like sweet old men, like Santa Claus even, you have to remember that in their DNA is the violent streak that put them behind bars in the first place.

"That is the place these defendants, these medical care-givers have chosen to work. They do so because they believe in the care they provide, and taking care of others. But they have chosen to do so in a dangerous place. Who would fault them for staying on edge in their job? They work under the ever-present threat that a prisoner will drive a shank into them. When they walk the units, they don't know if some prisoner will fling semen on them. The women that work there must do their job while men shout out the most awful sexual come-ons. In short, inside this complex facility, they work under enormous pressure, and they do their best.

"And Mr. Kendrick's response to all their efforts? He complains. You heard testimony that he complains all the time, even about the minor things. And when he doesn't feel he is getting fast enough service and that the prison staff failed to move quickly enough for his liking, he files griev-ances. He writes letters trying to get them in trouble. He sues these caregivers personally because he does not think they served him the right way. That is self-involved. That is selfish.

"In particular, it appears Mr. Kendrick has made Nurse Hatcher and Dr. Ralston the target of his ire. He wants them to pay because they didn't respond immediately to his every demand. But you heard them from the stand. You heard how seriously they take their job. They worked diligently to fix this problem, but they also can't fix something that is out of their control. If Huntsville does not send the medicines on time, then what can they do? They work the system. They make phone calls. They work to get the medicines as quickly as possible. But they can't make medicine appear out of whole cloth. They are caregivers not magicians. But

Mr. Kendrick does not seem to care about all those efforts. He works diligently at his complaint factory cranking out grievances about any little thing, all the way down to filing a formal grievance that he did not have a tube of foot cream delivered immediately for his athlete's foot. As if the staff was his own personal delivery service.

"And he has now called all of you here. Pulled you away from your families, your jobs, so you can give him his last hurrah. He actually has the gall to ask you to personally punish each of these public servants because he didn't find their service up to snuff. He wants you to put a permanent black mark on their work file, saying that they purposely tried to injure him in his cell by holding back medicines. You would have to believe that each defendant knew that by holding back the medicine it would cause him to suffer. And not only that, they knew he would suffer. That they intended to make him suffer. Hogwash.

"We ask only this. Tell Mr. Kendrick that enough is enough. His carnival is over. This distraction to the daily work lives of the defendants is over. Reject his claims, and by doing so, you will tell him that he should go back to Teton Springs, sit in his cell, and quietly serve out his time for the crimes he committed. Tell him to let these fine caregivers go back to the important work they do without threat of having their careers ruined by a selfish, cranky old inmate."

Rose finishes and takes her seat.

"Mr. Simmons," the Judge says. "You have ten minutes left for rebuttal."

I take a moment in my chair, letting the silence in the court focus the jury on what I might say, and then rise.

"It's Emmett's fault. . . . That's what Ms. Walker just told you. He is the one person in this courtroom with no control of when his medicines arrive and when they are distributed. But according to them, it's his fault. Why? Because he broke the law decades ago. He's an inmate. He's behind bars for a reason. So he should shut up, sit down. Take what comes because he deserves it as part of his punishment. My grandma used to phrase it, 'you get what you get, and you don't throw a fit.' Emmett robbed a bank. True. A jury sentenced him to jail. True. But they did not sentence him to an agonizing death for his crime. The jury did not, could not, impose that sentence. Since he came under the care of the Texas Department of Corrections, Emmett has suffered several heart attacks. In fact, as Dr. Ralston admitted, one of those heart attacks followed Dr. Patel discontinuing Emmett's Isosorbide. It's simple. He gets his medicine, he's fine. They take the medicine away. He has a heart attack. One follows the other as sure as night follows day. And they know it. *Nurse Hatcher knows it.*

"Emmett has undergone two open-heart surgeries and multiple bypasses on his heart. His sternum, as he told you, is nothing but wires and scar tissue. He described from the stand the anguish of an angina attack in his cell—no Nitro-glycerin on hand. Alone and unable to call out for help because the crushing pressure robs him of his breath. Instead, he waits. Hopes it passes. Hopes this is not his final heart attack. Someday, his heart may give out. But that decision belongs to forces well outside this courtroom. In the mean-time, the State has a responsibility to provide care for those it locks in a cage.

"I guess their answer to the question, 'why?' is that it's Emmett's fault, or he deserves it. That's a poor answer. That answer violates the United States Constitution and the Eighth Amendment's mandate against cruel and unusual punishment.

"You probably could ask the same question of us: 'Why?' Why would these medical professionals, prison officials ignore Emmett's calls for help?

"I would suggest that it's a primal response. Somewhere in our days of schooling, we've all heard that 'power corrupts, and absolute power corrupts absolutely.' And power can't exist in a vacuum. To have true power, you must wield it, to bend others to your control, to your will. And the prison system is all about power. The power to control. The power to punish. We give the prison system the power to take away a person's freedom, to make that person pay a debt to society. But that power can't exist unchecked. It must be used wisely.

"Did these defendants initially set out to harm Emmett? They 'didn't try to harm him' as Ms. Walker so eloquently would have you believe. No, that likely was not what motivated them. Rather, it was power. Think back to how many times the defense has fixated on what they say is Emmett's complaining. They fixate on the grievances, the letters, this lawsuit. They can't believe his persistence. They can't believe he dares raise his voice. Rather, they want him to shut up. Shut up. Submit. They want to bend him to their will. And the greatest source of leverage they have over him is the care they provide. Or fail to provide. They hold his heart in their hands. They control if he suffers in his cell. They control, literally, if he has a heart attack. All they have to do is fail to provide the Isosorbide or Nitroglycerin in a timely fashion, and they can remind him just how much power they really have."

I pause for a moment, so I can move beside Emmett and place my hand on his shoulder.

"Now, they would have you believe this is a case about mistakes, hiccups, and good intentions. That is wrong. This is a case about the United States Constitution and what you think is the proper use of power. Article I of the Constitution gives us the Congress. They write our laws. Article II, the President to execute those laws faithfully. Article III provides the courts, this court, and all its powers to mete out justice. But the Seventh Amendment to the Bill of Rights gives us you, the Jury. You are the great levelers. Today, you get to rebalance power; indeed, in this moment, for this case, you are the most powerful of all. The Eighth Amendment mandates that we, as a society, our governments, can't allow cruel and unusual punishment. That phrase, cruel and unusual punishment, includes ignoring—what the case law calls being deliberately indifferent to the critical medical needs of those we condemn to our prisons.

"Our justice system often favors the powerful. The state or corporations, they have significant resources. They can petition the courts for help with scores of lawyers writing fancy briefs. But as the Chief Justice recently pointed out in his confirmation hearing, sometimes—and case after case at the Supreme Court points out—sometimes the Constitution is on the side of the prisoner who's sitting in his cell and writes his petition out longhand. Sometimes it's on that person's side. It's on Emmett's side today."

As I sit down, the Judge turns to the Jury. "Ladies and Gentlemen of the jury, the case is now yours. You shall retire to the jury room and deliberate on the questions asked in the charge. If you have any questions, please write them down and submit them to the Marshal. He will bring them to me, and I'll provide an answer in writing. Good luck in your efforts. . . . All rise for the Jury."

Steve, Emmett, and I all stand in a line as the jury shuffles out. Some look at us, some focus on the jury room. As the large oak door closes behind them, I now understand how true the phase is "sweating the jury."

CHAPTER
FORTY-TWO

TWO HOURS LATER.

I stand in the courtroom's door. It's cavernous. The afternoon sun spills through the twenty-foot bank of windows that line both sides of the chamber. The Marshal sits quietly at his small desk in front of the jury room, chewing a sandwich. I wonder if it's bologna like Emmett's.

The jury door has a large seal of the United States District Court. The stillness of the room, the quiet of the room falls around me. Butterflies plague my gut. Two hours of deliberation—I have no way of knowing if that is good or bad for Emmett. I convince myself it must be good—or they would have found against him immediately.

I step into the hallway and walk a few doors down to a small conference room by the District Clerk's office. They were kind enough to let us use it for lunch and to wait for the jury verdict. Steve is inside reading the local newspaper, nipping at a cuticle with his teeth. Right there, below the fold is a headline. 'Prisoner's Trial Nears the End.'"

"Any sign?" Steve questions.

"Nothing. It's still as a desert in there."

"Well, that could a good sign. At least they are thinking it over."

"We'll see."

"You know, your closing might have done it. At least gave us a fighting chance." Steve sets the paper down and takes a drink from a soda purchased from the vending machine at the end of the hall. "Where did you get that saying from the Chief Justice?"

"A couple months ago, I was listening to the confirmation hearings in my office. He said it, and I wrote it down. Stuck it in the file for today."

"It came off well. Fit Emmett perfectly. You know, I'm still amazed he could get the District Judge reversed at the Fifth Circuit to get this far. No small feat."

"Yep. Preeminent jailhouse lawyer. Nothing about this has been a minor feat." I lean over and rest my hands on the back of a chair. "I'll probably sleep for a week when we get back to Dallas."

"Agreed. You think we'll be staying over tonight?"

"Can't tell. Who knows what the jury is doing. I hope they're giving Emmett a fair shake. Prison town. Prison officials on trial. Emmett an inmate in AdSeg. Not sure what they think."

"They were focused on every word you said. I think they know Nurse Hatcher was lying through her teeth."

"Let's hope."

"That one woman in the back, with the tall gray hair, she kept glaring at Nurse Hatcher while you spoke. At least I think she was glaring." Steve pauses. "Or, maybe she just had gas."

I smile and shake my head at Steve. "Maybe she just had gas."

"I'm going to go check on Emmett." I turn and open the door to the conference room.

"You know," Steve says, "I think you might have done it."

I step into the hallway. Steve's words echo in my ears. At the end of the passage, framed and back-lit by sunlight, is Ms. Walker. I watch as she paces the floor, her stiletto heels clicking on the tile. At this distance, her dark-suited frame looks more like a shadow than a person. Rose hunches over an old-time white porcelain water fountain and takes a drink, her pale skin fading into the surroundings. Looking up, she sees me. A cloud outside blunts the sunshine. Even at a distance, her hazel eyes framed in black bore into me. Her charcoal suit and severe angles exude power and certainty. She turns and acts as if she is reading the notices on the bulletin board. The tip of her high heel taps the floor, her only, almost imperceptible, sign of nerves. She's sweating the jury, too.

When I walk into the room, Emmett is brushing the shoulders of his suit coat. He lays it over the back of a chair next to him and sits down. Pulling up a chair, I join him. His ice-blue eyes pull me in. I wonder what got into him that he thought he could rob a bank. A different choice, and he would never have known a life behind bars. No AdSeg. No holding cell. No counting years by hamburgers.

We don't talk for a beat or two. The clock bangs out its seconds. The US Marshal in the corner stands, coughs, and steps out; giving us a moment alone.

Emmett speaks first. "You know, back home, back before I landed myself in jail, we had a preacher, Pastor Parsons. Young fellow, like you. He wasn't a fire and brimstone kind of preacher. He wasn't all, 'You're going to burn in Hell for this, or burn in Hell for that.' Didn't yell or look down on his flock. I actually liked listening to him. Only time I'd go to Church was if Pastor Parsons was giving the sermon. He told a good story. Then he helped you understand how to apply that simple story to your life. He told truths. You remind me of him. . . . Your closing today reminded me of him."

"That's high praise, Emmett."

"He told truths. You tell truths."

"Truths don't always sink in, Emmett."

"Well, he probably could have spent some more time on that Commandment, 'Thou shall not steal.' I should have heard that lesson a few more times."

"Maybe at least once more." We both chuckle.

"I sure didn't think I'd be here."

"Emmett, you robbed a bank," I say. "That usually leads to jail."

"No, not the robbing the bank. I was young. Stupid. I've come to terms with that a long time ago. I'm talking here." Emmett raises his hands and gestures at the wall of the court-house. "No way did I think, when I was scribbling out that lawsuit, that I'd actually make it all the way here, with lawyers to boot."

"Careful what you wish for. We don't have a verdict yet. You may change your tune if they come back with a decision against you."

"True, but I doubt it," Emmett says. "Maybe just one person will listen." After a moment, he starts back up. "You know the worst part about prison?"

"Lousy food?"

"No. They serve a mean grilled cheese at Teton Springs, and Thanksgiving is pretty good. It's kind of hard to screw up bread stuffing from a box."

"Tell me. What's the worst thing about prison?"

"Nobody listens. I mean, once you have that number stenciled on you back, it's like they turn down the volume on your voice. It's like you can hear yourself saying something in your head. And you can see the guard, or nurse, or whoever looking at you. You know they should be able to hear you. But no one does. It's as if they just reach in and turn a knob, and the sound of your voice gets quieter and quieter, year after year, until it goes silent. Like you're just mouthing the words, like one of those guys who pretends to blow around in the wind with those white faces."

"A mime?"

"Yeah. A mime. Mute, just like a mime."

"Well. Maybe the jury will listen. Maybe they heard you."

"They listened," Emmett says, and straightens his tie. After a few moments, he clears his throat, and says, "Did you always want to be a lawyer?" The chit chat an attempt to pass the time.

"Nope. I'm more of an accidental lawyer. I sort of stumbled into it. I was working a dead-end job, but my wife wanted kids, and I needed a different plan. In a way, I'm just a hillbilly with a law license."

Emmett smiles. The US Marshal knocks on the door; the deep echo pulls Emmett and me from our conversation.

"Come in," I say.

The Marshal pokes his head around the door. "We have a verdict."

CHAPTER
FORTY-THREE

MINUTES LATER.

Emmett, Steve, Ashley and I stand as the Jury walks into the courtroom, single file and take their seats in the jury box.

"Be seated," the Judge says. "Madame Foreperson, has the jury reached a verdict."

"We have, Your Honor."

"Hand it to the Courtroom Marshal please."

The Marshal steps to the jury box, receives the jury charge from the foreperson, turns, and walks it to the Judge. The Judge reads the first page, then the second. She flips all the pages in the charge to make sure the Jury has filled it out correctly and completely—no necessary question left unanswered. It seems to take forever. Then the Judge reads.

"Do you find the Defendants were deliberately indifferent to Emmett Kendrick's serious medical needs in violation of the Eighth Amendment of the United States Constitution? Answer. '*No*.'" My heart sinks. They didn't listen. Then the Judge continues.

"If not unanimous, list those who agree below." (In a civil trial the jury need not be unanimous).

The Judge reads off a list of juror names. Steve, Ashley,

and I look at each other. One Juror did not agree. *One Juror believed Emmett.* Someone heard Emmett and held out to the end.

"Ladies and gentlemen of the Jury, we appreciate your service in this matter. This concludes your duties. You may retire to the jury room, gather your things, and go back to your normal lives. Counsel, I would ask that you and all your clients remain in the courtroom until all jurors have left the building."

We stand as the Jury shuffles out. I turn to Emmett.

"Emmett," I say, "I'm sorry the result was not what you had hoped. We are just as disappointed as you."

"I'm a prisoner, you know that. We all knew it was a long shot. No, you, Steve, and Ashley did an excellent job. You should be very proud. Besides, one Juror heard me. That's a relief. Somebody out there doesn't think I'm a crazy old coot. That's a pretty big trophy for an inmate in AdSeg. The boys won't believe it."

One of the COs walks up behind Emmett, jingling the manacles, a sinister smile perched on his face.

"Kendrick. Time to go." Emmett reflexively puts his hands behind his back.

"Can we leave those off for just a minute?" I ask. "We would like a picture with Emmett, if you'll allow it."

Emmett pipes in, "Inmates aren't allowed to have pictures with other people. It's policy."

The CO looks at me, and then up at the Judge, who is still on the bench finalizing paperwork from the trial.

"I'm not sure they are just people," she says to no one in particular. "I believe they are his lawyers."

The CO lowers the chains to his side. "Be quick about it."

Emmett, Steve, Ashley, and I line up in front of the jury box and snap a few photos. Ms. Walker watches as she slides files into her briefcase. When we finish, the CO reaches out and places a single set of cuffs on Emmett's hands in front.

It's strange to believe that must be more comfortable for him.

"Emmett, we'll get back to Dallas and write soon. We have a few things to take care of to wrap this up," I say.

"I look forward to the letter. Steve and Ashley, safe travels. Daniel . . . just keep trying to ride those tractors." Emmett pauses, placing his cuffed palms on my forearm. He whispers, "You are no accident."

"Thank you, Emmett," pride washing through my chest.

Emmett turns to the CO. "Time to go, Boss." Emmett takes a few steps and then calls over his shoulder, "Brass, Daniel, brass." I watch as Emmett disappears through the door to the holding cell, his shoulders back, head held high. The heavy door shuts with a pronounced finality.

"He looks good in a suit," Steve says as if closing the back cover of a book, and we reach for the files on our counsel table and start placing them in boxes. On the way out of the courtroom, Ms. Walker stops by. She extends a hand, and I take it. Her skin warm, not exactly what I expected from the ice queen.

"Well-tried case, counsel," Rose says. A slight flash of respect in her eyes.

"To be honest, it was our first trial," Steve confesses, straightening his lapels and tugging on his shirt cuffs.

"That I would never believe." She looks at me, the black-framed hazel eyes more powerful up close. "You had me worried. They stayed out much longer than usual."

"How many of these do you try a year?" Steve asks.

"I'm usually in a different county every other week. Lots of prisoners. Lots of prisons." She pauses for a moment, looking all of us up and down as if taking our measure. She clears her throat. "I actually need to get going, I'm supposed to try a case in Nacogdoches next Monday. Got to find someone to feed my Siamese cat, who pretty much hates me because I'm rarely home." She shakes all of our hands in a business-like manner. Her gaze bores into me. "Nice to have tried a case against you. Look forward to seeing you in the future sometime." Steve and I watch her angular frame clad in a power suit walk the long aisle between the pews and then disappear out the tall double doors of the court.

"Mr. Simmons, Mr. Davis, Ms. Carmichael." It's the Judge; I'd forgotten she was still in the courtroom.

"Yes, Your Honor?"

A slight pause injects tension into the exchange that she finally releases. "Thank you," she says, "You have done a service for the Court. We'll see you back in Dallas." She stands and disappears through the door behind the bench.

For the next few minutes, it's just Steve, Ashley, and me in the courtroom, loading our stuff. We fill our boxes with files and exhibits; load up all our gear on a small folding dolly I borrowed from a paralegal at our office. We roll down the aisle and out the doors, headed for the elevator. We pass by the open door to the holding cell room, and I peek inside, hoping to see one last glimpse of Emmett, but the cell is empty. The room appears empty. We reach the elevators and push the "Down" button.

"Mr. Simmons."

I glance up and see the Marshal walking briskly toward me. He has Emmett's suit in one hand and his shoes in the other.

"Not sure what you want to do with these. We can't use them around here. Maybe give it to the Salvation Army or something."

I shift my briefcase, grab the suit, and flip it over my shoulder.

"Thanks. We'll do something with it."

The Marshal turns and heads down the hallway back to the door. "Nice work Mr. Simmons. Safe travels."

We load our gear into our cars; we'd driven up separately.

I look over the roof of mine and say, "It sure would have been nice to win."

"Depends on how you define, 'win,'" Steve says. "Maybe we did win, in a way." We look around at the courthouse; it's the tallest building in this part of town. "You going to the office on Monday?"

"We'll see," I say. "Hannah is still in the hospital."

Steve and Ashley hop into Steve's car and close the doors. I watch them back out, then turn out of the parking lot. For a second I wonder how much Steve might flirt on the way home before Ashely puts him in his place with a whip-smart comeback.

I get in my car, dreading the long drive: three hours or so. When I get out on the highway, I will call Hannah. I head out of Wichita Falls, away from Teton Springs.

In law school, one of my professors told me that trial lawyers do the best cross-examination on the way home. Your mind spins out all the things you could have said, the things you would have done differently. It already started for me in the elevator ride on the way down, perceived mistakes looping through my head. I turn off the radio, and head out in silence. Silence … except for the relentless cross-examination in my mind.

CHAPTER
FORTY-FOUR

FRIDAY NIGHT. Late October. Dallas, Texas. Seventeen weeks to a full-term baby.

When I get back home, I go straight to the hospital even though I'm exhausted.

Hannah's face floods with a mixture of joy and relief when she sees me. "Hi, Bear!" My wife pats her swollen abdomen with pride, as if she has done something miraculous. And she has. "Our baby's still in the right spot."

"Well done, Buzz." I breathe a sigh of relief, thankful that our baby didn't come prematurely while I was swamped at trial.

Dr. Phillips nods a greeting to me. As usual, the former Air Force doctor is pressed and starched, his bedside manner efficient but lacking warmth. I've interrupted them mid-conversation. Dr. Phillips is making his rounds through Labor and Delivery, checking in on Hannah after our terrified dash to the hospital a few days ago. It feels like weeks ago.

"Is she okay?" I ask.

"The bleeding appears to have stopped," Dr. Phillips says, briefing me. "She's moving to Antepartum."

"Antepartum? What is that?" Hannah quizzes Dr. Phillips apprehensively.

"You'll stay with us here in the hospital, and we'll keep you on bedrest until the baby comes. The antepartum nurses will keep watch over you. If the baby comes, or that previa bleeds we can rush you to the OR for a C-section." Hannah shifts nervously in the bed. Dr. Phillips continues. "They call a big bleed like the one she had a 'sentinel bleed,' a warning. If it bleeds again, it will be worse. And it *will* probably bleed again."

"Hannah's not going home at all?" I frown.

"No. She's with us for the duration." Hannah and I exchange a furtive glance. Dr. Phillips plows ahead like he's debriefing a military squad. "Our main objective is to keep that baby girl inside, healthy, and growing. Every day makes a difference. Frankly, every *hour* makes a difference. My job is to get that baby here safely. The best way to do that is to keep Hannah resting in bed. With a little luck and patience, we will make it to thirty-four weeks. Forty weeks is full term, but thirty-four weeks is acceptable."

"Dr. Abrams is on board with this?" I ask.

"Dr. Abrams does fertility, not obstetrics," Dr. Phillips snaps. "You are now with *me* to the end. I'll keep Dr. Abrams updated. In a minute, the nurses will move you down to the antepartum unit. Any other questions?"

Hannah and I both shake our head, "No," like cowed children.

"I'll go finish the orders." Dr. Phillips turns on his heal and leaves.

"What are we going to do about Lilly?" Hannah worries. "Who will look after her while you're at work?"

"Let's worry about that later. Once we get you set, I'll figure that out."

What are we going to do about Lilly?

My mind spins. I am now in charge of Little Bear.

Somehow I will have to balance taking care of a two-year-old with my demanding job. The portrait of William Paul Moore III flashes through my mind. I'm always drowning in work, and not sure how I will do it and keep my head from sliding below the surface. But I have to find a way, as my paycheck is essential to face the mountain of debt.

"Did my dad say how Lilly is doing?"

"I'm sure she's asleep. It's been a long week for all of us," I say.

Hannah says, "I'm sorry about Emmett."

I let that statement fall into the silence of the room.

We can hear the nurses outside the door talking about using a wheelchair to take Hannah to Antepartum.

"Seventeen weeks is a long time," I say. It's seventeen weeks until our baby is full term.

"I'd lie still a year if it keeps her safe," Hannah says, determined. She pats her swollen belly, looking in that moment like a ferocious Momma Bear, not a cute bumblebee.

The door opens, and a nurse enters with a wheelchair for my pregnant wife.

Seventeen weeks is a very long time.

CHAPTER
FORTY-FIVE

NOVEMBER. Dallas, Texas. Seventeen weeks to delivery.

Later that day, I call my trial practice leader, Connor, and explain everything that happened, and that Hannah is in the hospital for at least ten weeks.

"I'm now 'Mr. Mom' for Lilly. So I need to stay at the house, if possible."

"Do what you need to do," Connor says. "Just make sure your work gets done."

"I will. I'll have plenty of time to work at home."

"You sure?"

"I'll make it work. I'm sure. Positive." I try to make the tone of my voice match the certainty of my statement.

"If you need to take time off, take time," Connor says.

"Thanks. But I don't think that'll be necessary. I've got this. I'll keep you updated."

I disconnect the call with Connor. I can't stop working or stop my career. The debt we piled on during IVF and law school needs constant feeding. 'The only way out is through.' I have to keep grinding at work and also turn into 'Mr. Mom.'

New associates at a law firm must bill two thousand hours to advance, and at least that number or more to have any shot

at a year-end bonus. Even if I can be eighty-five percent efficient with my time in the office that means my job will
consume twenty-four hundred hours a year. Add in commute
time, non-billable training, and the minimum commitment to
stay on the path to partnership, and you arrive at fifty hours
per week, every week of the year. Associates climb that
mountain in six-minute increments, billing in tenths of an
hour. It's like any other endeavor. Work does not just materi-
alize. It's a pipeline. The firm assigns you to cases that last
months or years. If you can't do the work, the firm will
replace you. That's the reality. The machine must grind on.

To turn off my pipeline and let it run dry while taking care
of Lilly and Hannah is financial suicide. We are already
balanced on a knife's edge. Taking leave is simply not an
option.

I sit in a chair in Hannah's antepartum room and look out
the window. Dallas is peaceful outside. It's cold in November,
but the sun is out. Across the way, in all directions, buildings
loom with offices behind every window. Thousands of folks
mill about their workday. I'm sure some of them have family
members in the hospital or relatives that recently passed. My
life is not unique. Life happens.

I think of my grandmother, who lived through the Depression and myriad other hardships I can only imagine. So often,
when circumstances proved rough, she would say, "Well, just
get on with it." I let that phrase rattle around in my brain for
a moment or two.

I glance at Hannah resting in the hospital bed, some
mantra in her head. I have been married to her long enough—
seen her with Lilly long enough—to know she constantly
talks to Bailey swimming inside her. She will coach and
mother well before that kid even takes her first breath.
Grandpa Adam is probably playing dress-up with Lilly, or if
he is lucky, they have curled up for a movie and drifted off to
sleep.

For a moment, I imagine I'm at my office. I listen to all the commotion outside my door. Secretaries chatter on the phone. A file drawer opens and shuts. Phones ring down the hallway. I can even hear someone scooping ice into a cup in the break room. The office teems with activity and people to talk to about day-to-day events. It has its own heartbeat and momentum. I had not focused on it before. I look off to the horizon and think, "It's about to get really quiet for me for a while."

CHAPTER
FORTY-SIX

MONDAY. November. Dallas, Texas. Sixteen weeks to a full-term baby.

A few days after Emmett's trial, I head back into the office. Hannah has settled into antepartum at the hospital and I need to pick up some items from work and catch up on my inbox. Grandpa stayed in town, so I have a day to get some tasks done. I make some coffee in the break room, seeking some level of normalcy. I had arrived at my customary 6:30 am. The sun threatens to peek over the horizon at any moment. Only the hum of a few machines, computer fans, or the refrigerator compressor fill the air. Soon, the din of a law firm will drown out all that stillness.

"Did you win?" I hear over my shoulder.

I look back to see who is in at this hour. It's my early morning coffee companion, John. He, too, is an early riser, and his high-and-tight haircut is freshly shaved. We occasionally share a cup of coffee in the morning and watch the sunrise for a few minutes. All of Dallas appears calm and full of promise when the first band of sun peeks over the horizon. The practice of law disappears for a moment as sunbeams flood through the window.

All weekend I had dreaded that question. In trial law, only winners and losers exist. It's similar to sports. But even in sports you can have a tie, a draw. Never in trial. Someone goes out victorious; someone goes home on his or her shield. Always. In my mind, over the weekend, I had rehearsed what to say, probably a hundred times. I could tell people about Emmett, maybe a few war stories about what happened. I could try to spin it so a loss sounded like a victory. But the more I tried to color it, or explain the good we felt we had done, the more it sounded like excuses.

Excuses don't get you very far. No one hires a trial lawyer who *almost* wins. Hitch had told me that clients pay us to win. That is it. They pay us to win. Now, Emmett had not paid us as it was a *pro bono* case. But what kept looping through my mind is that true trial lawyers win.

"Nope," I say to John. One juror went with us, but the others found against us. Good experience, though."

"I'm sure it was. Maybe next time."

"Yeah, well . . . who knows if there will be a next time? Or if there is, when it will be. Crazy thing is . . . I keep wondering what we said that made that one juror hang with us. If we knew that, we might have hammered on that point. Who knows how many other jurors we could have brought along to our side?"

"I watch all the lawyers around here do that."

"Do what?"

"Wonder. Even when they win, you know. They'll mull over it, chew on it, and play it over in their head."

"I bet it stops after a while."

"Maybe. Don't know. I'm not a trial lawyer. But I don't think so. Seems they're always gnawing on it."

"Fabulous," I say sarcastically.

"I guess the sting might go out of it. Who knows? But I don't know how else lawyers could learn to master the courtroom."

I smile, a phrase from Hitch popping my mind, "The only difference between an old lawyer and a young lawyer, is the old lawyer has been kicked in the teeth more, and knows when to duck."

John shuffles out of the coffee room toward his desk. He calls back over his shoulder. "You did a good thing, Daniel. You did a good thing."

As John leaves, an attorney walks into the break room. "Did you win?"

"No," I take a breath. Only a few hundred more to go.

A couple hours later, I am at my desk. "Here's the return receipt on the petition you served in the Foster matter."

My secretary Ginny drops off the mail. A stunning red silk scarf from her collection drapes over her shoulders. "You want me to throw out all these legal periodicals, or are you going to read them."

"Who has time to read?"

"Right. Trash them." Her eyes tinged with amusement at my response. "You have a couple messages at my desk. I'll go grab them. . . . Oh, and this came today." Ginny hands me a letter.

I recognize it immediately. It's from Emmett. As Ginny leaves, I grab a small pocketknife, fold open the blade and carefully slide it into the envelope. The message is banged out on Emmett's manual typewriter.

Emmett E. Kendrick
TDCJ-CID No. 4483214
Teton Springs Prison

Dear Daniel:

First, let me tell you what I expected when I was noti-fied that Judge Navarro had granted my second motion for appointment of counsel: that I would be represented by a couple of attorneys who would be unwilling to invest the time (which would normally be billable hours) necessary to overcome my poorly crafted prior pleadings, and afford me the opportunity to confront my keepers and tormentors in the federal courtroom. I expected intellectual arrogance and little patience with me as a prisoner with no legal training. Instead, I got representation from a Dream Team of three intelligent attorneys and three of the most courteous, kind, and generous people I have ever had the privilege of meeting. I was most impressed that, during the whole proceeding, not one of you suggested that I should be less than completely truthful in my testimony or that I should misstate facts.

Second, while we are all disappointed at the jury's verdict, it was one we expected from the very first day. I was more disappointed for the Team because of the work and money invested and because you deserved to win the case. I can only imagine the efforts invested in organizing, for research and presentation, the chaos of papers dumped in your collective laps. If you will, please pass along my appreciation to Ginny and everyone else involved in such a Herculean task. Your, Steven and the team's presentations were clear, concise, articulate, and extremely professional. The Team's direct and cross examinations were sequential and supported by documents offered into evidence. Your arguments were articulate, supported by case authorities, clearly referenced, and relevant (your objections and pleadings seldom denied). Your closing was sincere, brilliant, and heart-felt.

And, finally, the four of us know the only reason the defendants were able to obtain a favorable verdict was:

(1) my errors in failing to adequately document events either in my medical record or the grievance record, and my poorly constructed pleadings, made before the Team came to my rescue; and, (2) the fact that I am a convicted felon, in a Texas prison. Daniel, truthfully, for my part, I am well satisfied. The Team gave me every opportunity to get all those folks together and confront them with the truth. Since the end of the proceedings, two of the LVN's assigned to work in segregation have confronted Ms. Hatcher and called her a "lying bitch."

On a personal note: I have never met anyone with whom I experienced such immediate and strong bonding as I did with you and, to a lesser extent, Steven and Ashley. When Ms. Walker sought to imply that the reason I may have been denied my medications was because I was one of the inmates that she was describing, it was far more important that you, Steven, and Ashley heard from the nurses that I was not one of those inmates, not for the jury to hear it. I seldom ever speak to the staff except about my medical needs, and I talk to very few other inmates. I shared more conversation and humor with the three of you than I have with anyone in the last seven years. For that, and for your many kindnesses, professionalism, and sincerity—for your caring and unstinting assistance and generosity, I am extremely grateful! AND, for the chance to wear a suit, tie, and white dress-shirt for the first time in decades.

In the white envelope I gave you on the last day of trial, I enclosed a copy of TDCJ's policy on organ donor procedures. I am going to sign up as a live donor for one of my kidneys because both of mine are super-healthy. If you happen to know of anyone needing a kidney, you can refer them to me. I am NOT trying to sell one. My heart will give out on me long before my kidneys start to give me trouble and, if I am still in TDCJ-CID, they won't comply with my stated desires to be a donor, so I'd like to do that while I am still alive. My next project is to convince the powers that be that I should have my good time credits restored, which would allow me to be released on mandatory supervision in eighteen months.

Again, please know that I am sincerely and deeply grateful for all your assistance and kindness. I wish for you the very best life has to offer and that your professional success is unlimited.

Cordially yours,

Emmett E. Kendrick.

Ginny walks back into my office with two small, square pink notes—telephone messages.

"Are you crying?" Ginny asks.

"No," I say, wiping my eyes with the back of my hands. "Of course I'm not crying."

"No, I think you're crying."

"I had to sneeze, Ginny. I'm just trying to hold back a sneeze."

"Well that would be the darnedest thing, if you were crying. In thirty years, I don't think I've ever seen a male attorney cry," Ginny teases, her wry smile framed by her bobbed gray hair.

Now the secretary who sits next to Ginny, the one right outside my door, peeks over the wall of her cubicle, looking at me with curious brown eyes, light glinting off the golden comb holding back her bangs.

"Is he crying?" Verna asks Ginny in an incredulous voice.

"I think so. I think he might be crying."

"Well imagine that," Verna says, "a grown man crying in his office." Her Southern drawl elongates the words.

"Ginny. Can I have my messages, please? I have to get in and out of here and back to Hannah. So . . . I need to focus."

"Okay, okay." She stands quietly for a moment. I look back to my computer. "You want me to get you some water?"

"Ginny . . ."

Ginny turns to leave and then turns back. "If you had been crying, and I'm not saying you were, but if you had been, what would it have been that may, or may not, have made you sad?"

I pick the letter up off my desk and hand to Ginny. "Emmett sent a letter."

Ginny reads the letter. I watch her face crumple as she pores over Emmett's words.

"Are you crying?" I ask with mock surprise.

"No, I'm not crying."

"You sure? Because it looks like you're all misted up over there."

"Well, maybe. I'm *not* holding back any sneeze, that's for sure." Ginny flashes a knowing smile. "Maybe I'm just very touched by Mr. Kendrick's desire to donate one of his kidneys. That's an awfully selfless gesture."

"Kidney donating is what got you?"

"I'm just funnin' you." She sets the letter down on my desk. "In all my thirty years, I've never read a client letter like that one. Y'all did a nice thing for Mr. Kendrick."

"Emmett."

"Emmett. You did a nice thing for Emmett. I'd frame that letter if I were you."

"Maybe I will."

"I'll go get you some water. That always helps me when I'm fighting back a sneeze or the hiccups."

"That would be perfect."

"Good. I'll get you some with ice. Ice water is the best for things like this."

"Thank you. I'm going to get back to my brief." I motion my head back toward my computer.

"Oh yeah, right, work, then wife. You better get working."

"I'm trying to, but. . . ."

"Okay, okay, I'll get out of here."

CHAPTER
FORTY-SEVEN

NOVEMBER. Dallas.

The next few days, the tasks Steve and I needed to complete for Emmett were mundane. We went over the trial at lunch, and could not find any grounds to appeal. But, we do not know whether Emmett wants to try to pull a rabbit out of a hat one more time. So we draft a notice of appeal for him to file on his own if he chooses. Our representation ended when the verdict came in. We write Emmett a letter to confirm.

My ever-faithful assistant Ginny packs it in an overnight envelope and mails it off. The trial has concluded for us; maybe it still goes on for Emmett.

A couple days later, I received another letter from Emmett, a package, really. It's the prepaid overnight envelope we sent him filled with papers, and a handwritten note:

Daniel:

Enclosed is the signed copy of the unopposed motion to withdraw. The other enclosures are to be disposed of however you wish. Again, I am deeply and sincerely grateful for your capable assistance and many kindnesses.

Sincerely,

Emmett

I leaf through the materials Emmett sent. He must have talked Officer Larkin into some library time because some of the pages are printouts from the Internet, or he's cleaning out his cell. He's included the story from *The Wichita Times Record*:

Man Loses Mistreatment Case Against Teton Springs.

October 28. All defendants in the Emmett Earl Kendrick v. Teton Springs Prison were exonerated today in a jury trial. Kendrick claimed that under the Eighth Amendment he was victim to "cruel and unusual punishment" by not receiving proper medical attention for his heart condition while he was incarcerated. He also said the prison officials were "deliberately indifferent" to his needs, a court document said. The trial, which lasted about three days, ended in the state's favor with no money awarded to Kendrick for damages.

No mention of the one juror that believed him.

Behind the newspaper blurb, Emmett has included an article about how to prepare my home properly in case of a house fire. A list of funny sayings, including: "Birds of a feather flock together to crap on your car," makes me chuckle. A parody of the President of the United States and his Secretary of State doing Abbott and Costello's famous "Who's on First" routine with the name of the leader of China. Some quotes from actual Federal Government employee performance evaluations: "Works well under constant supervision and when cornered like a rat in a trap." "Take it easy, Doc. You're boldly going where no man has gone before" tops the list of actual patient comments during a colonoscopy. Fifty nifty uses for a Bounce dryer sheet. "You walk to work and find your dress stuck in the back of your pantyhose," rounds out twenty-one ways to know it's going to be a rotten day. "Fifteen Immutable Laws of the Universe," includes the "Bath Theorem: When a naked body is fully immersed in water, the telephone rings." And Emmett has included three issues of "Prison Legal News: Dedicated to Protecting Human Rights." It's a hodgepodge of items I'm inheriting.

I flip to the last item. It's a copy of FORTUNE News. The title is, "Aging in Prison." Emmett has placed a note in front of it.

Dear Daniel:

Think you might find this of interest. I'll send it every month—the reason for the October delivery of the July issue is explained on page 6. I won't send it as "legal mail"—I understand we have had no attorney-client relationship since the trial ended, and I have no desire or intention of imposing on your kindness. I would like to keep in touch with the Team, just to track your careers.

Sincerely,

Emmett

At the top, in the FORTUNE masthead, is a saying by Fyodor Dostoevsky: *"The degree of civilization in a society can be judged by entering its prisons."*

CHAPTER
FORTY-EIGHT

NOVEMBER. Dallas. Fifteen weeks to a full-term baby.

It is a few days after Hannah settled into antepartum, and Dr. Phillips has sent us for a sonogram to check on the placenta previa. The orderly rolls Hannah's wheelchair down the hall and into the sonogram room. The specialist is young —too young for a doctor, in my view. His pale blue scrubs obviously are freshly pressed. He has a kind smile, but is all business. Once Hannah is on the table, he intently starts about his work, examining the previa. We have joked the entire ride with the staff and the orderly. A few days of calm have left us with a sense of success; we can breathe again. The previa has behaved, no added bleeding, and all of Bailey's vitals remain strong. The Perinatologist (a fancy name for a doctor who handles high-risk pregnancies) calmly performs the sonogram, measuring Bailey to see how much she's grown.

"She is doing well," he says. When he is done with Bailey's measurements, he probes around the previa. He stares at the screen which is a mishmash of undecipherable black and white static to me. Two pregnancies and countless sonograms have convinced me some of these doctors are just soothsayers reading runes.

"See that there," the doctor says.

I don't. "What do you see, doc?"

"Well, based on my reading of the chart and what I see here, the placenta has not migrated. It continues to rest flat against the bottom of the uterus right across the cervix. So it's definitely still a previa. . . . It's a vesa previa."

"A what?"

"A vesa previa. It's a further complication that can occur in pregnancy. Some of the blood vessels that connect the umbilical cord to the placenta are near the entrance to the birth canal. The risk is that these blood vessels can rupture when the membranes around the baby rupture. The baby risks losing a lot of blood." He takes a ballpoint pen out of his pocket to use as a pointer. "See these lines here?"

"Yes."

"These are the fetal blood vessels. Normally, these tuck inside the placental tissue and the umbilical cord supports them. Here, though, as you can see, they are exposed and run directly along the fetal membrane and across the cervical canal here."

All calm washes out of Hannah's face, and a whisper of panic rims her large, hazel eyes.

"So, what does that mean?" she asks.

"A Cesarean delivery for sure. And with the placenta failing to migrate, we can't rule out placenta accreta."

My quizzical look prompts him to explain.

"An accreta means the placenta has burrowed into the uterine wall—fused with it, making it almost impossible to remove. In most cases, they have to remove the uterus to stop the post-delivery bleeding."

"Remove my uterus? But then I won't be able to have any more babies!" Hannah protests.

"Can you tell if there is any accreta?" I ask.

"No. We won't know until the baby comes. But you should know it's a risk. If it's an emergency C-section . . . ."

He turns and looks intently at Hannah who nervously spins her wedding ring on her finger. "If it's an emergency C-section, and you are under general anesthesia, the doctor won't have time to ask. The uterus will have to be removed to stop the bleeding. He lets this sink in.

Hannah closes her eyes and takes a deep breath to calm her nerves, absorbing the possibility that such a procedure would gut her chances to have future children. "We plan on having four children, doctor," she says.

"Hopefully you won't require an emergency C-section," the doctor says. "Hopefully, they will have time to address any accreta without doing anything drastic. But at some point Dr. Phillips will want to take the child to avoid those blood vessels I showed you from rupturing."

"And if they rupture?"

"That's why you are in antepartum, so we can do an emergency C-section. If they rupture, if they pop like a hose, the bleeding can be uncontrollable. A risk of severe, or even fatal, blood loss to the child and mother exists."

"They could both bleed out?" A flood of remembered panic from Ithaca pours through me.

"Yes. They could both bleed out."

Hannah grabs my hand a little tighter, and I squeeze back —the only control I have over the situation.

I hear Dr. Phillips in my head.

It will bleed again.

CHAPTER
FORTY-NINE

EARLY DECEMBER. Dallas, Texas. Twelve more weeks to a full-term baby.

Lilly stirs in the bed as my alarm goes off at 4:00 am. I am tempted to hit the snooze, but that will only truncate the time I have to hit a deadline on a brief. I pull myself from under the covers and wait for the coffeepot to run while I feed our slightly obese polar-bear white Labrador retriever, Porter. Porter is usually lazy but always willing to eat as if it's his last meal. By the time I pour my first cup, Porter is already done, and dozes back to sleep with a full belly. On the kitchen table rests my laptop, beckoning me. I enjoy a few sips of coffee. Once I engage the office, it will suck me in and demand my attention. Finally, I sit down, answer a few emails, and then work on the arguments in my brief.

With Hannah at the hospital in antepartum, Lilly and I have settled into a reasonable rhythm. I will wake her and start her day at 7:00 am; she has to arrive at preschool by 8:00 am. For now, I have two uninterrupted hours to work before I have to get ready and then turn to Lilly.

I look up at the clock and drift into a daydream. The silence in the kitchen makes me want to call Hannah to check on her and baby Bailey. The fear of catastrophic blood loss has robbed me of any restful sleep. But just because I am up and anxious, does not mean she is. It's funny, when you wake up super early, you somehow think everyone else is awake. Hopefully, Hannah is sleeping solidly. I can picture every inch of her hospital room. Dr. Phillips has followed through vigorously on his orders for strict bedrest. The nurses have not let her out of bed for *anything*, even to take a shower or use the restroom. Emmett has an eight by ten cell and a chance to exercise in the yard once a day. Hannah has a three-foot by seven-foot mattress and no time outside. That is it.

Considering her conditions of confinement, my wife has remained in good spirits despite any indignities. Luckily, no further bleeding has occurred and Bailey's heartbeat chugs along. Today, they have us scheduled for another ultrasound to check on the previa. It's odd to exist as a hostage to dangers you can't see or feel. The uncertainty feeds anxiety constantly, so it takes effort to remain clearheaded and positive. At any second, the entire project could go terribly wrong . . . with fatal consequences.

My coffee is now cold and bitter. I have written only one paragraph in my brief. This new pattern, the new circumstances leak time all over the place. I worry I won't have sufficient focus to get it all done without spinning out of control. I stand up, replace my cold coffee with hot, and sit down, determined to focus on the legal brief in front of me. The only sounds in the house are Porter snoring and the clicking on my keyboard.

At 6:15 am, I log out, shut down, and get myself ready for the day. After a long, hot shower and then getting dressed, I attempt to pick out Lilly's clothes. She does not care, but I am sure that the teachers notice. She has not worn a matching outfit to school since Hannah went into the hospital. I concentrate on the basics: pants, shirt, socks, shoes, and—of course —underwear.

When I wake Lilly up, she is groggy for a few moments and then trundles out to the kitchen. I learned the hard way that it's best to get breakfast in her before dressing her in her school outfit. I stick a microwave pancake or two in the toaster, a shortcut Hannah has instructed me on for better tasting, out-of-the-box, ready-to-eat pancakes. I cut up some strawberries. Lilly might or might not eat them; Hannah will ask—for sure—if I provided them. I pack a lunch. Sandwich (no peanut butter and jelly or the school will freak because of nut allergies), chips, and the ubiquitous fruit. I toss in a juice box.

After breakfast, I get Lilly ready for school, changing her out of her pajamas and into her school clothes. I brush her hair, but am hopeless with anything fancy, so we made a compromise. Lilly is big into fish: clown fish, parrotfish, jacks, and sharks—anything with fins. We have devised a "Fish-Do." It consists of a short ponytail on either side of her head as pectoral fins, and a ponytail on the back as a tail. I know some of the moms stare, but in the chaos of carpool and drop-off, I don't notice anyone shooting me the evil eye. As I pull out of the parking lot each morning, I imagine the collective, "That poor man. Did you see how he dressed his daughter today?"

Lilly's school lasts until Noon, just a few hours, and certainly not sufficient time to jet downtown to accomplish anything productive. To bridge the time, I head to a local café and hang out with my laptop and a cup of coffee. Some days I eat breakfast, most days I don't. But the best upside is that the coffee is always hot, plentiful, and after a few hours, I don't have a burnt carafe of coffee that tastes like tar. The café comes with another benefit: noise and human beings. Porter is a fine companion, but if I'm honest, at his age and weight our dog is much more prone to sleep and snore than keep me company.

Plus, the house is too quiet to sit in alone for hours.

Besides, the couch always calls for a nap, and with no set schedule, I can persuade myself that I will sleep only a few minutes, but end up blowing hours of billing time. I also need the hustle and bustle to keep my mind from catastrophizing about Hannah and Bailey. I am alone, and my worst enemy is the question, "What if?" At the office, I would bury myself with activity and work. If the moments become too still, I could find someone to talk to about a case, or visit with someone while he or she pours a cup of coffee. With people around, the noise helps me drown out my own incessant worry. I use others to squelch my anxiety. But alone? The silence turns unbearable. There's no one to talk to about anything going on at the hospital. I keep these internal struggles from Hannah. She has enough to worry about without my burden.

I think about what she must feel stuck in antepartum on forced bedrest. She is never actually alone—nurses flit in and out, always checking on her. But mostly when Lilly and I can't visit, she is alone within those four walls—a captive of medical circumstance. It makes me wonder how prisoners, when the guards lock them up—especially those in solitary confinement—don't lose their minds. Silence and worry can work on a person like dripping water etches into stone.

If I am not careful, I can stew over why life wants our pregnancies to walk a crazed path. I am human, so I don't think it's fair. But I also know a delicate web of feelings around these journeys surrounds Hannah and me. Too much resentment, or "Why us?" and I know Hannah will blame herself. But Hannah is innocent. The only thing I am certain of, is whatever animates these journeys, they're mysterious. They remain as unexplainable and blameless to us as farmers watching a flood take away barns or crops. My grandmother has a photo someone took of my great grandfathers and great uncles during a flood in the Depression in Kansas. The photographer sat on a tall porch, and the men stand in the street. They form a line, shoulder-to-shoulder, arms around each other with the water lapping the chest pockets on their overalls, as the river slowly rises and lazily mulls through town. Every one of them is smiling, laughing almost, as they take the good with the bad. It's just life. Life happens. Get on with it.

For the next few hours, I work on a brief in a securities fraud case. Productivity translates to profitability and missing your billable hours requirement is the main reason associates don't advance in a law firm. I am unwilling to back off the work.

Pushing my career forward is the only way to keep the debt from law school and the IVF from sweeping us away. It's rising all around us like those waters around my great grand-fathers and uncles. My solution is the same: just get on with it.

The first diners for the lunch rush wander into the café, and that is my cue to head home to let Porter out of the house for a few minutes. He is happy when I first get there, lumbers out back for a few minutes, wags his tail, then quickly slides back into his lazy habits and curls up on the floor.

I check my email and answer a few. Then I head to pick up Lilly. When I arrive at the school, she is still in Ms. Susanne's classroom finishing a painting.

One of her classmates, Molly, a blonde girl with perfectly done braids, is barking at a kid in the corner. I remember Hannah telling me that Molly thinks she is a dog. Ms. Susanne spots me as she hangs up a couple old work shirts that dads have donated as painting smocks.

"She's just about done, if you can wait just a moment or two," Ms. Susanne says and then turns to Lilly. "Lilly, sweetie, your dad is here. Time to wrap it up." Susanne turns back to me.

"How are things at the hospital?" she asks, truly interested.

"Good, I think. Hannah is getting really bored sitting in bed. It's killing her not to be out here with Lilly."

"Well, *she* is doing fine," Susanne says, pointing toward Lilly. "She's adjusting. The baby?"

"Healthy. Doing well. Growing like they wanted her to grow."

Lilly hangs up her painting smock on a peg and trundles over to me with a folded piece of construction paper.

"She made another card for her mother today," Susanne says.

"Great, we'll find space to add it to the wall. Hannah's room looks like we are moving in."

"You did move in." Susanne smiles. "How many weeks now?"

"Let's see . . . we're at six. So we've made it to the magic twenty-eight week mark."

"Congratulations."

"Still a long way to go. Twelve more weeks to a full-term baby. But if the baby can stay put for at least six more weeks, we should be okay."

"We'll send good thoughts. If you ever need Lilly to stay late with the afternoon class, just let me know. I'm sure the school won't mind. I know I won't."

"That's very kind. We may have to take you up on that." Lilly hands me the card. "You ready to go see Momma?" I ask. That one query winds her up like a chatterbox. She grabs my hand and starts pulling me toward the door in a blaze of words. "Thanks Susanne. We'll see you tomorrow," I say as she waves to us on the way out of the classroom.

"Mr. Simmons," I hear behind me in the hallway.

"Yes."

I turn to see a prim thin woman, her head in a severe tight bun, her blouse buttoned to her neck. Her makeup functional, but not applied very well. The petty tyrant descends on me, her thin lips tight with disapproval.

"Mr. Simmons, I'm Ms. Harrington, the Head of School. Do you have a moment?"

"Yes."

"Mr. Simmons, I want to talk about Lilly's lunch."

"What? Did she lose it?"

"No, Mr. Simmons. There was a problem today. You see, you sent a bag of potato chips with her sandwich."

"Potato chips?"

"Yes. We don't allow potato chips in the children's lunches. They are not a healthy food or snack. And because we forbid them, they cause quite a stir when one child brings them and none of the others do."

"I apparently missed the potato chip prohibition." I try not to smirk.

"Well. Now you know. I'd ask that you not let it happen again."

"I'll do my best Ms. Harrington."

"Thank you." She disappears down the hall, scolding several Kindergarteners about running.

As I load Lilly into my car, I notice that her Fish-Do is still high, tight, and well-put-together today. I congratulate myself on a quality job. She looks healthy although I tried to poison the child with potato chips. As I drive by the prim Ms. Harrington on the way out of the parking lot, I resist the urge to roll down my window and yell, "Well at least my kid is not barking like a dog!"

The hospital is just down the road from Lilly's school. So like every weekday, we pull in, unload, and get ready to stroll up to Hannah's room. The first few days, I tried walking in, holding Lilly's hand. She likes to shuffle in by herself. But the hospital is a vast maze, and Lilly's little legs and ever-present curiosity slow the trip to a crawl. I have a trial bag—a giant box of a briefcase to hold binders, looks like something a salesperson would use to lug around sample kits. It has rolling wheels and a handle. I plop Lilly on top, seated with her back against the handle, and we roll inside, down the hall, and finally to the elevator up to antepartum. We scoot in and Lilly springs off the bag, crawls up into the hospital bed with her mother, and hands her the card of the day.

Hannah's beautiful hazel eyes flash with joy over the artisanship and message. She receives each card as if she has never seen one like it before. After that celebration, she hands it to me, and I take some tape out of my bag and hang it across the windowsill with all the dozens of others. I notice the smell of a bland hospital lunch in Hannah's room. Lilly notices a pudding cup on the tray next to Hannah and grabs up a spoon. She picks up the remote in the bed and starts flipping through channels looking for shows she likes. She digs into the pudding, sucking it off the spoon. A giant smile gives her pudgy cheeks an extra rosy glow. Of the three of us, she is oddly the most at home in this strange little room.

I pull out my laptop and spread my stuff out on the couch that is my afternoon office. I review the edits I made at the café this morning. Hannah runs her delicate fingers through Lilly's hair and lays her cheek on her head. One of the side ponytails tickles her nose and triggers a sneeze.

Lilly finishes the pudding and places the empty cup on the tray, intently watching a cartoon on the television. After a while, Lilly's eyes close, and she drifts off to her afternoon nap, curled up with her momma.

"We did it, Bear," Hannah says in a hushed tone. "It's twenty-eight weeks."

"Yes, we did it. But we still have twelve weeks to go to full term." I immediately regret pointing out the negative, as Hannah's smile fades. "Is Dr. Phillips happy?"

From the doorway I hear, "He won't be happy until she goes full term. But at twenty-eight weeks you have made it past a significant danger zone. Eight more weeks and we're golden. Twelve more to be full term."

I look up at the voice. It's Sabra, Hannah's favorite

antepartum nurse. She also works in the NICU (the neonatal intensive care unit). Sabra was a preemie, born at thirty weeks. She is smart, funny, and beautiful. She wears her waist-length auburn hair in an elegant double-braid. She has grown into quite a confidant to Hannah. It's comforting to watch Sabra move through the room day after day, knowing how successful she is after coming into this world early. She is petite, but strength radiates from her. Sabra checks the always-present fetal monitor tape.

"Everything is looking great. Bailey looks to be sleeping." Sabra talks directly to Hannah's belly, instructing the baby, "You stay in there at least eight more weeks." She runs her hand over Lilly's hair and then turns toward us, "Anything I can get either of you?"

"We're good," Hannah says.

Sabra tucks a bit of blanket around Lilly's shoulder and kisses her on the forehead. She turns a kind but stern gaze on Hannah. "Remember, Hannah: don't move." She rubs her palms together as if pronouncing all her work here is done and then strides out the door.

"Don't move," rings in my head, as I realize there is nothing I can do to change the state of affairs. Life is going to happen regardless of my wants or wishes.

Eight or twelve more weeks is a very long time when your wife and child can bleed to death at any moment.

CHAPTER
FIFTY

LATER THAT NIGHT.

When Lilly and I leave the hospital, I decide to do something special with her to celebrate twenty-eight weeks. I stop at the grocery store to pick up toaster pastries; she has been prattling about them every day as we drive by the grocery store on the way home from the hospital. Lilly has a sixth sense for where they rest in the aisles. She makes a beeline for the frosted, strawberry flavor. For a moment, I think, "This much sugar this late at night could prove a bad idea." But she already has the jumbo package in her hand and an enormous smile on her face, her eyes puddles of joy. I am now locked into whatever might happen.

At home, we sit down in front of the television as Lilly and I munch through the pastries. I had ordered a book on how to braid hair, which finally arrived. I think now is a good time to learn. With Lilly locked onto TV and her snack, she should be sufficiently distracted that I should have a chance at success. I am confident, with a little study and patience, I can make this happen. As I look through the book, I discover the directions look terribly complicated to a neophyte. By this time of day, Lilly's hair has wound itself into tangles. When I try to weave it into a braid, tiny yelps ring out from the kiddo as I accidentally pull and yank on sensitive hairs on her neck. For twenty minutes, I work the injurious puzzle. My first, and final, braid looks like a rope Porter has chewed on for a week. The science of braiding is simply beyond my grasp.

We abandon the braiding fiasco and start up the bedtime routine—pajamas, tooth brushing, reading a book. Unfortunately, the sugar has amped Lilly into a chattering wiggle worm with no interest in sleep. As she continues to refuse to doze off, I begin to hear valuable billing time ticking away. I decide to place her in my car and drive her around to lull her to sleep. Lilly, however, takes an interest in almost everything we pass on our journey, calling them out by name as she sees them. She has story after story from school, and a song or two she wants to teach me. After an hour, I declare the project hopeless and pull back into the garage. I curl up with Lilly in bed, trying to will her to sleep. I check I set my alarm for 4:00 am. Tomorrow will soon be upon us. I'm not sure who drifts off first. But I remember my last thought.

Eight more weeks to safety.

CHAPTER
FIFTY-ONE

JANUARY. Dallas. Nine weeks to full term.

The best part of taking Lilly to the hospital is the joy she brings Hannah—I can see a calm wash over my wife every time she snuggles up with that little girl. The worst part is that you can't keep a two-year-old from touching things. Lilly especially likes to push elevator buttons. The result, if you stay long enough in a hospital, is that you will get sick from something. For us, it's a high fever and lying in bed with the chills. Over the weekend Lilly, Grandpa, and I all go down with an ugly little virus with a persistent cough. Each hack seems to increase the pressure in my head and drives an ache into the sore muscles in my midsection.

I take Lilly to see the pediatrician, who says it should subside quickly. But the aches and sweating make every minute seem especially long. Luckily, the pediatrician is right, and after two or three days, all three of us rebound. After forty-eight hours without a fever, they clear all of us to see Hannah again in antepartum.

We have not seen Hannah for several days, wanting to keep her healthy. Any cold or virus will stress her and her body. I am sure any violent cough would tempt the previa's

291

blood vessels to rupture and a flood of blood to threaten to kill both Hannah and Bailey. We need everything to stay calm. But the separation took a heavy toll. Our only connection to Hannah the occasional cellphone call. It's hard to fight something together when life forces you to stay apart. Each day, I hear the loneliness and stress compound. Finally, we head to visit her. Lilly bounds down the hallway swinging her hands over her head and singing some song she learned on the playground.

As we round the corner, I am not sure who is more excited to see the other, Lilly or Sabra. Sabra eyes widen with joy, and she squats to receive a hug as Lilly admires Sabra's long, double-braided auburn hair. "Hey, little one. I know someone extremely excited to see you." Sabra opens the door, and Lilly bolts inside. I can hear the joy all the way in the hallway.

When I enter the room, I'm surprised. When I grew up, my dad would buy a premade treat of popcorn in a pie tin with a handle and foil on top. You would heat it on the stovetop and shake it until the popcorn would pop as the foil top expanded and stretched into a silver dome that looked like it was going to explode. We have been gone only a few days because of the virus, but Hannah's belly has ballooned like the foiled pie tin of popcorn. Last time we saw her, she looked pregnant but not "*pregnant*." Today she looks like she might be ready to burst. If she was a Thanksgiving turkey, I would be looking for the little red button that pops out when she is done.

Hannah's beautiful hazel gaze glows with excitement. She smiles at me, and then coughs and blows her nose. She has large bags under her eyes, and I can tell from years of being married to her that she is sick. *She has the virus that put us all down for a few days.* I think about my coughing, and how it rocked my body and my head felt like it would rupture. For a moment, fear floods through me as I think of similar pressure on those paper-thin, delicate vessels in the previa.

"You feeling okay?" I ask.

"I think it's just a cold. They tell me I'm okay." She smiles, coughs, and blows her nose again. "They don't want me to take any medicine because of my blood pressure." She notices my look of concern. "It's high," she says in a comforting tone. "But they check it regularly, so we're good."

She is trying to deflate my worry, but I know what high blood pressure means. Many women, late in pregnancy develop preeclampsia—high blood pressure that can cause risk to her liver and kidneys. Some doctors weigh the risk of delivering the baby early to forestall any risk to the mother. But we remain too early by many measurements for that escape route. Lilly crawls all over her mother as I plop down on the couch. I leave my trial bag untouched and close my eyes, savoring the sounds of them enjoying each other. Hannah is at risk of the vasa previa rupturing those major vessels and bleeding out. If they find an accreta, she will never have another child. If her blood pressure rises too high, the risk of damage to her most vital organs skyrockets.

She could die. They both could die.

I have no control—I can only wait and see where life takes us.

Silently, I say a prayer.

CHAPTER
FIFTY-TWO

PREDAWN. Dallas Eight weeks to full term.

The coffee pot barely pushes halfway through its cycle. My cell phone rings, and I can see it's Hannah calling to say, "Good morning."

"Hey, Buzz. Love you. How's your morning?" I say, knowing she is probably just lonely.

"She's coming, Bear!" Hannah blurts, her voice laced with panic. "They are taking her now. The vessels burst. I'm bleeding. It's a lot—the sheets are soaked. Sabra is wheeling me to the OR."

The phone goes dead. This is the moment I have been dreading. With a scheduled C-section eight weeks from now, Hannah would be safe. But a surprise bleed? That tosses everything into a chasm of uncertainty.

Blood pressure. Previa. Accreta. It's like tumbling over a cliff into a dark freefall. I call Adam, Hannah's father, on his cell phone. I try to keep my voice calm. But fear floods through the phone.

"Adam? Bailey is coming. . . . Yes, they just called. Hannah started to bleed. She says it's a lot. They just rushed her to the OR. . . . Okay, we will see you when you get here."

It's early and Lilly is still asleep. I can't bolt out of the house and leave her alone. I can't get to Hannah. Adam is at least a half hour away, and Hannah just went into the operating room for a surgery that may claim her life, and Bailey's life. All I can do is wait. Helpless, I grab a cup of coffee, although it is bitter and churns my stomach.

Lately, Adam, Hannah's father, has commuted to Oklahoma City so he can stay in town at night to help with Lilly and Hannah. His willingness to commute by car, three hours each way, makes him a saint. We can use all the help we can get. Adam's commute to Oklahoma City for his day job is helping the city rework its main Interstate exchange. After having kept Hannah company well into the night, I worry about him driving, about the fatigue. I try to push dark thoughts about his safety out of my mind. He has been a civil engineer all his professional life, mostly building roads for state governments. Adam loves to drive—he is like a monk meditating behind the wheel. He seems to take great solace in hearing the roll of asphalt under his tires.

Routine may help keep my dread in check, so I decide that taking a shower will make the time pass. Under the spray of hot water, my senses amplify. Time crawls to a stop. All I want to do is rush out the front door. I picture Adam gunning it down the highway. Mile markers zip past him. His little girl is bleeding, perhaps to death. His granddaughters also need him. I can't imagine the choices running through his mind. Lilly's silhouette keeps me running through the simple routine of getting ready for work. Just as I finish tying my shoes, Adam bursts through the doorway.

"I've got Lilly. Go!" I think of Lilly and how much I love my little girl, and wanting to protect her, I can't imagine the selflessness it takes for Adam to drive to the house and not the hospital to utter that one word, "Go." *Hannah is his little girl.*

The trip to the hospital is oddly calm. I don't speed—

much. I'm solely a spectator now. I have to believe that Hannah is in the OR with all the right medical professionals. The alternative is unthinkable; I force the image out of my mind of them pulling a white sheet over her face. I have no part in saving her and Bailey now. I am truly on the sidelines.

When I arrive, I run up to antepartum for an update. Hannah's room is empty. No bed—they must have wheeled it out with her in it. Lilly's cards and drawings hang all over the walls, but somehow this home for the past weeks is now empty, like a home after the movers have claimed all your belongings.

"They are down on Two in OR," a voice says over my shoulder.

I look behind me and see Sabra.

"We got her there as fast as we could. You better go. That kiddo is probably here."

I don't wait for the elevator. One of the odd things about living in the hospital for an extended period is you study shortcuts; you learn the stairwells. As I open the door on the second floor, a group of folks rushes by. One nurse recognizes me.

"Dad! You go with her." She points to a plastic bubble, an incubator, with a team of four clutching it, running down the hall.

"How's Hannah?"

"Just left, they are working on the bleeding now. They are working fast. Go with this kiddo."

She pushes me on my shoulder to follow the team rolling the incubator to the NICU. I can't see Bailey. All I see is a clump of striped blankets and an oversized stocking cap—red and white ringed like a bullseye. As I approach, one nurse turns to me.

"You Dad?"

"Yes."

"Up here at the hallway, turn right. There's a waiting room. The doc will update you as soon as they know more."

As I turn right and head to my appointed space, the crew and Baily turn left and then disappear through a set of double doors.

Then . . . silence.

CHAPTER
FIFTY-THREE

THE SAME DAY. Dallas.

In the waiting room just outside the doors of the NICU at the hospital, I find a couch and plunk down. Fish circle in the aquarium in front of me. I am alone—the only person here. A whistle emanates from the HVAC blowing air. I'm in the dark. I have no information about Hannah. No update about Bailey. Just these damn fish circling interminably.

Thirty minutes pass. I have finally consigned myself to flipping through well-dog-eared magazines when I hear a woman's voice, raspy with age.

"Are you Mr. Simmons?"

I look up and see a doctor's white coat. She wears her black and gray hair in a long braid that lops over her shoulder, dangling beside her stethoscope. The crow's feet in the corners of her steel-blue eyes speak of age and wisdom. A pack of long, menthol cigarettes in her lab-coat pocket explains the voice.

"Yes."

"I'm Dr. Suggs. We have decisions to make." The tone perfunctory and factual. The doctor grabs my forearm and quickly escorts me to a small brown table with two white, plastic chairs: a "consult room."

"The OR called. She lost a lot of blood. She'll be weak for a while. But Momma's doing fine. They're stitching her up now." My nerves, tight as a piano wire, relax for a moment. One bullet dodged.

"And the baby?"

The doctor's eyebrows draw together, and she drops her voice for emphasis. "Your baby's struggling to breathe." I rake my fingers through my hair and rub the raw pain of stress clawing into my neck. My nerves cinch instantly to the piano-wire-tight breaking point again. Dr. Suggs says, "I want to give her Surfactant."

"What does that do?" I say in a primal, protective voice.

Patience floods the doctor's tone as she explains. "When infants come this early, the inside of their lungs is still sticky. The lungs won't stay open, won't inflate. Surfactant acts as a lubricant. It keeps the lining of the lungs from sticking together." She pauses, allowing me to process her words. "*Mr. Simmons*, the drug will help the baby catch her breath."

The decision weighs too much for me alone, and I seek a lifeline. "Is my wife awake?"

"No. She won't be thinking straight until the anesthesia wears off." I look over the doctor's shoulder to a pastoral painting on the wall—a single horse grazing in the long timothy grass of a mountain meadow while a sunset paints the sky pink. The quiet swallows me, Dr. Suggs breaks my reverie. "We need to give the surfactant *now*. Will you consent, *Dad*?"

For years, Hannah and I have decided things together. But now . . . life has left all decisions to me. I envision tiny Bailey struggling to take her first breaths, and the answer is obvious.

"Yes," I say.

"I'll keep you informed," Dr. Suggs says, the urgency of the moment makes our conversation oddly transactional. She quickly disappears as a nurse brings me a pen and clipboard to sign a consent form.

When you go into a hospital, they make you sign forms that give you the power to decide treatment for a loved one when life or death balances on a razor's edge. But when you sign them, the paper never feels as heavy as the leaden moment when you truly decide.

I walk back to the waiting room, my gait awkward with fear. All I can do is wait. A brown and black spotted catfish sucks algae off the sides of the aquarium. I watch it work through my likeness in the glass. This journeyman fish is a Plecostomus. I know because of Lilly and her fish obsession. It's always working to keep the aquarium clean. He sucks his life away, grinding it out, hour after hour, minute by minute, sucking up sludge. No complaints. I imagine Hannah saying with an impish grin on her beautiful lips, "That's an ugly fish." I look at it a little longer. It really is an ugly fish.

After what seems like an eternity, a different doctor surfaces.

"Are you Mr. Simmons?"

"Yes," I say. This doctor wears the signature blue-green scrubs of a surgeon with the hat and booties still on, so I know she just came from the operating room.

"I'm Dr. Jones. I did Hannah's surgery." Her kind brown eyes radiate calm and caring, a slight sheen on her ebony skin from the focus and intensity of an emergency operation.

"How is she?"

"She is in the recovery room. It will take time for the anesthesia to wear off. But, she did well. Lost a lot of blood, so it will take some time to regain her strength. She'll also feel sore for a few days."

"Was there an accreta?"

"No, everything went fast . . . but fairly normal." Relief floods though me. They did not have to remove any part of Hannah. She is still whole. My rigid posture gives way to exhaustion for a moment, and tears rim the edge of my eyes. Dr. Jones cups her hand over mine, her dark, fingers strong but soft. "She will be fine," her tone calm, firm, and reassuring. "Hannah will wake up soon, and you can see her." Dr. Jones catches my gaze, and gives me a wide, kind smile of bright, perfect teeth. "Did they say how the baby is doing?" The joy of bringing new life into the world fills her voice.

"I haven't seen her yet. They came out and asked me for permission to give the kiddo some medicine for her lungs. She can't catch her breath." Silence passes between us for a moment. "I don't know anything else," I say.

Dr. Jones squeezes my hands. "I'm sure they'll update you soon. They really are excellent here in our NICU. I had a preemie. She was safe with our doctors, right here." She sits with me for a few moments in silence, her resolve buttressing mine, her firm grip full of caring. Finally she asks, "Do you have any more questions for me?"

"Bikini cut on the C-section?" I ask.

"Yes."

I nod. Two kinds of C-sections occur. A bikini cut, which is a small horizontal line several inches below the beltline. The other is vertical. The long vertical is an emergency cut and runs clean through the abdominal muscles. Dr. Phillips had explained the difference and told us, with limited time, he would have to do a vertical cut to be safe. The recovery is longer. It hurts more. It severs the abdominal muscles, often permanently altering them. Hannah worried about a vertical cut. She wants Bailey safe, but I think she also worries about potential permanent disfigurement and one-piece bathing suits to cover the enormous scar. In the silence between us, I realize that Dr. Jones took a risk with both my girls. Time was critical, but she let caring and foresight override panic. I imagine her grace under pressure in the operating room. Gratefulness floods through me.

"What does Dr. Phillips say?

"He wasn't here," Dr. Jones says. "I'm his partner and was on the floor monitoring another delivery when the previa burst. So they grabbed me."

"Does he know?"

"Yes. We just got him on the phone. He went jogging and forgot his pager. I briefed him. He concurs in everything we've done. Any other questions I can answer?"

"No, thanks, doc."

"Gotta go. That other baby is on the way." She pats my hand, stands, and then disappears down the hallway in a hurry.

I chuckle to myself, thinking about Dr. Phillips and all his conservative cautious ways, and he forgot his pager. Life is funny. That one mistake probably saved Hannah a long, arduous recovery from a much more significant surgery. We will take *that* doctor mistake.

I watch the Plecostomus circle for another thirty slow minutes. With Hannah and Bailey in limbo, other thoughts and exhaustion crowd in. It has been weeks since my trial in Wichita Falls, but my mind wanders back and forth over details. I rework each cross-examination in my head. Hindsight makes each one more crisp, and my choices seem more and more like mistakes and failures as my inner critic chimes in loudly. Soon my thoughts drift to Emmett and his small, sparse cell. The four walls around me close in, and I realize circumstances have placed me in a unique prison of my own, at the mercy of others who control what happens to Bailey, Hannah, and me. I close my eyes, and Emmett's ice-blue gaze appears above a wide grin. Cheeseburgers and brass.

I must have dozed off because a soft voice calls me back. "Mr. Simmons, you can come with me now."

A NICU nurse in purple and white scrubs decorated with images of zoo animals beckons me. Her short, blonde hair bobs as she leads me to the NICU double doors and points to a large stainless-steel sink.

"You'll have to scrub up. The directions are right there on the wall. Once you're done, we can go in and see her."

Above the sink, prepackaged sponges with disinfecting soap poke out from dozens of boxes. I tear one open and follow the pictures. The soap is industrial, pungent, and brown. I scrub my hands, fingernails, and forearms up to the elbow. The more I scrub, the more my nerves fray. The smell of the surgical soap coats everything with an air of danger. After I rinse, the nurse hands me a towel, and then leads me through the double doors. She points to a foam dispenser.

"That is hand sanitizer. If you touch anything, just get a little squirt and rub your hands. Most of these little ones remain at serious risk of infection, so we all have to do our part." I nod in agreement, and she leads me around the corner. "Do we have a name?"

"Bailey," I say.

"Beautiful name," she says, a quick glint in her eyes as she gives me a wide, bright smile. "There she is Dad. Don't touch anything for now." She points me ahead.

A NICU is one large room with premature babies lined up at workstations. It feels more like a science lab than a hospital. Nurses and doctors float through in a controlled hurry. Banks of monitors hang from the walls, all with a rainbow patchwork of lines and wires. Machines beep. Alarms chime. The raspy rhythm of ventilators keeps a beat on the floor. But the most striking feature remains the incubators. Each little human inside a plastic bubble clings to life. On three sides, circular cutouts rest with plastic gloves attached so the doctors and nurses can perform treatments without touching the babies.

My baby is tiny. Bailey's head with a wisp of dark hair is smaller than an apricot—her skin is almost translucent. Veins float just under the surface, and her petite frame would fit the palm of my hand. They have taped various blue, red, and black leads for monitors to her hands and feet. Her diaper looks no bigger than a folded cocktail napkin. Mostly, though, I see her struggle to breathe. Each breath requires all the effort in her minuscule frame to suck air into her little body, almost as if she is drowning. I look up at the monitors, hoping to decipher some thread of color to help me understand what is going on. Panic rises in my soul.

"The surfactant is working," I hear Dr. Suggs's familiar raspy voice over my shoulder. "But it may not be working as well as we need. She'll become exhausted under the effort to draw in breath. We'll likely need to place her on a ventilator. Is that okay with you, Dad?"

"How long?"

A slight smoker's hack delays Dr. Suggs's response. "Until she picks up breathing more easily on her own. No real timeline. But she is expending too much effort to breathe by herself right now. That's stressing all her systems. Her heart rate is way too fast. I'd like to help her some. Plus, we can supplement with some oxygen, more than is in the room air."

The word "oxygen" strikes at me, as I know from conversations I had long ago that the proper mix of oxygen is essential for preemies, especially the eyes. Too much or too little, and the child can grow up blind. I look down at my baby daughter fighting to breathe and whisper, *"You will always be safe, and I will always love you."*

I give a single nod. "Do what you need to do," I say to Dr. Suggs.

"Okay. Give us some time. Maybe about an hour to get her on the vent and stable. You can wait outside. You're not going to want to stay around for this."

I cautiously back away from the incubator and take one last look at Bailey before I head out the double doors. I can't do anything to help her for a while, so I snake my way through the stairwells and along hallways to the recovery room to see my wife. Hannah is awake, but groggy.

Her eyes widen as she recognizes me. "Hi, Bear, have you

seen her? Is our baby okay?" Hannah's sweaty, flaxen hair is plastered to her face. She reaches for my hand, her movements disjointed and frail.

I struggle to wipe any concern from my expression. "Yes. I just left the NICU. She's doing fine. They are going to help her breathe for a short while, but the doctors are pleased. How are you?"

Hannah lets out a long slow breath. "I'm not feeling much right now. But they say I'm going to feel pretty sore for a while," she says. "Thank God Sabra and Dr. Jones were here. Sabra was incredible; she moved so fast, there was blood everywhere."

A voice floats over the beeps of the monitors. "We're going to move her soon to a room in postpartum," a red-headed post-op nurse says as she scribbles notes into the chart.

"When can I see my baby?" Hannah asks.

The nurse flicks the IV bubble on the tube running into Hannah's arm to encourage it to run faster. "Let's get you moved into a room. Then, when you are steadier and feel like sitting up, they will wheel you over to the NICU," the nurse answers. "We'd better get you ready."

Hannah stares at the ceiling for a moment, dampness around the edges of her eyes. Finally, her voice comes more like a resigned sigh, "Will you go take care of her until I can see her?" The after-effects of surgery exhaust her, and she fights to keep her eyes open.

"We'll be set up in the room downstairs in about an hour," the nurse says to me and flashes a large, calming smile. Freckles grace her nose and cheeks of pale skin. "You might want to wait down by NICU in case they need you."

As I walk out of recovery, nurses gather the equipment and cables that will follow Hannah to her new room. She has fallen asleep, her expression peaceful.

I jam my hands into the front pocket of my jeans and walk back down to the waiting room near Bailey. Not able to focus on any more magazines, I call Adam and give him an update on his daughter and new granddaughter. Lilly is up, and he is preparing her for school. I mention, "no potato chips." I end the call, and the silence floods in all around me again, I wait.

A young couple in sweatpants and T-shirts shuffles into the hall and then to the sink. A haze of exhaustion emanates from the young woman's eyes. Her blonde hair hangs in a functional but messy ponytail high on her head, the muscles around her jawline tight. No words pass between them as they both take out sponges and scrub methodically, that tells me they have scrubbed a lot. It has now become rote. I wonder how many days, or weeks, they have come to see their child in an incubator, and it hits me. We now face several weeks of watching and waiting, while Bailey struggles to build strength inside that magic bubble.

You will always be safe?

CHAPTER
FIFTY-FOUR

EVENING SAME DAY.

As I round the corner in the hallway, a fluorescent light with a dying ballast flickers in the ceiling. Twenty feet ahead, a heavily accented voice spills out of a doorway and snaps, almost like a drill sergeant. With a few more strides, I step into Hannah's postpartum room.

"If you don't move, then you will hurt more and for longer," the nurse scolds.

Hannah's jawline is tight, and I know curse words rest on the tip of her tongue behind those clenched teeth. Hannah groans from the pain of the C-section, her legs weak and out of practice from the blood loss and lying in a bed for weeks. Exhaustion has deepened the fledgling crow's feet at the corner of her eyes, framed by tendrils of hair plastered to her temples with sweat. Hannah protests. The nurse won't have it. She insists that Hannah "get up and walk around" to "start healing." That nurse is close to drawing the ire of my sweet wife, whose temper blows fierce once she loses it.

Oh boy.

"Hey, Buzz," I say.

The nurse looks annoyed at the interruption. "I'll come

back later." As she moves toward the door, she scolds Hannah over her shoulder, "Ms. Simmons, you are going to walk when I get back."

I miss the sweet, supportive Sabra.

"How's Bailey?" Hannah asks.

"She is breathing well. We can go see her if you like. I'll wheel you down." I turn to the nurse, catching her before she scoots out the door. "Could we get a wheelchair, so I can take her to see the baby?"

"She's going to have to walk," the nurse says.

"I know, but not right this minute. Okay? We'll work on it, but if we could have the chair, that would be wonderful." The nurse stomps off to grab a wheel chair.

The nurse is still within earshot when Hannah says, "I don't think they have to be nice."

"We get you home and with Lilly, and you'll feel better."

After a few minutes, the nurse rolls in the wheelchair. Hannah gets out of bed, refuses the nurse's help, and makes her way into the seat with a few labored, tiny steps. I wheel her out of the room and down the hall. As we leave, the nurse warns, "She will have to walk soon."

The trip to the NICU is short. I teach Hannah how to scrub her hands, and help her reach the water from her wheelchair. I pat her fingers dry, then I scrub up. With trepidation, I push the large button that says, "ENTER," to swing open the doors to the NICU. I'm not sure how Hannah will react to the clinical, sterile setup in the NICU or not being able to touch Bailey. We roll past a few machines. Hannah's eyes widen at all the chirping equipment and the silhouettes of incubators in rows. My heart rate quickens as we turn a corner and pull up to Bailey's magic plastic bubble. In the wheelchair, Hannah is eye level with our premature baby. Hannah's beautiful, hazel eyes widen, and her smile soon morphs into a tense line. Hannah sits, perfectly still, as if absorbing all the details of the situation. A few times she opens her mouth as if about to speak, but words elude her. Finally, she finds her voice in a whisper.

"She's so tiny."

I stare into the bubble, taking inventory of all the details. Bailey is resting more comfortably. The struggle to breathe has dissipated. She lies motionless except for a rhythmic rising in her chest. The ventilator and tape supporting the tubes obscures her face, a slight calm surrounds her closed eyes. The nurses have placed little mittens on her hands to keep her sharp fingernails from scratching herself. I grab Hannah's shoulder softly as she absorbs the precarious situation; she grabs my fingers, holding on.

"She is doing really well," a deep, solid voice says behind us, dragging us from our reverie. A bald man in jeans, sneakers, and a simple button-down shirt stands a few feet away. "I'm Dr. Wexler," he says, "I'm watching your kiddo tonight. Her vitals are good. Her breathing seems stronger. Hopefully, we can wean her from the vent tomorrow or the next day." He flashes a comforting smile at Hannah, whose maternal protectiveness has hit overdrive, painting her expression with worry. "Your baby is responding to stimuli,' he says, "so we take that as her brain function is normal."

His phrase, "brain function is normal" drives home the seriousness. You can't assume everything's okay with a premature baby. Bailey came eight weeks early.

"So she's safe?" Hannah asks, pre-tears rimming her eyes.

"Time will tell," Dr. Wexler says in a calm and noncommittal physician's voice. "She's what . . . thirty-two weeks. So, she'll probably stay with us for about six to eight weeks. We'll just take it day by day for now."

"Can I touch her?" Hannah asks, a hitch in her voice.

The corner of Dr. Wexler's mouth turns up in a kind grin. "Sure," he says. "Preemies love their mother's touch."

He grabs a sanitizing wipe for Hannah to clean her hands one more time. Then he opens a small door in the incubator.

Hannah reaches inside and places Bailey's hand in hers; it's no larger than a coin. Hannah starts rubbing Bailey's palm with her thumb. Peace washes over Bailey's face.

Hannah bites her lower lip. "When can I hold her?" Her words lined with impatience.

Dr. Wexler stares at the monitors as if collecting data for his answer. "Let's give it a few more hours, make sure she's stable on that vent or even until she comes off." Hannah slumps in the chair as disappointment floods over her. She grips Bailey's hand ever so slightly. Dr. Wexler pipes in. "Have you heard of kangaroo care?"

"No," Hannah says.

"Well, something tells me you're gonna like it. When she's ready to hold, we bring you down here, sit you in one of these rocking chairs, and then lay that kiddo on the bare skin of your chest. We'll give you a blanket to cover up, of course. But some preemies really respond to that closeness. They can hear their mother's heartbeat."

"I would like that very much."

Hannah and I stay for a few minutes longer, the noises fading into the background as we both stare at Bailey. After a few minutes I roll Hannah back toward her room.

"She's in danger, Bear." Her voice catches. "I wish I could have kept her inside just a little longer."

CHAPTER
FIFTY-FIVE

JANUARY. Downtown. Dallas, Texas. Weeks have passed since Ashley, Steve, and I arrived back in Dallas.

The questions from others about whether we won or lost Emmett's trial have evaporated. Occasionally someone will bring it up, but the outside interest has waned quickly. Shiny objects fade fast, but the questions constantly churning in my mind still haunt me. Often, I think about Emmett, trial, or what I could have done differently to get to a win. Every trial breeds a minefield of "if only" residing in your head. The rhythm of a big law firm has swallowed some of the time for second-guessing. But I am learning no such thing exists as getting over a loss, just different degrees of living with it. I've stopped by the office to pick up some papers. Ginny, my cheerful secretary, hands me my messages as I head into the office, one of the blue, silk scarfs she loves elegantly looped around her neck. As Ginny exits, the phone rings, and I pick it up.

"This is Daniel."

"Daniel, it's Rose Walker, from the State Attorney General's Office—I'm calling about Kendrick."

I picture her hazel eyes outlined in black projecting that

severe, raptor-like gaze but something in her voice sounds off. "Rose, I didn't expect to hear from you."

"Well, I didn't expect to be calling. It's not the best of calls." After a pregnant pause, she says, " Mr. Kendrick died of a heart attack two days ago."

A sudden flash of Emmett's ice-blue eyes above that huge smile pulses through my mind. Then comes an image of Nurse Hatcher's smirk on the witness stand. I close my eyes and pinch the bridge of my nose. All I can see is Emmett's peaceful, pale corpse under a shock-white sheet as they tie a toe tag on his lifeless body. *She finally got him.*

My voice loses its power as I probe, "What, how?"

The tight voice on the end of the line signals angst, "I'm trying to get more details for you. I know this will not sit well. Frankly, it doesn't sit well with me either. No matter what happened, it doesn't look good."

After an uncomfortable silence, I say, "Can you get me the autopsy report, the details?"

"I'm checking into that. I saw the Judge granted your motion to withdraw. So, technically you are no longer his lawyer. And since he's passed, you'd have to be the lawyer for his estate, and you're not."

"But . . ." Frustration punctuates my protest.

"I know. I want to get you some facts, so you'll know. I want to know. I'm checking to see what we can release under the Texas Open Records Act. I mean if you'd made a formal request under the Act as a member of the public what documents could you get yourself. Those I can send, and I will send as soon as they're on my desk."

"Do you know anything else?"

"All I know is he was alive after trial, went back to Teton Springs, and he's dead a few weeks later. I'll do my best to get you something."

"I'd appreciate that."

"Shouldn't be long. I'll see if I can get it rushed."

"Many thanks."

"Talk soon."

The line goes silent as Rose hangs up the phone. I replace the handset and drop my face into my palms. The slump of my shoulders obvious. Ginny walks in my office.

"You holding back a sneeze again?"

My voice catches in my throat, "Emmett's dead." The words suck the oxygen from the room, and I try to rub away the headache rushing on me. "Dead of a heart attack. Two days ago."

"Well, . . ." Ginny pauses, "that would be a good reason to cry." A twinge of sadness in her eyes as she tucks her bobbed gray hair behind her ear on one side and tugs gently on her blue scarf.

"A damn good reason," I say in a voice devoid of energy.

"You don't think they . . . ."

"I don't know what I think," I say as I turn from Ginny, the desire to hide and collapse into myself overwhelming. A hawk floats on the updrafts between the skyscrapers outside my window.

At least Emmett is finally free.

CHAPTER
FIFTY-SIX

FEBRUARY. Dallas, Texas.

The hardest part of having family in the hospital is going home without them. Lilly and Grandpa Adam came to see Hannah in the hospital. Lilly was brilliant, pouring childish generosity and peace into Hannah. Adam was jovial and positive. Bailey rests safely in the NICU. Hannah is finally safe with us at home. No one bled out. In short, no one died, which seems like an incredibly low bar to set, but these are our current mile markers.

But, at some point, you have to leave. With Hannah no longer a patient in antepartum, she spent all her time in the NICU. The hospital has been pestering us to gather Hannah's things, and the task of cleaning out her hospital room falls to me. Sabra is off duty when I arrive, and a sense of aloneness washes over me.

The hospital lends me a cart to gather Hannah's things and roll them out to my car. Flowers threaten to fall off and Lilly's stick-figure pictures flutter in a breeze, at risk of blowing away. Halfway through the parking lot of rough asphalt, an email dings on my phone. It's an email from my boss announcing Bailey's arrival to the department. It's a standard announcement. "We joyfully welcome Bailey to this world," and as is customary, it included her dimensions, along with the obligatory, "Mom and baby are resting and doing well." One of my fellow associates, pure of heart but ignorant of circumstances, chimed in, "Are we sure the length is right, that sounds very small." Standing in the middle of the parking lot, loading Hannah's room into my car, I toss the phone into my trunk. I rant to no one in particular. A couple headed to their car give me an odd look. That one statement, "that sounds very small," pushes me into realizing how isolated we are. No one truly knows the journey we have traversed. The chill air swirls around me. I finish loading Hannah's things, sit down in my car, and I cry. Months of angst and effort pour out in the silence as I pound my flat palm against the steering wheel. *She's in danger, Bear*, ricochets through my head.

After a few moments, I feel calm enough to head home. As I carry things from the garage into the kitchen, the silence in the house amplifies. The image of Bailey on the ventilator plagues me. When you get pregnant as a couple, no one prepares you for moments of helplessness. With both babies, I had almost lost Hannah. With both babies, she put herself at risk without thought for herself. I could tell she was scared but determined. Fear is healthy, but desire can bulldoze any fear. As I sit down on the couch and pet Porter, I realize I have always been along for the ride. This has always been Hannah's mission, her core reason for being. To be a mother overrides every other warning sign. Passion drives people who are truly connected to their reason for living. Bailey and Lilly remain her reasons, even if it meant sacrificing herself.

"Are they safe?" I ask Porter. He yawns, his white jowls flapping, and lays his fat head in my lap, as if to answer, "Yes," and he's known it all along.

CHAPTER
FIFTY-SEVEN

LAST WEEK OF FEBRUARY. Dallas, Texas.

I scrub Lilly's hands, and we head into the NICU. As she waddles in front of me, I congratulate myself on the fact that her outfit matches today. Lilly has been bouncing around all morning, waiting to meet Bailey. Her excitement puts a little pep in my step too. Buzz has kept vigil in the NICU for hours, seemingly immune to exhaustion. When I round the corner, we see them sitting in the rocking chair. Lilly skips ahead to get there first. Hannah squeezes my hand with her delicate, warm fingers as I pass by.

Bailey did well on the ventilator, and the Surfactant performed its magic. The doctors weaned her to room air quickly on the vent and then removed it much earlier than expected. Hannah smiles as she turns that beautiful gaze from her large hazel eyes down at Bailey sleeping on her chest, enjoying some "kangaroo care." That little girl has her ear pressed to Hannah as if greedily sucking up the sound of her mother's heartbeat. Her tiny fingers grab at Buzz's skin like a rock climber clinging to a cliff face for dear life. The monitors above show an even, steady rhythm of vital signs.

Hannah beams as she drinks in Lilly's smile—shakes her

head slightly at the fish-do pigtails that are dramatically crooked today.

But look at the outfit

Lilly takes her pudgy little toddler hand and pulls the blanket back just enough to see her little sister's face. Joy and curiosity flood her expression. Hannah grins at me, and then Lilly. Joy envelopes them.

"Do you like your baby sister?"

"She's cute." Lilly rubs the faint wisps of hair on Bailey's head. In a determined and confident voice she pronounces, "She will be a good baby sister."

Hannah grins and kisses Lilly on the cheek as my little girl rests her head on Hannah's shoulder and looks at Bailey. Their features soften as they all relax into the thought of our new full family.

Suddenly, behind us, an alarm emanates from a monitor. Hannah's shoulders stiffen, and a primal, protective nature brings me to full attention. With wide eyes, a nurse stares at the digits on the monitors. She tells us nothing, but jogs down the aisle and retrieves a doctor. The alarm continues its insufferable rhythm. The doctor rubs his forehead, and with pursed lips and a furrowed brow, his gaze passes repeatedly between the screen and Bailey.

Finally, he mutes the alarm and reaches for Bailey. With a steady voice he says. "Alright Mom, I must steal her for a little bit. We need to do an ultrasound *now*."

"Why—what's going on?" The calm that surrounded her just moments ago shatters. Lilly tucks into my body, grabbing onto my thigh.

"Let's not worry yet." The intensity in his eyes contradicts his statement. "But, I need to get a better look. We may have a brain bleed going on."

I'm rocked to the core.

A brain bleed.

CHAPTER
FIFTY-EIGHT

LATER THAT DAY.

Time drips past us as Lilly and I head home. Hannah stayed at the hospital while the doctors conducted the ultrasound on Bailey's brain, planted like a protective grizzly sow over her cub. I could tell the doctor was going to ask her to leave, but then thought better of it.

"My baby sister will be okay," Lilly pronounces from the backseat.

"Yes," I say, "She will be fine." My reflection in the rearview mirror not convincing, even to me.

Four stages of a brain bleed exist in a premature infant. We pray for the least complicated. The blood vessels in a preemie's brain remain very fragile and vulnerable to rupture. Stage I and II bleeds often have no side effects almost like a simple, internal bruise. Stage III and IV may lead to excess pressure in the skull and developmental difficulties that can last a lifetime. Uncontrollable bleeds lead to death. I shake my head, trying to erase the parade of horribles.

No treatment exists. Medical science has no direct way to stop a brain bleed in a preemie once it starts. They can only treat any underlying condition. The sole rescue surgery to save her would be to place a shunt in her skull to drain excess fluid and pray the bleeding stops. We feel hopelessly helpless, as we wait for the results from the ultrasound. Hannah and I decided it was best for me to take Lilly home and leave her with Adam. I'll return when I can. Hannah promises to call with any news, or if she needs me. But the ride home splits me in two. One kiddo needs me to get her to the house. The other is undergoing an ultrasound trying to survive and grow healthy enough to come home.

My prayer circles in my mind:

You will always be safe, and I will always love you.

Staring out the windshield, I realize I will have to truncate it. Indeed, I can't control anything, so I simply whisper the short version under my breath, "I will always love you."

As I pull into the garage, Hannah calls.

Her voice tight, she provides me the information in short bursts. "Bear, they say, right now, it's a Stage I, at worst a Stage II. They hope it has stopped. But they can't be sure. The doctor scheduled another ultrasound in the morning."

"So all we can do it wait?"

"We wait and pray for our little girl."

CHAPTER
FIFTY-NINE

LAST DAY OF FEBRUARY. Downtown. Dallas, Texas.

"You got a minute," a voice says outside my door. I look up; it's the Managing Partner of my firm, William Paul Moore III. His impeccably tailored bespoke suit accentuates his athletic frame and tanned face from his obsession with the golf course. I'm perplexed why, with his perpetually busy schedule, he would show up in my office. I really only know him from his picture hanging on the wall in the lobby. He is not carrying an empty cardboard box, though, so I am hopeful the news is not a catastrophic end to my short legal career.

"Absolutely, Mr. Moore. Come on in." He walks in and sits down in the chair in front of my desk. His deep brown eyes focus on me intently. Then he flashes me a friendly smile.

"Call me William. I've got something you should see." He hands me a paper. It's a letter from Judge Navarro.

United States District Court
Northern District of Texas
1100 Commerce Street
Dallas Texas, 75242

U.S Magistrate Judge Carmen Navarro

William Paul Moore III
Managing Partner
2300 Main Street, Suite 3300
Dallas, Texas 75201

Subject: *Pro Bono* Representation of Emmett Kendrick
by Daniel Simmons, Steven Davis, and Ashley
Carmichael

Dear Mr. Moore:

Enclosed please find a copy of a letter which I received
several weeks ago from Mr. Emmett Kendrick
concerning his representation by Mr. Daniel Simmons,
Mr. Steven Davis, and Ms. Ashley Carmichael of your
firm. Mr. Simmons had graciously accepted an
appointment by the Court to represent Mr. Kendrick at
trial of his claims for unconstitutional denial of
medical care. Several weeks after trial, and shortly
after sending this letter, Mr. Kendrick passed away. As
he eloquently sets forth in his letter, these young
lawyers made a tremendous impression on him. Their
efforts and dedication to this difficult case were highly
commendable and obviously would not have been
possible without the support of your firm. Thank you
for the commitment by your firm of its resources,
including the time and talents of these three attorneys,
to this *pro bono* case.

Sincerely,
Carmen Navarro.

I'm nervous to turn the page. It's been several weeks since

Emmett died, but every day seems to have some flashback to the trial, or some phrase of wisdom: "You're no accident." The off-the-rack suit we bought Emmett hangs on the back of my office door. I tell myself I should give it to charity, but I can't seem to lift the hanger off the hook. I look up at William, who gestures for me to go on, and I flip the page.

Emmett E. Kendrick
TDCJ-CID No. 4483214
Teton Springs Unit

Honorable Carmen Navarro
United States Magistrate Judge
Northern District of Texas
1100 Commerce Street
Dallas, Texas 75242

Dear Judge Navarro:

Ma'am, I am not petitioning the Court for a new trial or appealing the verdict, the judgment, or anything about the proceedings. I am no longer a plaintiff or have any business before this Court. So, maybe, this letter is not too inappropriate. If it is, then I beg the Court's forgiveness.

I want only to express my deep appreciation for my treatment by the Court since your assignment to the case last year, and, especially, during the trial of this matter. I have, at all times, been treated fairly and given ample opportunity to present my claims in an environment of equality, where I was treated with the same graciousness and professional conduct as the defendants.

I was ably represented by a team of attorneys
(Mr. Daniel Simmons, Mr. Steven Davis, and
Ms. Ashley Carmichael). The attorneys were, at all
times, very professional in their representation, always
well prepared and unfalteringly courtly and kind. I am
convinced their representation exceeded the representation normally accorded a billable client.

It's my personal opinion that these attorneys are a
credit to their profession and set standards that every
member of the bar should strive to achieve.

You have been more than fair in your rulings, and
ensured that I was given an opportunity to present my
claims. For that, and all your other professional kindnesses, I am sincerely grateful.

Sincerely,

Emmett Earl Kendrick

I place the letters on my desk in front of me.

"Those are quite a couple of letters," William says.

"It was an amazing experience. We appreciate you letting
us do it, the firm supporting it."

"You know, I've practiced law for nearly forty years. I've
never seen letters come across my desk like these or the
others Mr. Kendrick sent."

"Emmett was unique," I say, keenly aware I'm using the
past tense.

William stands up, adjusting a bright-red silk power tie.
"I'm hoping you'll let us make a big deal about this, so others
might understand the importance of *pro bono* work."

"Sure, not a problem. Whatever I can do to help the firm."

"We'll put something together, run it by you, Steve, and Ashley."

"I look forward to it."

As William leaves my office, Ginny comes in, passing him, a long white scarf with its fringe swaying in rhythm as she walks. She pauses a moment and then, "Wow. Managing Partner in your office. Look who's hit the big time."

CHAPTER
SIXTY

MARCH. Dallas, Texas.

Over the next few weeks, with Bailey stable in the NICU, we settle into a routine, and I can go back to work regularly to keep pushing my career forward, and to keep the debt at bay. But sitting in an office amplifies my worry.

In contrast, Hannah subjects herself to the worst of schedules. She rises before dawn and goes to the hospital to spend time with Bailey in the NICU. After an hour or so, she comes home to care for Lilly until Adam or I can relieve her in the late afternoon. She'll take a power nap, then rise, shower, and dress in jeans, a T-shirt, and tie her hair in a ponytail—her simple uniform for this effort. On her way out, she kisses me goodbye with her soft lips, flashing a warm smile, and then she disappears back to the NICU to stay with Bailey until well after midnight. She comes home, sleeps for a few hours and then gets up to do it again.

Day after day she marches off full of determination. And it pays off. We had expected Bailey to remain in the NICU six to eight weeks, but Bailey progresses quickly. At thirty-seven weeks, and only a few weeks in the NICU, they transfer her to the PICU—pediatric intensive care unit—the final stop before she can leave. Hannah increases her tireless efforts to spend as much time at the hospital as she can. The PICU stay is short-lived, and the hospital discharges Bailey within days.

Shortly after Bailey comes home, late at night, I stand in the doorway of our bathroom as the light spills from behind me and over the bed. Our dog Porter has commandeered my side, although I'm not sure how he hefts his polar-bear-white girth up on the mattress. He rests his head on a pillow, a quiet sentry protecting my wife and two daughters. After the final horror of the brain bleed subsided, Hannah and I agreed that two kiddos would be the right number—no need to keep tempting fate.

Lilly sleeps behind Hannah, her tawny hair splayed on a pillow, holding onto her like a human knapsack, curled up against her warmth. I don't have to check to know that Lilly has wriggled her pudgy toes under Hannah's legs to stay warm. Bailey is asleep in Hannah's arms, her forehead resting against Hannah's lips. Joy radiates from Hannah. She is sleeping, but for the first time, in a long time, I see no worry lines on her face. Nothing is missing; she has her daughters, the full family she wanted. In that moment, I realize, not for the first time, she is the stronger of the two of us. She knows her purpose in life every minute of every day.

I shuffle to the kitchen and brew some coffee. I have a draft brief due before the partner arrives at work tomorrow. It will be a long night. As the coffee pot chuffs the final sounds in its cycle, I wonder about *my* purpose. Perhaps I will find it someday in the gaps between billable hours. Time will tell.

I sit down and think, "It has been a long, strange trip to get here."

CHAPTER
SIXTY-ONE

JUNE. Downtown. Dallas, Texas.

Months have passed, and I am thinking the State of Texas will never send me any details about Emmett's death, when an envelope arrives. Inside is a transmittal letter from Rose Walker's secretary. She has forwarded a few Attorney General Opinions on the public accessibility of records about the death of a prisoner under the Texas Open Records Act. The body of her letter is to the point, factual: "Please find attached a copy of the documents we received in reference to your client's death. It's our understanding an autopsy was not done at the request of the family. Hopefully this is the information you were looking for." They dated the letter June 22, which feels especially meaningful as that's my birthday. The next page is entitled "DEATH SUMMARY."

I read, looking for answers. Emmett died at 4:38 p.m. on November 20th at Hendricks Medical Center in Abilene, Texas of an Acute Myocardial Infarction. His heart finally broke. He had been recently transferred to the AdSeg Unit at the Robertson Unit, also in Abilene. His only family, a deadbeat brother in Maine, declined an autopsy, declined to retrieve any of his personal effects, declined to claim the body, and declined any responsibility for his estate. Prison officials transported Emmett's body to Lubbock, Texas, to the morgue at the University Hospital there and then notified the main prison mortician in Huntsville.

I am not sure why they transferred Emmett from Teton Springs to Robertson; I can only guess it was for his safety or because Teton Springs was tired of dealing with him. I will never really know. With his family not claiming the body, I am sure Texas buried Emmett in a prison cemetery grave marked solely by a four by six-inch shank of granite with a stainless-steel tag that reads simply: Emmett E. Kendrick, TDCJ-CID No. 4483214.

Over the past few months, I have thought that I would like to get Emmett a headstone. It would read: "Emmett Earl Kendrick, Preeminent Jailhouse Lawyer and Friend."

But that may remain a pipe dream. Texas is a big state, and if anyone thinks prisons care little for prisoners, I am positive a dead, unclaimed prisoner disappears altogether like a whisper in the wind. But still, I think about placing that stone.

I picture a nice, sunny spring day, breeze rolling across my face, large pecan trees leafing out. I kneel on the dew-covered grass. I know the headstone is made of bronze, but if I try hard enough, I bet I can polish the lettering to *shine like brass*.

———

BOOK REVIEWS

BOOK REVIEWS REQUESTED

Reviews are the lifeblood of authors. Your book review will help other readers discover a new book by a new, award-winning author. You will be encouraging Michael Stockham to write more novels for your reading enjoyment. Please leave your book review online on Amazon or Goodreads. Thank you!

This book has already attracted many 5-star reviews and book awards.

INTERNATIONAL IMPACT BOOK AWARDS, Gold, 2022

AMERICAN FICTION AWARDS, Finalist, Thriller & Mystery/Suspense, 2022

LITERARY TITAN, Silver, 2022

AMERICAN WRITING AWARDS, Finalist, 2022

FIREBIRD BOOK AWARDS, Legal Thriller, 2022

#1 NEW RELEASE, AMAZON, Legal Thriller, 2022

———

A SAMPLING OF RAVE REVIEWS

Michael Stockham is a real craftsperson who gives impeccable attention to his writing.

—JOHN NICHOLS, BESTSELLING AUTHOR, *THE MILAGRO BEANFIELD WAR*

Confessions of an Accidental Lawyer by Michael Stockham is exceptionally well-written. The writing is beautiful, clear, and concise, and the author's knowledge of medicine and legal commentary is impressive. … *Confessions of an Accidental Lawyer* is a domestic and legal thriller that has been inspired by a true story. Readers will be given a look at the challenges faced by those in the medical and legal fields, as well as the prison system.

— LITERARY TITAN REVIEW

Confessions of an Accidental Lawyer is a page-turner, combining two suspenseful stories. One story is a legal thriller with courtroom drama. The other storyline is a domestic thriller with medical drama. The young hero is a lawyer defending a prisoner in solitary confinement, and they become improbable friends. The lawyer is also fighting for the life of his wife and unborn child. I won't give any spoilers. Highly recommended!

—AURORA WINTER, BESTSELLING AUTHOR, *TURN WORDS INTO WEALTH*

Confessions of an Accidental Lawyer by Michael Stockham is an award-winning finalist book in the mystery and suspense category for 2022. The author is a litigation attorney and public speaker, who masterfully delves into the world of suspense and intrigue in this legal thriller. I found the writing style exceptional, with an in-depth, detailed story about the characters. Stockham keeps the narration straightforward yet descriptive and elegant at once. The author showcases his professional skills and knowledge, which is reflected in this impeccable tale.

Real events inspire this story, the story focuses on a young lawyer, Daniel Simmons, who struggles between his career and his family. On one hand, his inmate client manages to keep things interesting and unpredictable while his wife is facing her truncated dreams of a healthy baby and a family. The feelings and experiences are well reflected, with flawless character description and development. All the characters in the story are richly complex and mysterious, drawing the reader in for more.

Overall, I found the book exciting, gripping, and action-packed throughout. As soon as I began reading, I couldn't put it down. I highly recommend Confessions of an Accidental Lawyer by Michael Stockham and rate it 5 out of 5 stars for its brilliant reflection of anguish, nostalgia, and legal system frustrations that make this a compelling read.

5-STAR AMAZON REVIEW

I absolutely loved how the author told two stories here. He combined what was going on in the lawyer's personal life and also professionally. Both stories were amazing to read about and the bravery in both is undeniable. Loved this book solid 4.8 rating. Would love to read other books by this author.

—GOODREADS REVIEWER

IT. BLEW. MY. MIND. I want to read EVERYTHING from this author now. The book is gripping to say the least. I cried, I laughed, I felt anger, I felt despair and I was on the edge of my seat…I couldn't read this book fast enough! If a book makes me FEEL emotions while reading, I'm hooked for life. It eloquently ties two worlds together through the eyes of a new lawyer and draws you in to each side of the story. What really does it for me is that it's based on events that really happened. I'm hooked. Everyone should read this and the author needs to make this a series. I want MORE!!

Confessions of an Accidental Lawyer by Michael Stockham is a mesmerizing thriller that tells the story of Daniel, a young lawyer that must fight two major battles on his own, but this time, it involves his family. This story is based on true events and focuses on the life of a promising attorney who must balance a difficult juggling act while absorbing the weight of his one client, an elderly man in solitary confinement, and his wife, who is coping with mental health challenges.

As Daniel's wife, Hannah's lifelong dream is to have a large family, she quickly becomes depressed when this possibility diminishes, causing a major rift in the marriage and declining health. It's a strong, solid read that's fascinating and engaging.

Michael Stockham is a true professional who integrates his knowledge into the heart of this book, focusing on the human side of working in the legal field, which is a nice change from the cold courtroom dramas. I enjoy the author's perspective on a delicate topic while focusing on the often-harsh results of a controversial prison and legal system.

I rate Confessions of an Accidental Lawyer by Michael Stockham a solid 5 out of 5 stars as a unique take on the challenges of working as a lawyer and facing extenuating circumstances that complicate his life in unimaginable ways.

———

SYNOPSIS

Battling against a Texas prison, a young lawyer fights for a fair trial in a prison-friendly town as witnesses and evidence evaporate.

Scarred physically and emotionally by a botched delivery, his wife struggles to realize their dream of a healthy baby and a happy family.

Trapped in solitary confinement, an inmate fights for medicine to keep his failing heart pumping.

Torn between career and family, with the lives of a prisoner, his wife, and his unborn child on the line, the young lawyer struggles to ensure that his client, his family, and his integrity all survive.

MICHAEL STOCKHAM takes us on a page-turning journey in this novel inspired by actual events. He is a litigation attorney, award-winning author, and speaker.

———

ACKNOWLEDGMENTS

Writing a book has been a long-time goal for me, but the task was daunting, especially with my schedule as trial lawyer. Thankfully, I found Aurora Winter, MBA, Founder of www.SamePagePublishing.com. Collaborating with Aurora makes the process of writing a book fun and interesting.

Aurora is intensely curious, listens deeply, and coaches with compassion and skill. She helped me discover and structure a gold mine of content. She is also there to catch me and coach me when the goal seems too big (or an overly critical inner voice tells me it is impossible). I appreciate working with Aurora and want to acknowledge her contribution and support.

It is a blessing to have someone so thoughtful and kind to work on the project of launching as a Thought Leader, speaker, and author. If you would like to write a book but have no idea how you could find the time, I recommend Aurora Winter's VIP solutions for busy experts and entrepreneurs, as well as her award-winning books, which include Marketing Fastrack and Turn Words Into Wealth. To learn more, visit www.AuroraWinter.com.

ABOUT THE AUTHOR

Michael Stockham has worked as a big-firm lawyer for over twenty years after receiving his law degree from Cornell Law School. He's a sought-after litigator and speaker.

Confessions of an Accidental Lawyer is Michael Stockham's first novel. It has been honored with several book awards, including: American Fiction Awards Award-Winning Finalist, Literary Titan Silver Award, and International Impact Book Awards, Gold.

A life-long lover of books, Michael received two degrees in creative writing: a Bachelor of Arts from the University of New Mexico and a Master of Arts from Texas A&M University.

Blessed by two grown daughters who are Clemson University Tigers, Michael lives in Dallas with his wife of twenty-four years, Kiersten, along with three dogs and two potbelly pigs.

www.MichaelStockham.com

Made in the USA
Columbia, SC
01 February 2023

11417636R00209